THUNDERHEART HAS COME AGAIN ...

The old man's black eyes bore relentlessly into Ray's. "The blood of the holy man is in your veins," Grandpa said, "the same blood that spilled on the grass and snow at Wounded Knee. It runs through your heart like a buffalo. Can't you hear it drumming?"

Ray looked away, not wanting to face the old man and the even older truth he was speaking.

"Look at me, Thunderheart," the old shaman commanded.

"My name is Raymond Levoi."

Grandpa jabbed his long finger at Ray, nodding with conviction. "It is Thunderheart."

The drumming in Ray's mind increased, ripping through his objections, smashing the truths that he had always known ...

THUNDERHEART

A NOVELIZATION BY
LOWELL CHARTERS

BASED ON THE MOTION PICTURE
WRITTEN BY JOHN FUSCO

PENGUIN BOOKS

PENGUIN BOOKS

Published by the Penguin Group
Penguin Books Ltd, 27 Wrights Lane, London W8 5TZ, England
Penguin Books USA Inc., 375 Hudson Street, New York, New York 10014, USA
Penguin Books Australia Ltd, Ringwood, Victoria, Australia
Penguin Books Canada Ltd, 10 Alcorn Avenue, Toronto, Ontario, Canada M4V 3B2
Penguin Books (NZ) Ltd, 182–190 Wairau Road, Auckland 10, New Zealand

Penguin Books Ltd, Registered Offices: Harmondsworth, Middlesex, England

First published in the USA by Avon Books, a division of the Hearst Corporation, 1992
Published in Penguin Books 1992
1 3 5 7 9 10 8 6 4 2

Penguin Film and TV Tie-in edition first published 1992

Printed in England by Clays Ltd, St Ives plc

))) PROLOGUE

THE SOUL-SEEKERS WERE restless.

It was almost dawn and they still had not acquired the newly dead brother they sought. Like the wind, the seekers passed over the long, saw-toothed prairie grass, parting it, seeking him. Dressed in their Ghost Dance shirts, they lingered in the willows beside the milky little river and played in the branches of the black-trunked cottonwoods.

The spirits were confused. Had Leo Fast Elk not heard the owl call his name? Did he not know that his time was at hand? Did he not know that resistance was as useless as singing against the wind?

The sun rose like a ball of fire behind Red Deer Table, and still the high plains of South Dakota were as empty and quiet as death itself. A round-tailed raven called once in the cottonwood; a false alarm, for no one was there.

The soul-seekers searched the grass again, showing themselves in the retreating shadows as a small band of Minnicojou Sioux warriors in full ceremonial dress. That was only fitting; Leo Fast Elk was an important man. He should be welcomed into the netherworld with proper dignity.

Then the shadows shifted in the light and disappeared. Somewhere far away, the seekers heard the rhythmic sound of the heartbeat drum.

Their brother was coming to them at last.

Once, Leo Fast Elk had been worthy of his name. He had run with tireless grace on the flat, ragged track of an

Indian high school in Sioux Falls. But that had been years ago. Now he was soft and fat from an easy job and the laziness that overtakes all men in middle age.

As a boy, Leo Fast Elk had never run in cowboy boots and blue jeans. As a boy, Leo Fast Elk had run for prizes. Now he was running for his life. That fact gave his feet wings and his body the kind of stamina he thought he had lost.

After the first half mile, Leo was amazed at his own prowess. He thought he had lost this ability to cover ground with tireless strength. He felt like a bull elk with stately antlers and the next generation flowing through his loins. He felt potent, balanced, powerful, on the edge of something incredible.

I will do what I never have done. I will shape-shift right in front of my pursuers. I know it can be done.

It was what the man with the gun did in front of me. That is why he wants to kill me.

I have seen.

Now I must be as my brother the elk. I must be fleet and fast and powerful, outrunning my puny two-legged pursuer.

But the feeling of being on the edge of something incredible slid away, leaving Leo to run alone. In the next quarter mile his strength failed. His arms sagged. His breath caught in his throat. His heart began to beat wildly, faster than a man could drum.

Leo stole a quick glance over his shoulder. The pursuer was there, growing closer, seeming to fly, awesomely fast with that gun in his hands. It felt like an eagle at his back. Leo could not outrun him.

The dirt banks of the gully loomed in front of Leo. The polluted creek ran sullenly within. There was no bridge, no path of stones. The gully would slow him too much. Flying was his only hope.

A crow, perhaps. No. A red-tailed hawk, broad-shouldered and strong. On his wings I will fly to safety.

As the edge of the gully hurtled closer, Leo gathered

himself in one final effort, preparing to fling himself into the sky like the hawk he must become.

It will happen this time. It must.

As Leo ran the last few steps, peace spread through him. It was an extraordinary sensation, like getting drunk, only much more gentle, more inevitable. He had never shape-changed before. He wondered if this was how it always felt. He gathered himself for the leap, sure now that he would make it, sure that he would soar away from the man with the gun.

When Leo reached the edge of the bank, he leaped off with the assurance of a shaman or a child. He unfolded his wings, floated, and then beat his wings once. The ground fell away beneath his feet . . .

. . . and at the first moment of flight, a bullet caught him in the back. It was followed instantly by six more, small and fast, tumbling violently. The bullets hit like thousand-pound clubs, generating hydrostatic shock that passed through Leo Fast Elk in a simultaneous wave more powerful than any earthquake. His body was in shock while he was still in the air, his heart overwhelmed, his brain numbed.

One instant Leo was a hawk soaring. The next he was a man who had run headlong into an invisible brick wall at a hundred miles an hour. A red mist of blood enveloped him. Wrapped in his own shroud, he fell soundlessly. Pain washed over him like the opaque waters of the dead creek.

The soul-seekers gathered around Leo. He recognized them instantly, lifted to them, leaving pain and life behind. Once again he shape-shifted and soared, spiraling higher and higher into the arching sky.

The man with the gun hovered over Leo Fast Elk face down in the water and knew that he was dead.

>>> ONE

RAYMOND LEVOI NEVER felt better than when a deal was going down. When that happened, he was alive and free. The sensation was like flying.

This morning, a deal was going down.

Ray found Vivaldi on the FM, listened a minute, then stabbed the seek button again. Vivaldi was all wrong. He needed something that snapped.

He stopped the seek at Steely Dan. Then he jabbed the accelerator on the red Mustang convertible until the five-liter engine slammed him against the back of the seat. The Mustang growled like an eager wolf. He fought the understeer through the curving on-ramp and hit the approach to the Arlington Memorial Bridge at sixty miles an hour, shooting past a startled tourist with Georgia plates and two smoking National Airport cabs.

Smiling, Ray kept it in third and let the tach climb to four grand, eighty miles an hour. The guy he was going to meet was a nervous sort; Carl thought Ray lived in Crystal City, so he would be watching the approaches from Virginia for the red Mustang. Ray wanted to give Carl a real show, make him feel good, keep his mind off all the things that could go wrong.

He wanted Carl nice and relaxed when it all went from sugar to shit.

The Potomac was muddy and unappetizing, a slowly moving cesspool. Ray liked the river, but only in the wintertime, when it was overlaid with ice that at least looked clean. Now, in the height of summer, the river was like the city, hot and sticky and rotten.

Ray had often thought he would like to leave summertime Washington behind, but he never had. Washington was the most exciting place in the world, the one place where he had a license to do exactly what he wanted, when he wanted, however he wanted. Just like he was doing this morning.

As Ray slowed for the Lincoln Memorial exit, he lifted his foot off the accelerator and let the big, well-tuned engine back down loudly. Carl would hear that, no matter what direction he was looking. So would everybody else at the Memorial.

Ray pulled into a handicapped parking spot and shut down. Carl was waiting on the sidewalk, a blue knapsack slung over one shoulder and a folded *Washington Post* in his free hand. He looked nervously at the blue and white sign in front of Ray's car.

Poor dumb Carl. He just didn't have a crook's outlook. Even in the middle of a deal he'd still worry about a lousy parking ticket.

Ray grabbed the green gym bag from the seat beside him and stepped out of the convertible without opening the door. Carl would like that. He thought Ray had great style. That was one of the reasons this deal had gone so smoothly.

"Hey, Carl, how's it going?" Ray said.

"Shitty," Carl replied. "Birds lost again last night."

Carl was trying hard to look relaxed but he was not making it. He clung to the shoulder strap of his knapsack like he thought it would fly off his shoulder.

"You get the paper?" Ray asked as he walked past Carl, headed for the Reflecting Pool.

Carl looked sourly at the *Post* in his hand. "You don't want to read it. 7-0. Shit, even Ripken went 0-4."

Ray looked back and shook his head. "Not the bad news. The good news." He looked at the green bag.

"Oh, yeah," Carl said. He hustled to catch up with the other man.

The two of them walked past a National Park Service maintenance van that stood with its hood up on the access road halfway down the Reflecting Pool. Two park workers, a black man and an Asian, both in grimy khaki work clothes, argued over who was responsible for checking the steaming, obviously overheated radiator. Ray led Carl to a bench out of earshot of the park workers and sat down.

"How many?" Ray asked pleasantly. His tone was casual, like they were still discussing baseball.

Carl looked around furtively. The Memorial was starting to fill with summer tourists, but the only people close enough to hear anything were a dumpy couple in matching Smithsonian T-shirts and shorts. The woman was trying to work the video camcorder and position her husband in front of the Memorial at the same time. The man's legs looked like they hadn't seen sunlight in years.

"Seventy-five," Carl said. He grinned, proud of himself.

"How bad are they?" Ray asked dismissively, bad-mouthing the merchandise even before he saw it.

"Nuthin wrong with them!" Carl said defensively. "They're just as good as the Government Printing Office can make them. There was a fuckup over at Treasury, that's all. The goddamn geeks just ordered five sheets too many. They sent them back over so we could destroy them. I dug them out of the shredder bag last week but I couldn't get at the destruct log until last night."

Ray shook his head. "Doesn't anybody ever check on you janitors?"

"Custodians," Carl corrected him in a sulky tone. "I'm a goddamn GS Five, you know." He looked hard at Ray. "Nobody's going to try cashing these damn things, are they?"

Ray hesitated, as though he didn't want to discuss the rest of his business. Finally he shook his head.

"Nobody's going to cash them," Ray said. "I'm going

to sell them to a banker who needs collateral to pretty up his loan portfolio. Nobody's ever going to see these bonds again, except maybe a bank examiner, and he's not going to check serial numbers."

Carl still looked real worried. Ray grabbed the other man's shoulder and gave it a hard, manly squeeze.

"Relax, for Chrissake," Ray said. "You look like you're going to have a heart attack."

Carl sank back against the bench and rotated his head like a pitcher trying to shake the nervousness out of his arm.

"That's the way," Ray said. "Now let me see the damn things."

Carl unzipped the knapsack and laid it on the bench between them. Ray reached inside and pulled a sheaf of bond certificates out of a folder. Carl watched as Ray thumbed through them, running a quick total in his head.

"Chrissake, Richard, move over," the woman tourist in the Smithsonian T-shirt ordered as she squinted through the camcorder. "I can't get you and the Memorial in the same picture."

She had a thick Puerto Rican accent.

"The zoom, hon," her husband said patiently. "That little button under your thumb. It makes the lens go in and out."

"Oh," the wife said. "What they think of next."

Ray shoved the bonds back into the knapsack.

"Okay?" Carl asked anxiously.

"My hero," Ray said with a grin. "I make it seventy-four good ones, but I'm not going to bitch. At a penny a point, that's seventy-five hundred bucks, which is just exactly what I happen to have in this bag." He unzipped the gym bag and held it out toward Carl. "You want to count it?"

Carl stared inside and started to reach greedily.

"Now walk, Richard, like you're going up to Mr. Lincoln himself to shake his hand." The woman was backing toward the Reflecting Pool, camcorder covering her face.

Carl glanced in her direction, remembering he was in public. The greedy look vanished from his face. "Naw, Ray, that's okay. I'll owe you the C note, okay?"

"No problem."

Ray zipped the blue knapsack closed, dropped it casually on the ground at his feet, and stretched. A few seconds later a sweating jogger in shorts and a Georgetown Hoyas T-shirt approached the bench. He looked leg-sore and was breathing hard, as though he had just finished a ten-k workout.

"You mind?" the jogger said, stripping a blue knapsack off his back.

"No problem," Ray said, sliding over, making room.

The jogger pulled a plastic sports bottle from his blue knapsack and took a quick drink. Then he shoved the bottle back in his sack, which was identical to the one that contained the stolen bonds. He dropped his own sack on the ground, picked up Carl's, and slipped it onto his shoulders.

"See ya," he said, heading across the grass in the direction of the Washington Monument a half mile away.

Carl followed the jogger with his eyes, then glanced at Ray with real admiration. "You're one smooth son of a bitch."

Ray nodded agreeably. "You ain't too bad yourself. You just made yourself a nice little vacation bonus." He nodded toward the green gym bag. "Go ahead, pal. Pick it up. You've earned it."

Carl started to reach for the bag, then hesitated. He looked around the Memorial, suddenly wary again, a frightened rabbit who had just heard a suspicious noise. He stared across the Reflecting Pool, his gaze fixed on a tourist in a ten-gallon straw hat.

"Something doesn't smell right, Jenks," Carl said.

Ray followed Carl's gaze. The tourist in the straw hat had turned and was walking away.

"You're paranoid, Carl. You're watching too much television,'' Ray said. ''Grab the bag and let's get the hell out of here.''

But Carl's nerve had deserted him entirely. He stared uneasily at the bag, as though it were ticking. ''You grab it,'' he said.

''Fine,'' Ray said sharply. ''You want me to grab it, I'll grab it.'' He stood up and snatched the pack from the ground. ''There. All right? Now take it and let's go.''

Ray tossed the pack to Carl, who caught it by reflex, then stood there staring at it uncertainly.

Before Carl could move, the two men from the broken-down van appeared beside him from nowhere. One man took him by each arm. Carl dropped the bag, but it was too late.

''Easy now, Carl,'' the first man said. ''We're going for a little stroll. Just keep walking . . .''

''What the—'' Carl objected.

''He took the bag,'' Ray said. ''Did we get that on film, Anabel?''

''Got it,'' the woman with the camcorder replied. She kept her camera rolling, aimed now at Carl as her ''husband'' slipped in behind him and pulled out a pair of handcuffs.

Ray sauntered across the broad cement promenade to another bench. He was joined quickly by the jogger, who handed Ray the blue knapsack. A red-haired man with an Igloo cooler and a camera with a long telephoto lens cracked a joke. He laid the camera aside and opened the cooler, handing Ray a cold can of Coke. Anabel shut down her camera. She and her ''husband'' went over to Ray. She snapped the video cassette out of the camera and handed it to Ray. He put the evidence in the knapsack with the stolen bonds and offered the woman his drink.

''Anabel, you're outrageous,'' Ray said appreciatively. ''Do you always work surveillances so tight?''

''My momma always told me it's gotta be tight to be good,'' Anabel said.

Ray laughed as he marked the cassette with a grease pencil. He was floating now, enjoying the adrenaline rush.

"Hell of a job, you people," he said, looking up. "You all do real nice work."

The truth had finally dawned on Carl. He tried to twist away from the two agents who held him.

"Jenks, what the fuck is this?" Carl demanded. His voice was a mixture of pain and rage.

For a moment Ray glanced over at the manacled prisoner, the man who had been transformed from crook to defendant in a matter of seconds. This was the instant Ray relished, when the truth smacked the bad guy in the face like a dead fish.

"What is this?" Ray mocked slowly as he walked back toward Carl. "This is a bust, that's what it is."

Ray produced a leather credential case from the pocket of his jogging suit and let it fall open to reveal the badge and identification card inside.

"My name isn't Jenks, it's Raymond Levoi. . . . Special Agent Raymond Levoi. I'm an FBI agent, and you're under arrest for theft of government property, conspiracy, and embezzlement."

Carl's complexion went from red to purple. "Why you lying son of a bitch! I trusted you, goddamn it! We got drunk together, you scumbag!"

Ray felt a sudden blinding flash of anger. He took a step forward.

"You're the scumbag," Ray snarled in Carl's face. "You're the one who stole from your own country. You wanna stand here and discuss loyalty, asshole?"

Carl flinched and looked away, shaking his head. "I don't believe this shit," he mumbled.

"Shut up and take it like a man," Ray said, disgusted. "You're bought and paid for."

The two arresting agents led Carl away. Ray watched, surprised at his own outburst. He drew a deep breath and looked around, centering himself in the real world.

There was always an awkward moment at reentry, when

he stepped back from an undercover role and became an
FBI agent again. Carl's accusation had caught him in tran-
sition, that was all. That's why he had reacted so fiercely.
He had no qualms about lying to a defendant. He had no
reason to be sensitive. The guy was a thief, after all.

Anabel Huerta, the fishwife with the camera, brought
Ray the rest of his Coke. She looked at him closely, catching his mood. They had been on the same squad for four
years. They were closer than friends; closer even, in some
ways, than lovers. They trusted one another with their
lives. Anabel had been the closest backup position. If the
arrest had gone sour and Carl had pulled a gun, it would
have been up to Anabel to take him out.

"You okay, Rowdy?" she asked softly. She was a cop,
through and through, but she was also a woman, less afraid
to let her feelings show than were the men on the squad.

"Fine," Ray said. "I just don't need lectures from
clowns like Carl."

Anabel laughed. "Have you ever known a crook who
was happy to get busted?"

"Levoi!"

They both turned as an undercover van pulled up. The
driver, a black man, waved Ray over. "They want you on
the seventh floor, Levoi. Right away."

Ray and Anabel traded looks.

"The seventh floor," Ray said, trying to figure it out.

"Dawes," Anabel said. "The director himself. Poor
Rowdy Ray. What have you done now?"

Ray shook his head. "Damned if I know," he said.
"But I suppose I'd better go see."

"Spell my name right if he's handing out commenda-
tions," the black agent in the van called out. "I've got six
months in on this case."

"What about if he's handing out transfers to East Bumblefuck?" Ray called back over his shoulder.

"Forget you ever heard of me."

))) TWO

As THE UNIFORMED security guard led Ray down the long, wood-paneled hallway, he felt like a country priest in the Vatican. He was a street agent, a "brick," assigned to the Washington Field Office. Although WFO was in the same city as the Hoover Building, FBI headquarters, WFO might just as well have been Billings or Idaho Falls.

"I'll bet I could find the director's office myself," Ray said. "It probably says 'Director' on the door, right?"

The guard gave him a sideways look.

Ray shrugged. "It's easy. I'm a trained investigator."

The security guard gave him another look. Ray gave it back.

"Nobody comes up here without an escort," the guard said. "Not agents, not supervisory agents, not seniors, not even assistant directors. That's the way it is."

Ray smiled wryly. His buzzer—the badge and credential in the leather case in his breast pocket—would get him anywhere in the world except the White House and the seventh floor of the Hoover Building.

There were four secretaries and two executive assistants in the director's suite. Ray was passed smoothly from one to the other until the chief assistant escorted him into an office the size of a conference room. There were papers scattered across the big cherry wood desk. A coffee mug with the Bureau seal rested on a blue and white ceramic tile bearing the Department of Justice seal.

"The director will be along in a moment," the aide said. "I'll bring you some coffee."

"Black, no sugar."

From the corner of his eye, Ray checked his reflection in the glass over a photo on the wall. Brooks Brothers worsted properly squared, silk four-in-hand properly Windsored, blue oxford-cloth shirt spotless. Ready to fly.

Ray had been in the director's office once before, with the other forty graduates in his Quantico class. This time it was going to be harder to blend into the woodwork.

He looked through the glass to the photo beneath. It took him a moment to recognize Allan Pinkerton, Lincoln's bodyguard and chief intelligence operative during the Civil War. Ray smiled to himself. Director Dawes had a good sense of history, or a bad sense of bureaucratic turf. Pinkerton had been the first head of the United States Secret Service. J. Edgar Hoover would never have allowed such a photo on an FBI wall.

Ray inspected the rest of the photos on the director's wall, searching for more insight into William Dawes. There were political photos—a portrait of the President, a staged still photo of Dawes receiving the oath of office from the attorney general, and several of the director with foreign dignitaries, including Prince Charles and Mikhail Gorbachev.

But most of the photos were candid photos of FBI agents in action. Ray recognized one of five G-men escorting a Nazi saboteur to a court hearing, and another of two foreign counterintelligence specialists arresting a Soviet diplomat as he emptied one of Joseph Walker's dead-drops. The most vivid photo was a grainy blowup of a motion-picture frame showing FBI agents in raid jackets outside a burning house—the South Los Angeles bungalow where five members of the Symbionese Liberation Army had died.

An odd, sepia-toned photo puzzled Ray. There were five men in thirties suits, straw boaters, and felt hats stiffly facing the camera like men confronting a firing squad.

J. Edgar Hoover was in the center of the photo. He had been a short man, and Ray recognized him instantly. Next to the Bureau's first director stood his aide and confidante, Clyde Tolson. But the other three men were strangers. They looked lean and tough, almost leathery, particularly in comparison to the round-faced, corpulent Hoover. Ray studied each man individually. All were dark and clear-eyed. All three looked faintly familiar.

Ray was still trying to place the faces when the corridor door opened and William Dawes strode in.

"Levoi," the director said.

"Sir."

Dawes was the first career FBI agent ever to become director. A tall, aggressive, well-tanned athlete who still played power tennis with agents half his age, he crossed the office with the kind of patrician self-confidence that was the result of breeding or long association with power. He offered Ray a hand. The grip was firm and dry and practiced.

Dawes looked at the wall of framed photos. "Like my little gallery?"

Ray nodded. "I recognize everything except this one," he said, indicating the sepia print.

"That's the squad that conducted the only field opera-tion Mr. Hoover ever took part in," Dawes said. He chuckled. "He thought it would look good in the press, so he waited until his street agents got a line on a high-profile suspect down south somewhere, then he and Clyde flew in and made the arrest themselves."

Ray looked at the picture with more interest.

"Hoover and Clyde had the help of some backup men, of course," Dawes added dryly.

The director pointed to the three strangers in the pic-ture. "You may not hear of these guys in the official Bu-reau histories. They were called the Hat Squad."

Ray had heard about them, but all that showed on his face was interest as he turned to Dawes.

"The Hat Squad," Dawes continued, "was recruited by Mr. Hoover to make deals with men like Dillinger and Pretty Boy Floyd. They were the toughest men the Bureau had to offer, and they went along to make sure nothing went wrong when Mr. Hoover made his first arrest.''

Ray started to say something but thought better of it. Dawes read his reaction quickly and nodded.

"Exactly," Dawes said. "It was very nearly a disaster. The agents spotted the crooks' car and got it pulled over. Mr. Hoover leaped out, gun in hand, and shot himself in the foot. Literally."

Ray looked at the director, astonished.

Dawes nodded his head. "That's right, Levoi. It was not one of the Bureau's brightest moments. The Hat Squad spent more time making sure the press never found out about it than they did apprehending the suspect.

"I keep this picture on the wall as a reminder to myself. I'm the director, now. I'm not a street agent. I let the men in the field take care of the operational details. Then I back them to the hilt.''

Dawes gave Ray a thoughtful look, letting his message settle in.

The director turned and went to his desk. As he sat, a change seemed to come over him. He settled into the high-backed chair, gestured for Ray to take a seat across from him, and picked up the first memo from a stack on the gleaming cherry wood.

"Sit down, Levoi." Dawes's tone was formal, businesslike, as though the two men had never spoken before. "Do you like to fish?"

Ray sat down.

"I don't fish, sir," Ray said, his own tone as formal as the director's.

"You used to fish. As a boy."

Suddenly Ray felt uneasy, as though he were on a witness stand, being quizzed by a defense attorney.

"I fished a time or two, yessir."

"With your father?"

"That's correct."

"Your real father?"

Ray hesitated, suddenly recognizing the trap. Then he barged ahead, getting it over with.

"I didn't know my real father, sir," Ray said with outward calm. "He died when I was a baby."

Dawes glanced up from the memo sharply. "No. He died when you were seven."

Ray met Dawes's gaze and said not one word. After a moment, Dawes looked back to the memo.

"Your father had a very interesting lineage, didn't he? French, Scots . . . and Indian. Sioux Indian, I think."

The subject was one Ray had spent more than thirty years trying to forget, ever since he had been old enough to know his father was a drunk.

"Well, I know I've got French, Scots-Irish, and Lithuanian," Ray said. "Somewhere back there is some Sioux, I was told, or maybe it was Cherokee." He shrugged. "I forget."

Dawes shook his head with disapproval. "Sioux. Your paternal grandmother. Come on, Ray. You know better."

Ray shrugged again. "I've never dug too far into my background, sir, one way or the other. A man makes his own life. It's the American way."

Dawes started to respond, then seemed to think better of it. He went back to the memo. When he finished, he looked up with unreadable gray eyes.

"I'm pulling you out of the Washington Field Office for a couple of days," the director said. "I have a special assignment for you."

Ray felt a sudden rush of adrenaline. Then he remembered the director's interest in his Indian background and his enthusiasm faded.

"Sir, I just made an arrest this morning," Ray said quickly. "We grabbed a janitor who had stolen a couple million dollars' worth of Treasury bonds from the Government Printing Office burn bag. It's going to be a fairly high-profile—"

Dawes interrupted. "Somebody else can take the case,"

he said flatly. "I have a job that needs someone with a special background. I need you."

Ray swallowed his objection and said nothing. Only a fool or the President argued with the director of the FBI.

"You'll be part of a two-man team," Dawes continued, "working under Frank Coutelle, Assistant Special Agent in Charge, an ASAC, in Denver. You know him?"

For an instant Ray remembered the hard-faced men beside Hoover in the sepia photo on Dawes's wall.

"They call him Cooch, don't they?" Ray asked.

Dawes nodded.

"I met him once, on the range at Quantico," Ray said. "I've studied his case abstracts. So has everybody else in the Bureau, I guess. The guy's kind of a legend."

"That he is," Dawes said approvingly.

He smiled at Ray, grateful that the other man was finally falling into the expected patterns of response. Ray smiled in return, keeping his uneasiness to himself with the ease of a lifetime of practice.

"You'll be meeting Cooch in South Dakota. You're both going into an area called the badlands. Indian reservation."

Ray didn't say anything. He had connected the dots the moment the director mentioned South Dakota. He put on his game face, the one that gave away nothing, and settled in to hear about the assignment he knew he was going to hate.

Dawes leaned back in the tall chair, folded his hands on the rich, well-polished cherry wood, and watched Ray like a gray-eyed hawk.

"There's been a homicide," Dawes said after a moment. "Actually, there have been several deaths over the years. They seem to be the work of a militant Indian group operating on the reservation. They call themselves ARM, the Aboriginal Rights Movement, and they are as much at odds with tribal authorities as they are with us."

Ray shifted his lean body and tried to look a lot more interested than he was.

"The place is a tinderbox," Dawes said flatly. "There's been a good deal of violence. We're going to go into what amounts to a foreign country, trying to serve as peacekeepers."

The certainty grew in Ray that this speech was a condensation of one Dawes had already given, or was about to give, probably to a congressional committee. Ray nodded to show he was being properly attentive.

"It's my belief that with an American Indian representative out there, we can diffuse some of the tension, improve relations," Dawes concluded with a meaningful look at Ray.

"Sir, I understand what you're saying," Ray said, "but I'm not an Indian. I mean, I may have a little Indian blood in me somewhere, but so do a lot of other people. I know less about being an Indian than I do about being Lithuanian. And I'm—"

Dawes cut him off. "You have enough Indian blood for our friends in Congress," he said flatly. "And enough to satisfy the media."

Ray's game face slipped.

The director drew a deep breath and started over. "Look, Levoi. Nobody is asking you to weave baskets or make rain. We're just trying to take some of the heat out of the situation."

"I appreciate that, sir," Ray said evenly, "but I'm not sure I'm your man. I've never made a big deal out of my ethnic background in the past, and I'm not interested in being somebody's token buck now, not even the Bureau's. I'm a street agent, not a public relations gesture."

Dawes's gray eyes turned glacial. "Then look at it this way, Levoi. It would do any street agent's career good to spend a little time with someone the caliber of Frank Coutelle. The man has been in Special Operations almost as long as you've been alive."

"I'm older than I look. Sir."

Dawes ignored him. "And remember, a coin has two sides. A negative evaluation from a senior supervisor like

Cooch has a nasty way of sticking in an agent's personnel file for a long time."

The director's tone said he had been pushed as far as was prudent. Farther, actually; but then, Ray had never been known for his prudence.

"I understand, sir," Ray said. He stood to leave.

"Draw your travel vouchers from the girls outside."

As the director spoke, he put aside the Levoi memorandum and reached for another from the neat stack on his desk.

Ray turned and had his hand on the door when the director stopped him.

"One more thing, Levoi. If Cooch seems a little testy, a little impatient, just remember that he's under the gun. He has three days to wind this thing up."

"I understand, sir."

And Ray did. Cooch's balls were in a real nutcracker. The murders had been going on for years, and now Cooch was expected to wave a magic wand and solve the whole mess in three days.

"That means you have three days, too," the director added. "Close the door behind you."

As Ray passed the little photo gallery, he stole one more glance at the faded sepia print. This time he realized that Dawes looked a good deal like J. Edgar Hoover, after all.

))) THREE

THE CORN-FED BLOND United Airlines flight attendant
gushed with Chamber of Commerce enthusiasm, even
though her flight was the functional equivalent of a red-
eye, the first daily arrival into the Rapid City Airport.

"Ladies and gentlemen," she said breathlessly as the
airliner touched down, "welcome to the regional airport
at Rapid City, South Dakota, out where the Real West
begins."

As though to punctuate her words, the plane shivered
and shuddered subtly, as though caught in a strong prairie
wind. Gradually the vibrations subsided as the plane
slowed and taxied toward the terminal.

With no eagerness, Ray Levoi peered out of the dark-
ened cabin window at the landscape of the place where he
had been born. He didn't need daylight to know what was
out there. Beneath the shelter of the night were muddy
ravines, muddy hills, gritty buffalo grass and cottonwood.
Mud in all colors and shapes, streams too thick to drink
and too thin to plow. That was where there was water.

Where there was no water, there was dust—dry, gritty
dust and a wind that droned on forever like an old woman
with nothing new to say.

Welcome to South Dakota. Welcome all to hell.

Closing his eyes didn't shut out the view. Ray had seen
it too many times as a child, remembered it too well despite decades of trying to forget. Once a teacher had told
him hell was a place of fire. Ray was certain that hell was
built from layers of reservation mud and dust.

20

Grimly Ray opened his eyes and peered out the airplane window, trying to see if anything had changed since his mother had shaken the dust of the reservation from her shoes and headed for Chicago, taking her six-year-old bastard with her.

In the west, backlit by the setting moon, the Black Hills rose gaunt and barren, blunted by time and erosion. Once they had been mountains, then they had been grains of silt washed down to the bottom of an unbelievably ancient sea, then they had been grassy plains at the foot of a monstrous sheet of ice, then the land had risen and streams had eaten down through eon after eon of mud, carving mounds from the flats.

The Black Hills were like Ray's memories, badly eroded shadows of too many yesterdays.

Off toward the north and east, where the sky was beginning to show light, the Great Plains fell away in a rolling, undifferentiated landscape that was dotted here and there with the dark green. The green came where river bottom stands of cottonwoods or box elders had managed to take root in the hostile, crumbling soil.

Trees marked the presence of water. Sometimes the water took the form of sloughs big enough to survive from one wet winter to another. Sometimes the water was captured in small streams that braided their way across the land like lost children seeking a home. Most often there was no water, which meant there was no life, nothing moving but the wind rasping away at eons of dried mud.

On the flats and eroded hills, away from the watercourses lined with green, the land was brown and spare, as though it had been cleared with a gigantic blowtorch. There was a little grass and a lot of dirt. In some places wind and water had cut deep gashes in the face of the land. Time and the elements were still at work in those places, deepening the scars, carving the grassy highlands into smaller and smaller pieces. The best of the land was barely marginal. The rest was frankly useless.

Ray stared out the window and wondered what in such

a place could be worth enough to make men and women kill one another. There was no answer but the obvious one—in Washington, people killed each other over five dollars' worth of crack. Why should Sioux Indians be any smarter?

As the United jet made a slow turn onto the taxiway, its landing lights picked out the shadowy form of a coyote loping off across the sparse grasslands. Trash from the airport Dumpster showed in the animal's muzzle like an oversized smile.

"Eat hearty," Ray muttered. "Cold fries and grease-burgers have to be better than anything you'll catch on the open land."

Ray jerked down the window shade, shutting out his view of a land that was so depleted it couldn't even support scavengers.

The plane eased to a stop. Slowly the jetway was wheeled up to the nose of the parked aircraft. The door popped open. There were only a dozen passengers on the flight.

Ray let the other civilians deplane before he got up and went forward to collect his service revolver from the captain. Even FBI agents had to abide by FAA regulations regarding transportation of firearms.

Feeling better with the familiar weight of the revolver back in place, Ray stepped out into the jetway. He had expected his new partner to be waiting, but a sleepy passenger agent was the only other person in sight. The agent gave Ray a quick once-over, noting his summer suit, his briefcase, and the trench coat over his shoulder. All of it classified him as an Easterner, a tenderfoot, a foreigner; in short, no one to care about. The agent looked away.

Ray took some small pleasure in the reaction. At least his dirt-poor South Dakota origins no longer showed on the outside.

Looking neither right nor left, Ray walked down the long carpeted jetway. Once inside the deserted terminal building, he searched for a pay phone. A glass display case distracted him. The case was a Chamber of Commerce project, packed with tourism advertisements and local exotica like a stuffed ring-necked pheasant, a stuffed walleye pike from one of the Missouri River reservoirs, and glossy color photographs of Mount Rushmore.

Ray's glance quickly went to the glass shelf below, where Indian artifacts were displayed. There was a deerskin Ghost Dance shirt, a willow coup stick, a choker made of the hollow wing bones of geese, and a skin drum whose head was painted with what had once been bright designs. The drum was obviously quite old, for the designs had faded to their darkest primary colors.

Yet for an instant the instrument seemed vivid to Ray, as familiar as the faces in the sepia picture in the director's office, as familiar as the landscape he had seen from the window of the plane. Ray stopped and stared intently at the drum.

Ray went closer, drawn by something he couldn't name. In his mind he heard a distant thunder, a gigantic heartbeat, and his own heartbeat shifted to keep time. Ice prickled and slid down his spine, yet he couldn't bring himself to look away from the medicine drum.

"LEE-voy," a hard, flat, uninflected voice said. "Or is it Lay-VWA, like the French?"

Ray straightened up and whirled around. The man facing him could have stepped from the sepia photo . . . or from Ray's own mirror.

Reality shifted like cards in a deck, lifting and shuffling, revealing and concealing faces while a medicine drum thundered with a primal beat. For a few spinning instants Ray didn't know whether he was himself or a long-dead agent in a photo or a wild young kid or an old Frank Coutelle—or a lean coyote running into the dawn with a McDonald's bag clenched in his jaws.

Ray hated those amorphous instants when nothing was what it should be. He thought they had ended with his childhood nightmares.

He had been wrong.

Deliberately Ray focused on Frank Coutelle. The man was tall and dark, darker even than Ray. He had the hard, clear eyes of a hawk. His body was whip-thin, the build of a horseman or a distance runner. His face had the leathery look of a man who spent a lot of hours in the sun and the wind, a Gary Cooper face with harder angles.

Dressed in a business suit, Coutelle lounged against a pillar with his hands in his pockets, giving the impression that he had materialized there from one instant to the next. It was an old trick among FBI agents of a certain type. Ray had used it himself.

"Works better with brimstone and a red flash," Ray said, stepping forward and holding out his hand. "Ray Levoi, Mr. Coutelle, and since you're the case agent on this one, you can pronounce it any way you want to."

Coutelle straightened up and shook hands.

"Cooch," he corrected Ray. "And haven't we met somewhere between here and there?"

"Quantico, a dozen years ago. You lectured my new agent class on the Hobbs Act and labor racketeering. I'm surprised you remember."

Coutelle shrugged, as though his memory was nothing unusual. "C'mon. It's eighty-seven miles to the reservation. Let's hit it."

He stepped onto an escalator and rode, seemingly occupied with his own thoughts. Ray, a step below, let a few seconds pass before he tried to make conversation.

"We have any field agents out there?" Ray asked.

Coutelle shook his head. "Just you and me. That's why they call it the lone prairie."

"Who found the body? Locals?"

"I'm going in as cold as you are."

Ray got the message and shut up. He watched the walls slide past for a few seconds. Then Coutelle broke the silence.

"Turn your head to the right for a second," the senior agent said softly.

Ray looked to the right, searching for whatever Coutelle

had seen. There was nothing but wall. He looked at Coutelle, who gave him a sardonic grin and a nod of his dark head.

"They were right," Coutelle said. "In the right light, with your head turned like that, and if I squint just a little, you do bear a slight resemblance to Sal Mineo in *Arrows on the Prairie*. You ever see that one?"

It was an old game that agents played among themselves and against others. Ray called it the mouth game. He treated it like the semi-serious contest it was, bull elks shouldering to assert dominance. That kind of shouldering was routine to Ray. He usually won the brief contests because he had the good sense to choose his battles carefully. This was a contest he knew he couldn't win, so he let the challenge pass.

Coutelle waited for a response. When he realized there wasn't going to be one, he nodded as though he thought Ray had shown good sense.

"That's right, Sal," Coutelle said. "Other than your straight hair and the shape of your features, you being out here is sort of like pissing into the wind. So drop probing-investigative-questions bullshit and stick to your public relations assignment and we'll get along just fine."

Coutelle dug a package of Lucky Strikes out of his shirt pocket and shook one out.

"You want a bull?" he said, just to show there were no hard feelings.

Ray looked at the Luckies casually. "I haven't seen those things in a while." He shook his head. "No, thanks, I don't smoke."

Coutelle nodded, not bothered by the implied insult.

"Good for you," he said. "Good for you."

Then Coutelle turned and walked through the revolving terminal door to a Diplomat four-door parked in the red zone. Ray tossed his gear in the back seat and climbed into the passenger seat, the wife seat, the one reserved for the junior agent.

Coutelle snapped the shifter into gear and pulled away

from the curb with enough force to push Ray back into
the seat.

"Go to sleep, Sal," Coutelle said. "It could be the last
you get for three days."

))) FOUR

RAY AWOKE ON the moon. The summer sun reflected off barren mud dunes and crumbling buttes and flooded the car with heat and light. The air was stale and as close and unwanted as bad breath. The atmosphere reminded him of Washington at its worst, just before a thunderstorm. He looked around, trying to orient himself.

Yeah, South Dakota, just like in my childhood nightmares where men turned into wolves or birds and then back again.

Shit, Ray thought, rubbing his arms against a chill that had nothing to do with the weather, *I could have gone the rest of my life without remembering those damn dreams.*

Frank Coutelle drove like a man on autopilot. Ray glanced at the Rolex on his wrist; he had slept for almost exactly an hour. He looked up at the speedometer. The needle was nailed at eighty-five mph, as it had been when he fell asleep. They had to be getting close.

A bullet-dimpled roadside sign flashed past as though to confirm his hunch:

ENTERING RESERVATION

Ray stretched and tried to work the knot out of the back of his neck by rotating his head.

"Jesus but it's wonderful to be a federal agent," he muttered. "The work takes you to such wonderful places."

"Hell, Sal, ain't it nice to be home?"

"The name is Ray, Cooch."

27

"I know, Sal."

Ray shut up and looked at the stark landscape.

A hundred yards onto the reservation, the blacktopped state highway became a dirt road. There was little difference in dry weather; the clay surface was packed brick-hard by the sun and the wind. The road traveled along the edge of a broad, flat table for a mile, then dropped down the face of a mudstone bluff into the heart of the badlands.

Coutelle slowed, watching the roadside for something. A pair of dirt tracks broke off to the left and disappeared behind a line of slumping crags. He braked and turned onto the track. The Diplomat's suspension hit bottom once, then settled into a steady thumping as the sedan found the track and followed it.

They drove for almost a mile. It was long enough for Ray to begin feeling lost in the bleak landscape. The badlands seemed to stretch to infinity in all directions. The heat went from uncomfortable to oppressive. The air was too sultry to breathe. After a few minutes Ray loosened his tie and opened the top button of his white shirt.

Coutelle caught the motion from the corner of his eye and said, "Old J. Edgar never knew about the badlands when he designed the Bureau dress code, did he?"

Before Ray could answer, Coutelle pulled off the road and stopped.

"Showtime, Sal."

Coutelle turned off the engine, stepped out of the car, and set off across the cracked gumbo landscape without looking back to see whether Ray was following.

The body lay on a flat little spot atop a nose of high ground. The view would have done credit to the moon-blasted earth and ravines, nothing green, nothing human. The body had been covered with a yellow plastic groundsheet that was held down by a dozen heavy rocks.

"I told 'em to leave the crime scene alone until we got here," Cooch said, disgusted. "Tribal cops don't know shit about gathering evidence. But I figured the stupid bas-

tards would know enough to leave somebody at the site to
keep the coyotes away.''

Cooch threw his smoking cigarette butt onto the ground.
''Give me a hand with these rocks.''

The hot wind lifted one corner of the groundsheet the
moment Ray took away the first rock. The foul smell of
death and decay slid out from under the waterproof
groundsheet like an invisible, oily river.

Ray tried not to react. Crime scenes were an exercise
in the suspension of normal human emotions. He stacked
the rocks to one side. When he was finished, he and Coutelle peeled back the groundsheet.

The body lay face down on the barren ground. The
blood-caked wounds were dark and dry. Horseflies, drawn
by the smell, had crawled in under the edges of the sheet
and were at work on the wounds.

''You can have the honor of making this poor devil's
acquaintance,'' Coutelle said.

Ray drew a deep breath before he knelt down beside the
body and waved a hand across the wounds to scatter the
flies. Trying to touch as little as possible, he fished a flat,
sweat-darkened wallet from the left hip pocket of the dead
man's jeans. The wallet yielded a South Dakota driver's
license and several other pieces of identification.

Ray read the license aloud. ''Leo Fast Elk.''

Coutelle grunted. ''Not fast enough.''

''DOB of seven, three, fifty-two,'' Ray said. ''That
makes him thirty-seven.''

''Immaterial,'' Coutelle said.

''Single.''

''Immaterial.''

''Mailing address is Box Twelve, Community Three,
Badlands Reservation.''

''Cheap digs, Sal. Penny ante.''

''This other card identifies him as the fifth member of
the Tribal Council.''

Coutelle looked up from the body. ''An investigative

key, Sal," he said, deadpan. "Maybe what might be called a clue."

Ray ignored him and read further on the card. "Head of the Water and Land Resources Committee."

"Immaterial," Coutelle said. "What do you make of the wounds?"

Ray studied the pattern a half-dozen bullets had stitched across Leo Fast Elk's back.

"Automatic weapon, small to medium caliber, M-1 carbine, maybe, no bigger than that, certainly." Ray shifted his view and continued, "Maybe as small as a .223, which could make it an M-16 or its civilian equivalent."

When Coutelle said nothing, Ray bent down and tried to see the front of the body without disturbing the scene too much.

"No through-and-through," Ray said. "That means high-velocity rounds with soft tips. Armor-piercing round would have passed through him and ended up in the next county."

Coutelle looked at him thoughtfully. "Very nice, Sal. Very clinical. But probably wrong."

Coutelle dug a pair of half glasses out of his breast pocket and perched them on the end of his nose. He waved a persistent fly off one wound and read the pattern himself.

"Did you know that double-ought buckshot pellets are precisely .32 caliber, Sal? One round from a twelve-gauge would explain this pattern as easily as a burst from an automatic weapon."

Ray closed the wallet and stood up. "Look, I never claimed to be a homicide dick or a forensics expert, okay? I'm just a brick agent. I didn't ask for this job and I sure as hell didn't ask to be sent out to East Bumblefuck, South Dakota, to take a ration of shit from some supervisory ASAC who has a case of the ass."

Coutelle listened to the outburst with an expression of polite disinterest on his face. Then he reached over and took Leo Fast Elk's old wallet out of Ray's hand and dropped it into his own coat pocket.

"Take a walk," Coutelle said. "Do a spiral from here. Brick agents do know how to do a ground-search spiral, don't they? Look for shell casings, anything. Maybe you can pick up enough for a merit badge in crime scenes."

Coutelle moved off in the opposite direction, starting a search spiral of his own. Ray watched him for a moment, trying to understand the older agent's purpose in riding him so hard. Maybe Coutelle had just been out on the range too long. Maybe he was permanently field-sour.

Or maybe he was digging to see what kind of agents headquarters was dispatching on temporary duty, nowadays.

Ray turned his back on Coutelle and started his own search pattern. He had covered fifty or sixty feet when Coutelle called out from beside a patch of buffalo grass at the edge of the drop-off. Ray marked his own position, then crossed to where the other agent stood looking down at the ground.

The soil beside the patch of buffalo grass had been loosened by the last rain. Someone had etched a deep circle in the soft gumbo with a stick. A single white eagle feather stood upright, its quill embedded in the mud at the center of the circle. The hot badlands wind caught the vanes of the feather and made it dance slowly, as though it were alive.

"Now, Sal, that's what you call a clue," Coutelle said. "Get the camera. I want shots of that feather from every point of the compass."

Ray started for the crime scene kit next to the body. After two steps he stopped dead. The wind had suddenly shifted, bringing a distant sound with it.

Ray and Coutelle heard the sound at the same instant. They stood silently for a moment, turning their heads, trying to locate the source.

"Company," Ray said, pointing out over the mudstone landscape. "There."

Coutelle followed the gesture and squinted.

Ray's eyes were younger, stronger, quicker to change

focus. It was a long five-count before Coutelle picked out the tiny plume of dust that rose like a dancing eagle feather from the flats to the west.

"Motorcycle," Ray said. "One man, riding alone. He's headed this way."

Coutelle squinted into the distance for a moment, watching until he was certain.

"Maybe it's another clue, Sal."

"And maybe somebody is coming back to the scene of the crime," Ray retorted.

Coutelle had already thought of that. "Grab yourself some cover. Fast."

Ray and Coutelle headed for the rocks.

The motorcycle came on fast. Within thirty seconds, Ray could see that it was old, mud-caked, and hard-used; a 500-cc Triumph trailing an oily blue exhaust cloud. The rider was a big man, as heavy through the middle as a side of beef. He wore a big black Stetson, a black shirt, jeans, boots, and dark glasses.

At the base of the bluff, the rider turned the bike and aimed it at the slumped slope. The exhaust plume turned to a cloud of dust as the tires hit the loose clay. Casually the rider took his boots from the pegs, using his feet as outriggers while he nursed the throttle to keep the back wheel turning but not spinning.

The engine complained and choked and seemed on the edge of dying all the way up the hill. The engine cut out once, but the rider kicked it back into life with one stroke and kept on coming, headed right toward Leo Fast Elk's body.

When the machine crested the slope, Ray saw that the rider was an Indian. He had strong, almost Asian features and skin that looked like a Frederic Remington bronze.

Sitting Bull wearing Ray-Ban aviators.

Ray wondered if his first impulse had been correct, if this was the cool killer coming back to tidy up.

The big Indian certainly didn't seem surprised to find Leo's body there. He punched the kill button and kicked

off his bike like he was dismounting a horse. He took a
rolled quilt from the saddle seat and walked to the body.
There he squatted with his back to Ray's hiding spot, in-
specting the corpse and looking around.

Behind the sunglasses, his features seemed carved from
stone. If the sight or smell of the corpse was bothering
him, it didn't show. After a moment he reached into the
pocket of his black shirt and pulled out a white cloth bag.
Then he bent over the body.

While the cyclist was distracted, Ray pulled his gun,
slipped from the shelter of the rocks, and started forward.
He was twenty feet away when he recognized the cloth
bag. Bull Durham.

The guy was rolling a smoke.

Then Ray realized that the big Indian was scattering
pinches of the shredded tobacco.

What the hell?

Suddenly the big man froze, as though he sensed the
cold, one-eyed stare of Ray's .357 Magnum.

"Hands on your head," Ray barked. "Now!"

The big Indian didn't listen. He started to turn around.
He had made a few inches when Ray's foot caught him in
the middle of the back and shoved him face first into the
cracking, dry gumbo. The Ray-Bans were knocked off.
They lay face down like a large, dead insect.

"Move and you die," Ray said roughly. "You're bought
and paid for."

"Okay, okay, man," the big man muttered. "Take it
easy. Don't shoot."

The Indian showed no signs of wanting to fight, but Ray
moved carefully. He looked over to make sure Coutelle
had moved into a covering position. Coutelle nodded.

Ray shoved the Magnum into his belt, snatched the
handcuffs from their place on his belt at the small of his
back, and dragged the prisoner's arms behind him. The
bracelets were almost too small to fit on the burly man's
wrists.

"Jesus, he's a big bastard," Ray said.

"Take it easy, Sal," Coutelle said. "He's under control now."

Ray gave Coutelle a hard look but said nothing.

Despite his words, the senior agent kept his gun out while he walked over to inspect the motorcycle. He reached beneath the rider's seat and dragged a short-barreled pump shotgun from a leather boot.

He held the gun up so that Ray could see it.

"What do you bet this thing is loaded with double-aught buckshot?" Coutelle asked.

Ray didn't bother to answer.

The senior agent walked over and hunkered down beside the handcuffed prisoner. "You come back to clean up, pal?"

The big man rolled his head to one side and glared at Coutelle. "Leo's been out here too long, man. I was just gonna take him home for a decent burial ceremony."

"This is a restricted area, Geronimo," Ray said.

"Not restricted for Indi'ns," the man said calmly.

"What's your name?" asked Coutelle.

"Ain't Geronimo, chief."

Ray and Coutelle traded looks of mild surprise. Murder suspects weren't usually so confident, once they were in handcuffs.

Ray dug a wallet out of the man's hip pocket. The wallet was newer and better stocked than Leo Fast Elk's. Ray tossed it to Coutelle and went on frisking the prisoner.

The big Indian twisted his head around and stared at Ray with eyes that were cold and angry.

"Look, I think maybe you two guys got off at the wrong exit, yeah? You were looking for Mount Rushmore, right?"

"Cut the bullshit," Ray said. "What's your name?"

"I'm a full-blooded Oglala Sioux, born and raised on this reservation. My friends know my name. I don't have to explain myself to no one."

"Wrong," Ray shot back. "You're a murder suspect

and you're under arrest. Now answer up. Who the fuck are you?''

It was Coutelle who answered. "Bad news, Sal. He's a cop.''

Ray looked up, stunned. Coutelle let the Indian's wallet flop open, revealing an old, somewhat battered badge.

"Tribal cop," Coutelle continued. "His name is Walter Crow Horse.''

Ray looked down, suddenly realizing that his knee was firmly planted in a brother officer's back.

"Shit," Ray said.

He slid the offending knee off onto the dirt and dug a handcuff key out of his watch pocket.

"Sorry, man," Ray mumbled. "I thought . . .''

Ray's voice died. It was obvious that he had thought the tribal cop was a tribal crook.

Once the cuffs were off, Crow Horse rolled over, grabbed his sunglasses and hat, and struggled to stand up. Coutelle was there instantly, helping him up, dusting him off, and handing him back the wallet and badge.

"You'll have to forgive this agent, Officer Crow Horse," Coutelle said smoothly. "He's just a little aggressive. He didn't mean any harm.''

Crow Horse knocked the dust out of his Stetson and put the glasses back over a faint smirk. He tossed his longish hair and fitted the hat back in place. Then he looked at the two FBI agents.

"Coutelle, right? We got the wire you were coming. And this must be the Indian official.''

Coutelle stepped forward, as though handling a diplomatic introduction. "Yeah, this is Ray, uh, Ray Little Weasel. Yeah, that's it, Little Weasel.''

Ray shot Coutelle a disgusted look and started to correct the introduction. Then he met Crow Horse's gaze head on and decided to leave the question of his name—and his Indian blood—alone.

The Sioux officer nodded and Ray nodded back, mim-

icking Crow Horse in case it was the Indian way of doing
things.

"Oh-han, Kola," Crow Horse said formally. Then he
nodded toward the dead body. "Leo's gotta get to burial.
He's gotta make the journey."

"Huh?" Ray said.

Crow Horse looked at him, surprised, and Ray immediately realized he should have kept his mouth shut.

"Oh, uh, the journey," Ray said quickly. "Right. Right.
Don't want to get in the way of that."

Crow Horse nodded, mollified. "It's time."

Ray stared at him for a moment, unsure how to respond.

Cooch stepped into the gap. "I understand the journey
is important, Crowfoot, but—"

"Crow *Horse,"* the Indian interrupted, correcting Coutelle.

"Yeah, well, I'm afraid the only trip Leo's going to be
taking for a while is to see the medical examiner in Rapid
City. In case you didn't know, officer, violation of the
Major Crimes Act on—"

"Yeah," Crow Horse interrupted again. "I know the
reservation is within the jurisdiction of the Federal Bureau
of Intimidation. I know all about that." Behind his glasses,
Crow Horse's face was cold and impassive.

"Good," Coutelle said. "Then if you'll stand aside and
let us get on with it . . ."

Crow Horse said something to Ray in a language that
was like the landscape—alien and familiar in the same
instant.

Ray turned his head, as though he hadn't heard clearly.

"I just asked when we could have the body for the ceremony," Crow Horse said.

His expression said he knew full well that Ray had heard
but did not understand the spoken Lakota language.

Ray felt a momentary irritation at being so transparent.
Crow Horse was no bumpkin, regardless of his looks.

"We'll have to let you know on that," Ray said carefully. He tried to relax a little, hoping to turn the dynamics of the situation in his favor. "I know it must be hard for you to see Leo like this. Have you known him long?"

Silently Crow Horse stared at Ray for several seconds, as though deciding whether to answer. Behind the Ray-Bans, the Indian was studying the FBI agent from dusty Bally loafers to dark suit, rep tie, and on up to the sunglasses which were, ironically, nearly identical to Crow Horse's.

"Nice shades," Crow Horse said.

With that he turned away and strode toward his motorcycle. Interview over.

But Crow Horse wasn't through with Leo Fast Elk. He pulled something from a bag on the motorcycle and went to the corpse. With the quickness of a cat, Crow Horse bent over Leo's body. As he moved, he broke open a locking Buck knife with a five-inch blade. With one deft pass of the blade, Crow Horse sliced off a short hank of the dead man's hair.

For an instant, Ray thought Crow Horse had actually scalped Fast Elk.

"What the hell do you think you're doing?" Ray yelled.

Crow Horse stood, blade still in his hand, and showed Ray the lock of hair in his hand.

"His mother needs a piece of his hair. It's for the Keeping of the Souls ceremony."

He gave Ray a bitter, scornful look before he folded the blade into the handle with one hand and returned the knife to his saddlebag. He fished a leather pouch out of the bag, put the lock of hair into it, and snapped it into his shirt pocket. With a quick flourish, he settled the black Stetson on his head, slung his leg over the bike, and rocked it off the kickstand with one continuous motion.

The bike rolled forward over the edge of the mesa and onto the slope he had just climbed. Crow Horse freewheeled down the steep slope for a hundred feet before he engaged the clutch and started the engine on the roll. He was doing forty miles an hour when he hit the bottom.

With a roar he accelerated into the distant heat waves and vanished.

"So much for ethnic solidarity, huh, Sal," Coutelle said when the sound of the Triumph had faded away.

Ray didn't reply. Instead, he turned away and listened for a moment to the sound of the wind in the badlands. His eye fell on the white tail feather inside the deeply traced circle. Its meaning was as enigmatic as the strange, guttural language Crow Horse had used to test him.

Welcome to Indian Country, Ray. Welcome home. Jesus.

))) FIVE

THE SPEEDOMETER WAS pegged at eighty, but Coutelle lounged like he was on a Sunday drive, watching the passing landscape. As Ray studied the lanky agent, he realized that Coutelle's casual style behind the wheel was the result of long practice. He had worked out of the Denver Field Office for most of the last decade—ten years in a region where the only route from point A to point B was a blue-line highway. No interstates, no four-lane highways, no commuter airlines, no helicopter junkets, just four rubber tires and a pair of hands on the steering wheel.

Not even much of a landscape to keep you awake, judging by the scene that unrolled in front of the bug-stained windshield. Crumbling clay hills, barren flats, muddy ditches, empty sky.

As the miles rolled by, Ray tried to decide whether the badlands were more ugly in their natural state or when they were adorned with the detritus of modern life. Finally he decided that the places where man had been were the ugliest. There was an almost subliminal dignity to the untouched land.

But not where man lived. There, the austere, seamed landscape was replaced by short-grass plains and scattered reservation settlements. Modern life had taken the elegant lines of the tipi from the Indians. In its place were tar-paper shacks with broken windows and flapping shingles. The shacks were surrounded by flimsy, half-fallen buckrail fences and by front yards littered with rusting, wrecked automobiles and bright plastic wading pools. Stunted chickens, skeletal horses, and hip-sprung beef cattle all competed for grass on threadbare pastures.

And everywhere, eyes peeled for the main chance, there were hungry dogs, animals so painfully skinny and furtively predatory that they would have made a mother think twice about allowing her child outside to play.

That was one of Ray's distant, buried memories, a vivid image of fear that had leaked out from his past in the hours since he landed.

It wasn't the presence of poverty that triggered his unhappy memories. He had seen plenty of hard times and harder places as an adult. He had been raised in the slums of the District of Columbia, and the tenements of New York had been his first FBI duty assignment.

But the Sioux reservations of South Dakota put new meaning on the idea of "dirt-poor."

Trash and an unidentifiable road kill were being picked over at the side of the road. The crows were nearly as big as the mongrels that flashed savage snarls over scraps even a ghetto rat would have scorned.

"Jesus, would you look at that," Ray said, thinking aloud. "Hard to believe this is America."

"That's right, Sal," Coutelle said, shaking a cigarette out and lighting it with the Zippo he carried in his shirt pocket. "We're well and truly stuck in the Third World, out here. When you think of all the money we spend on starving Albanians . . ."

Coutelle shrugged and said no more as another collection of diseased-looking shacks and dirty children flashed past like fast cuts from a *noir* movie.

"The whole country used to be theirs, clear up to Canada," Coutelle said, exhaling a rush of smoke, "and this is all they have left."

Ray watched a bent old woman in a bandanna kerchief and a cheap wash dress shuffle across the dirt yard in front of a tar-paper shack.

"And now they're killing one another," Coutelle continued, shaking his head at human stupidity. "Civil war."

"Over what?" Ray asked, looking around the impoverished little settlement.

Coutelle took a drag on his smoke and glanced at Ray, trying to decide whether Ray was asking as a human being or an FBI agent looking to solve a case.

"Well, Sal, I wouldn't think I'd have to educate a man whose blood is as red as yours, but I guess you've been away for a while," Coutelle said sarcastically.

Ray ignored him.

"You see," Coutelle said, "most of the dustups pit the traditionals—people who want to go back to the coup stick and the buffalo hunt—against the progressives, the progovernment Indians, the folks who have sided with the tribal corporation."

"Guys like our dead body, Leo Fast Elk?"

Coutelle nodded.

"Tribal Council member," Ray said. "Offing him would be a major coup for a bunch of militant traditionals, I suppose."

"Yeah," agreed Coutelle. "The traditionals want to overthrow the council system and go back to the old ways, with chiefs and tipis and the whole nine yards."

"I'll vote for the tipis," Ray said. "Those shacks are butt ugly."

"You ever try to stay warm in a tipi while a Dakota blizzard is blowing?" Coutelle asked sarcastically. "Try it, city boy. After one night in a tipi, those old tar-paper shacks will look like the fucking Taj Mahal."

Ray smiled slightly. "Yeah, I suppose so."

Coutelle grunted. "After they've frozen their nuts off in a blizzard, the traditionals are going to ride out and reclaim the Americas, from Alaska to Argentina."

"How?"

"Old treaties, medicine prayers, and New Age film stars." Coutelle made a disgusted sound. "Shee-it. Folks that dumb deserve whatever happens to them."

Ray looked at the yards that were littered with discarded

automobiles on cement blocks and empty five-gallon pails that had once held axle grease.

"You'd think that if they wanted to reclaim the land, they'd start by cleaning the trash out of their front yards first," Ray said, not bothering to hide the contempt he felt for people who would live in their own garbage.

Coutelle looked over, surprised by Ray's vehemence. "Hey, Sal, there's nothing out there for you to be ashamed of. They may be your folks, but nobody's holding it against you."

Ray stared out the window through narrowed eyes and said distinctly, "These are not my people."

"Oh, that's right. You were raised by that Air Force colonel, Director Dawes's fishing buddy. You're a true-blue Washington white boy, aren't you?"

Ray glanced at the other agent. His eyes were expressionless. "You have a problem with that, Cooch?"

Coutelle grinned and shook his head. "I've been sent into Indian Country at a time when it's open season on federal agents. I just want to know who's covering my ass."

Ray looked away, back at the land. Coutelle's concern was understandable enough.

"So you figure you're safe or not?" Ray asked after a minute.

Coutelle stared down the road. "I'll know as soon as you tell me your version of March 1980."

Ray kept his gaze fixed on the middle distance, even though Coutelle had just caught him flat-footed again. "What's so interesting about March 1980?"

"You tell me."

Ray glanced at Coutelle, not eager to lie and not willing to tell more of the truth than he had to.

"It was my third month in the Bureau," he said finally. "I spent it in the basement of the Hoover Building, typing summaries of wiretap logs from a white-collar case in Chicago."

"That was during the days," Coutelle said. "Nights

you spent banging one Ann Marie Beltone, computer systems analyst on the Bureau's support staff.''

"So?"

"So you had her open your background file."

Ray was silent for some time, waiting, wondering if that fact had been included in the director's briefing memo as well.

"Seven hundred words were deleted from that computer file," Coutelle added. "You wiped out your old man and your childhood. Why?"

Ray still sat silent, watching the badlands, wondering how much to say and what it would cost him to say nothing at all. Coutelle was an ASAC, and the Bureau was the closest thing in the civilian world to a military bureaucracy. One bad word from a ranking supervisor and Ray's career would be over.

The thought made Ray cold. For all his frustration with the Bureau's hidebound, unimaginative ways, Ray loved it. The FBI was the family he had never had. It was the center of a life that would otherwise be rudderless. Without the Bureau, he would be nothing more than a cop with a college degree and less future than past.

Ray was in trouble and he knew it.

Coutelle dragged on the Lucky and fired the butt out the open window, heedless of the dry grass in the ditches.

"Do you know what Indian Country means among field agents west of the Mississippi," Coutelle asked. "It means No Man's Land. Out to pasture."

Ray shrugged and said nothing.

"I think you've been sent to Indian Country because you fucked up somewhere along the way," Coutelle continued, "and I want to know how and where and how bad before I decide whether I want to keep you as a partner."

Coutelle couldn't have made the choice clearer. Ray stared into the badlands for fifteen seconds, as though he were deciding what he would say, what secret fears he might share with Coutelle.

When Ray looked across the car again, he wore a grin a mile wide.

"Nice try, Cooch, but that's an unethical, manipulative interrogation technique that most of us quit using two months after we learned it in Quantico. It's particularly nasty, coming from an agent who joined the FBI 'to serve God and country and protect the integrity of the American Dream.' "

Coutelle's face stayed blank for a slow three-count. Then he glanced at Ray carefully.

"That's how your application essay was worded, wasn't it?" Ray said.

Coutelle's leathery face broke into an appreciative smile. "Very good, Sal," he said.

Ray dragged a Halliburton hardcase into the front seat, snapped open the catches, and admired the broken-down NATO-green Remington .308 rifle and night scope that were nested carefully in the foam.

"Is this the same gun you used when you grouped three-eighths at a hundred yards on the Quantico range?"

Coutelle's right eyebrow rose. He nodded. "You really did do a job of crashing my file," he said.

Ray smiled. "Me? Crash an ASAC's file? No, sir. I *consulted* it. It told me that you've been out here a long time, and that you've spent most of the last nine years investigating reservation violence all over the West."

"No secret there, Tonto."

"So what did you do, Cooch? How did you screw up so big that you were sent out to Bumblefuck, South Dakota?"

Coutelle ignored him.

"Was it that entrapment charge in 1971?" Ray asked. "Was that it? You tell me your secrets, boss, and I'll tell you mine."

Coutelle's wind-burned face turned a darker shade. For a moment he looked more like an Indian than Ray did.

Reluctantly Coutelle grinned. "Pretty sharp, Sal, pretty damn sharp."

Before Ray could speak, the speeding Diplomat crested a small rise. The road ahead was blocked by fifteen heavily armed Indians.

It was a well-designed roadblock. There was no place to go, nowhere to hide, and barely enough time to lock up the brakes to avoid smashing into a truck. Before the tires stopped screaming, the Diplomat was surrounded by men with rifles and shotguns.

Adrenaline pumped through Ray in the instant before his training took over. By reflex he pulled his Magnum as he assessed the opposition.

"Automatic weapon on the right," Ray said tightly. "The rest of them look like civilian guns. A shitpot full of them, though. Which ones you want?"

"Steady, Tonto."

Ray looked around slowly, taking the time to digest details more subtle than the guns that were aimed at him. The armed men were all young and fit. In fact, they had the look of a gang or an irregular army. They carried mismatched weapons, but all of them were uniformly dressed in blue jeans, western shirts, and baseball caps that were all the same dark blue color as the pickup blocking the road.

Beyond the pickup, more armed men surrounded a battered station wagon that had approached the roadblock from the other direction. The occupants of the station wagon—four young Indian men with long hair in tightly plaited braids—were braced at gunpoint against their vehicle while the armed men searched inside.

Moving carefully, Ray stepped out from behind the car door and moved to back Coutelle up. The Indians had begun to shift from their own positions. Fifteen Indians and two FBI agents met uneasily in the center of the highway.

"Ray, let me introduce the Guardians of the Oglala Nation," Coutelle said, still holding his credential open like a talisman. "Better known to reservation riffraff as the

Goon Squad. A vile nickname but not entirely unfair. Ain't that true, Jack?''

Coutelle's last remark was aimed at a thin, hard-faced Indian in a white straw cowboy hat and Pendleton shirt. He was older than the armed men, who all stepped aside deferentially as he pushed through to confront Coutelle.

"So, Coutelle, you managed to find your way back," he said. *"Washte',* then."

"Yeah. Same to you, Jack." Coutelle turned and motioned Ray forward. "Ray, meet Jack Milton, tribal president."

Milton squinted at Ray and then turned to Coutelle. "This is the Native American agent that Washington sent us?"

"That's right. Meet Ray Little—"

"Ray Levoi, Mr. Milton," Ray said, cutting Coutelle off.

Ray holstered the pistol he had been holding at his side, then held out his hand to shake Milton's.

"What's with the roadblock?" Ray asked. "You caught us by surprise. Looks like we aren't the only ones, either."

Ray nodded toward the station wagon. Three armed men were pulling what looked like household goods from the back and tossing them on the roadway—blankets, clothing, jugs of water. One of the men held up an intricately beaded deerskin dancing costume for the other men to see.

Everyone watched as the man wadded the traditional clothing into a ball and tossed it carelessly toward the ditch.

"Wait," said one of the young men who was braced against the car. "That belonged to my—"

The youth was hit sharply with the butt of a shotgun, drawing blood from the corner of his mouth. When another traditional objected, a Guardian slapped him into silence.

Ray's mouth flattened. He glanced at Coutelle. No

reaction. Then he looked at Milton. The tribal president looked away from the violence, as though it didn't exist.

"We're just looking for some people," Milton said.

"How about Jimmy? You haven't seen him, have you?" Coutelle asked.

"We're still looking," Milton said. "This time it's gone too far. We're gonna catch those murderers, take care of them. Indian way." He looked directly at Ray, as though challenging him. "You know what I mean, *Kola?*"

Coutelle shook his head before Ray could speak.

"These things have to be taken care of in the legal way," Coutelle said. "Federal jurisdiction."

"Tribal jurisdiction, tribal Guardians. That's the law. Me and my Guardians have been employed to run all those so-called warriors out before more of our good people die."

Coutelle moved until he stood directly in front of Milton. "Tell them to put their guns away, Jack. You don't need more shooting out here."

Milton met the agent eye to eye. The Indian was a man used to having his own way. He clearly didn't like his prerogatives challenged.

"It's gone way too far," Milton said flatly. "You federals can't get them off the res, so we will. The ARM is going to be the busted ARM, right, Lewis?"

One of the Guardians stepped forward, lifted his Winchester carbine, and levered a shell into the chamber to voice his approval.

Milton nodded, then glared at the two federal agents. "Move your car, Coutelle. You're blocking a tribal highway."

Milton turned and moved back into the midst of his men, muttering to them in the language that Ray didn't understand.

"Welcome to Indian Country, Sal," Coutelle said. "Let's get the hell out of here before you get us shot."

))) SIX

As HE STEPPED out of the Diplomat in front of the ram-shackle, six-unit motel, Ray thought he heard the throbbing, elemental sound of the heartbeat drum once more. The sound had haunted him from the moment he had touched down in these godforsaken badlands, but he hadn't known what it was until he saw the ceremonial skin drum in the airport.

The motel was not the kind of place to have a display case. Ray glanced around intently, seeking the source of the sound. Suddenly the heartbeat drum was swept up in a rambling bass guitar and Merle Haggard's thin, reedy tenor. The music was pouring out of a grimy building at the far end of the motel parking lot.

A jukebox inside the bar had just opened up with "Okie from Muskogee." The sound was loud enough to rattle the Grain Belt, Hamm's, and Coors signs on the windows. A flashing arrow pointed toward the red neon script over the door that read The Buffalo Butte Bar.

"The locals call it the Buffalo Butt," Coutelle said. He grabbed the Halliburton case and his duffel from the back seat of the Diplomat and headed for Unit 6, still talking. "There's a sign on the front door. 'No Indians Allowed.' "

Coutelle looked over his shoulder. "They probably weren't thinking of white Indians with badges in their pockets, Sal, but I wouldn't drink alone in there if I were you. Some of those cowboys don't care much for FBI agents, either."

48

Ray grabbed his own gear from the trunk and followed
Coutelle. He had developed some immunity to the other
agent's barbed humor in the past twelve hours. Cops with
thin skins didn't last long in any squad room, not even a
button-down FBI bullpen. But Ray did feel a sudden, surprising stab of irritation at the idea he might not be welcome in some redneck bar, whether it was because of his
profession or his parentage.

*Maybe I'll just slide on over and have a drink. Might
be kind of entertaining to find out whether my badge or
my blood would upset them more.*

The screen in the door of Unit 6 had been kicked out
some time ago and not replaced. The room itself suffered
from the same lack of maintenance. There were two sagging single beds, a rump-sprung easy chair, and a television set that was probably black and white, if the age of
its plastic cabinet was any clue. At the back of the room
was a small kitchenette and a door that led to a closet-
sized bathroom.

"Welcome to the FBI's Oglala Field Office," Coutelle
called out from the bathroom. "You can bunk here or next
door. The beds will kill you either place."

Ray dropped his gear on the bed closer to the window
and turned on the television. He had been wrong; the
screen glowed not in black and white, but in an unhealthy
shade of purple. Not that it mattered. He went around the
dial and found only one station. Ray shut off the set and
wandered into the kitchenette.

Coutelle had turned the tiny alcove into a makeshift
field office, complete with cardboard box files, a small
computer terminal and modem, and a rogues' gallery that
took up the entire back wall. The centerpiece was a surveillance photo of a handsome Indian with dark braids as
long as the ones worn by the two young traditional Indians
the tribal Guardians had rousted.

Ray recognized the surveillance subject as Dennis
Banks. The photo had been taken from a Bureau bulletin
issued after the Wounded Knee shootout. A second photo

showed Banks and other long-haired men shouting angrily at the camera. A third showed police officers in a pitched battle with Banks and his men on the streets of a small town somewhere in the Dakotas.

Coutelle came out of the bathroom and noticed Ray studying the pictures. He went to one of the files and dug out a thick folder.

"Read it and weep," Coutelle said, thumping the file into Ray's hands.

Ray thumbed through the file, which was filled with photos and Xerox copies of local police and FBI reports. Several ID photos were clipped together with thick reports under a covering note that read "Primaries." Ray removed the clip and started to leaf through the documents.

The name on the bottom of the first photo was Severt Clear Moon.

Coutelle flopped in the rump-sprung chair and lit a cigarette. He saw the photo that had caught Ray's eye.

"Clear Moon's in the pen," Coutelle said, blowing out smoke. "Forget him."

"He have any family in the movement?" Ray asked.

"A cousin. Next in line. William Stands."

Ray shuffled to the next photo. A pock-marked young man with a black eye and bruises on his face glared into the camera lens. The caption beneath the photo indicated Stands was being booked into the Custer City Jail on a rioting charge.

"Must have resisted arrest," Ray said. "Did the attitude adjustment soften him up?"

"Lightweight," Coutelle said.

He stared at the water-stained, fly-specked ceiling and blew rings with the heavy blue smoke from his Lucky, waiting for Ray to ask more questions.

Ray looked at the next photo in line, a light-skinned Indian with collar-length hair and a calm expression. He flipped the photo over and read the background material on the back.

"What about this guy Buffalo Dreamer? Says here he's an ex-cop from Sioux City. Can we turn him?"

Coutelle shook his head. "There's no true believer like a recent convert."

"Maybe he believes in money. Cash has been a regular miracle on the streets I've worked."

"Make an ex-cop into an informant? He'd be the first suspect," Coutelle said. "Even trying to turn him could blow us right out of the water."

"We have anybody at all inside?"

Coutelle shrugged. "There's always somebody that can be twisted. Just a matter of finding him."

"Somebody close to the leadership?" Ray persisted, trying to draw Coutelle out.

Ray tried to keep the eagerness out of his voice, but it was hard. He had been keyed up and jittery all day, feeling as though he were on the outside of the case looking in; or as though he were on the edge of a waking nightmare, drums beating relentlessly, telling him things he really didn't want to hear.

But seeing the files and folders, computer and phones and modem, all the tools of his trade, had both relaxed and revived him. He loved the old pattern of cops and robbers, good guys and bad guys, everything defined and tangible. This was where he belonged, where he was accepted, and even an acid-tongued Coutelle couldn't change that.

Coutelle flicked the ash from his cigarette on the floor and stared out through the tattered screen door into the distance, apparently considering Ray's question.

"No, Sal," he said finally, "we don't have a single informant, confidential or otherwise."

"After nearly a decade of work?" Ray asked in disbelief.

"Listen up, little white Indian," Coutelle said. "ARM is on its last legs. Most of the leadership is in jail. Or dead. There are only three key activists left, three real extremists. Maximum hardcases. Take a look."

He pointed off-handedly toward the grimy door of the old refrigerator in the kitchen. There were three mug shots taped at eye level.

Ray went over and examined the first, a young, dark-eyed woman with straight hair down to her waist and clean, regular features that were surprisingly finely drawn.

"The good-looking one is Magdalena Eagle Bear," Coutelle said. "Don't fall into those deep, dark, sexy eyes. She's part of the leadership, she loves armed protest, and she has a positive genius for inflammatory acts."

"Full-blooded Sioux?" Ray asked.

Coutelle ignored him. "She was born up north of here but she got most of her education on the East Coast, some Ivy League school that was looking for scholarship kids to fill out their affirmative-action enrollment."

"Not too bright, huh?"

"Brighter than you, Sal. But not bright enough to see through the radical bullshit they fed her."

Ray studied the photo again, intrigued by the clean features and direct glance of Magdalena Eagle Bear. Coutelle was right about her intelligence. It showed in her eyes and in the calmly defiant way she stared at the mug-shot camera.

She knew exactly what she was doing. She realized full well that every new cop that ever looked at her file would form his first impression from this mug shot.

Reluctantly Ray moved to the next photo.

"The one in the center is Thomas Deer Shield," Coutelle said. "There's a better picture of him around here somewhere. It shows him with a thirty-aught-six in his hands and two bandoliers of ammo across his chest."

"Sounds like the Frito Bandito."

"Try looking at him when he's shooting back. See how funny he looks then." Coutelle flicked ash on the floor. "Tommy's a dog soldier rather than a thinker. He's tied up in the courts right now, pretty much dormant."

Coutelle stood up and came over to where Ray stood.

He tapped the third picture on the refrigerator door hard, once, right in the middle of the subject's forehead.

"And then there's Jimmy. He's the bad boy of the lot."

The Indian in the photo didn't look like a bad boy. A bad man, perhaps, with penetrating almond-shaped eyes that met the camera's gaze calmly and a scar above one eye that looked like it had been inflicted in God's own bar fight.

Ray read the caption aloud. "James Looks Twice." He frowned at the picture, doubting that the man was called Jimmy by anyone but his mother and Frank Coutelle.

The man had a thick bull's neck and broad shoulders, suggesting formidable physical strength. He wore a bright blue velvet shirt, a white eagle feather in his long hair, and a choker dressed with porcupine quills and beads that would have looked effeminate on anyone less masculine and self-assured.

"Bit of a dandy," Ray suggested.

"That's charisma, Sal," Coutelle said. "Jimmy's the last messiah of the Aboriginal Rights Movement, a genuine national leader. 'Course, what he's leading those poor devils to is another century of eating shit."

Coutelle took one last drag on his cigarette, then flicked the butt in the direction of the screenless door. It struck the cement pillar outside and exploded in a shower of sparks.

Ray flipped the photo over and read the identifying information on the back.

"Messiah with a felony record?" he asked skeptically.

"Ever read your Bible?" Coutelle said dryly. "Comes with the territory. Jimmy has a felony record *and* a history of violence."

"What's he done lately?"

"Burned the American flag in front of the council offices. More recently he's pledged to overthrow Milton's tribal Guardians."

"That stuff in affidavits?"

Coutelle looked at Ray sourly, as though his skills as an investigator had been questioned.

"Five affidavits on the flag," Coutelle said crisply, "two on the overthrow, and two more that document Jimmy's history of assaultive behavior aimed at one Leo Fast Elk."

"Two assaults on Leo?"

"That's just in the last month."

Ray stared at Coutelle, wondering what else the senior investigator had withheld from him.

Coutelle dug another folder out of the file, flipped it open, and showed Ray FBI field reports.

"Three assaults, if you count the one that ended up with Leo Fast Elk face down in the clay."

"Those are what I'd call clues, all right," Ray said.

Coutelle went to the kitchen sink and turned on the cold water. The plumbing knocked and sputtered before spouting a rusty flood of water. Coutelle looked at the water distastefully, rinsed his hands, then shut the faucet off.

"It's common knowledge around the reservation that Jimmy wanted Leo out of the picture," Coutelle said.

"Why?"

"Who the hell knows? Tribal politics are about as byzantine as the political games on the seventh floor of the Hoover Building."

"Any theories?" Ray asked.

"My guess is that Leo had been tabbed as the next tribal president and Jimmy figured to off him before he takes Jack Milton out."

Ray said nothing, filing Coutelle's theory with the other facts and gaps in the case.

"Whatever the motive," Coutelle continued, "Jimmy's my candidate for hip-shooter of the week. That's why we're going to move on him. There's a guerrilla camp west of here. I'm guessing that's where he'll be."

Ray looked at the photo again. "You think you could get a federal magistrate to issue a warrant on the basis of those facts?"

"We're too far from Rapid City to go after a magistrate's warrant," Coutelle said bluntly. "Besides, look at the arm. How much more probable cause do you need?"

"ARM's a political organization, not probable cause, Cooch."

"Jesus, Sal," Coutelle said, stabbing angrily at the photo. "Not ARM. Jimmy's arm. There. Chrissake, use your eyes."

Ray stared at James Looks Twice's powerful forearm. There, clearly visible in the cold blue-white flash of the mug-shot camera, was an inked jailhouse tattoo: an eagle feather inside a circle.

Turning the photo over, Ray looked at the official report on the back. There, under "identifying marks," he read: "Tattoo, left forearm, eagle feather inside circle, believed to be the insignia of the Aboriginal Rights Movement."

Ray looked at the photo again. There was no question. It was the same symbol he had seen that morning, etched in the soft soil beside Leo Fast Elk's body.

Coutelle gave Ray a cold, humorless smile.

"Gotta keep your eyes open all the time, Sal. Otherwise those clues get by you."

The late afternoon sun had lost its strength by the time Ray pulled in behind the three tribal police squad cars parked beside the dirt road.

Coutelle got out and conferred with the six uniformed Indian officers who stood around, waiting for the feds. Ray waited in the Diplomat, listening to the sounds of the prairie that was both unfamiliar and deeply known, the landscape of his childhood and his nightmares.

The wind was the land's only voice. It moaned across the ground in a low, sustained cry that was so relentless the mind simply stopped hearing it, accepting the wind as background. Only silence would draw men's attention, making them look around as though to ask what was missing.

Ray turned his attention back to the cops. Tribal or municipal, they were all of a type. He had worked with local officers dozens of times in his career. He had been on raids with them, had ridden patrols, had drunk their strong coffee and their warm beer. Some local cops were good, some were bad; but none could be trusted because you never knew what kind of training they had.

Frank Coutelle had a great many drawbacks as a partner, but at least Ray had a good idea how the caustic bastard would react in a crisis. The FBI's training was nothing if not thorough.

That was the genius of the Bureau. It selected intelligent, shrewd people, men and women both. Then it trained them hard and imposed the sharpest kind of discipline imaginable. The point was to instill a measure of uniformity in a diverse and self-assured group of human beings, to make them as close to interchangeable as possible without completely destroying their initiative. In many ways it was a good system, one to which Ray willingly submitted because he liked the result.

Ray thought of the picture of James Looks Twice. In an odd way, the result of FBI training was something close to tribal, binding members together with shared icons and goals and the belief that they were the best of the best.

The Bureau is my tribe. Button-down and wing-tip and close-cropped rather than unbuttoned and barefooted and long-haired. Badge instead of necklace.

The guns stay pretty much the same, though.

The idea both amused Ray and made him uncomfortable. One of his former girlfriends had once told him the Bureau was the family he had never had—and the wife he never would have if he didn't watch it.

Ray hadn't "watched it" and his girlfriend's prophecy had come true. The Bureau was the only family he had. That was why he put up with being a public relations gesture, a sop to the ethnic sensitivities of the Sioux Indians.

After a few more minutes, Ray got out of the car. The familiar hot wind tugged at his body like an invisible lover, triggering memories that were both old and new, whispering to him of heartbeats magnified by callused hands beating on drums.

Ray went to the trunk and broke out the short-barreled riot shotguns. He loaded each carefully, comfortable with the familiar routine, glad to have something he could control.

But as soon as he finished, he heard drums again. They were both inside his body and far in the distance.

It's just the wind and my imagination. I'm used to urban noise, so I'm inventing sounds to fill the silence and the wind.

He shouldered one shotgun, carried the other in his left hand, and went to join Coutelle and the Indian officers.

"It's loaded," Ray said as he handed the second riot gun to Coutelle.

"Don't ever give me one that isn't," Coutelle said.

Ray nodded to the officers.

The men nodded back. They were rumpled and a little seedy, but somehow he felt more comfortable around them than he had around Jack Milton's Guardian squad. Vigilantes went against everything the FBI had taught Ray.

The tribal cops all inspected the FBI shotguns with open interest. One of the Indians carried a double-barreled twelve-gauge that looked like it had been designed for ducks and pheasants rather than law enforcement work. The rest of the men carried nothing heavier than revolvers, most of them so old the blueing had worn off cylinders and barrels.

"The camp is in a little draw just below that next rise," Coutelle said to Ray. "We'll make a skirmish line when we get there, you and me in the middle. Let's hit it."

Ray fell in behind Coutelle as they moved out. While they climbed the small rise, the sound of drumming got louder. At first Ray thought his imagination was getting out of hand. Then he realized that the men around him were hearing the drums too.

As the raiding party approached the brow of the hill, Ray began to pick out the sounds of several individual drums. Weaving through them was a faint keening sound, like a bird of prey somewhere far up in the empty sky.

One of the officers listened carefully to the songs and said quietly, "They must be in the sweat lodge."

"*Inipi,*" another added. "Maybe we should wait."

The cop looked at Coutelle quizzically, as though he thought the agent might attach some significance to the term.

Coutelle shrugged. He was in no mood to wait. "Skirmish line. We go now."

The sounds of singing and drumming swelled as the skirmish line crested the hill. The camp lay in a gentle depression below the crest. The only permanent building was a small round hut with a large circle of fire-blackened rocks. The hut was covered with a patchwork of quilts, canvas, and shaggy buffalo hides.

The officers spread out on either side of the two agents. When Coutelle dropped his hand, they all started down the hill together.

The skirmishers were ten yards from the edge of the camp when they saw a teenager in long hair and skivvies reclining by a small campfire. The youth began to shift on his side, covering his eyes in the late afternoon sunlight. He groped around behind him, found a broken pitchfork, and began to stir the fire.

As the boy sat up further, he found himself staring into the muzzle of Ray's shotgun.

"On the ground, son," Ray said softly.

The boy dropped like a boot camp recruit and lay still.

Coutelle slid past and approached the hovel. For a moment, he looked confused, as though he couldn't figure out how to open it. Then he found the canvas flap. He touched one edge, motioned Ray into position, and held up three fingers.

On the count, just as they both had learned at Quantico, a dozen years apart.

Ray nodded, understanding perfectly. He counted silently, mouthing each number so Coutelle could see it. On three, Coutelle threw the flap aside . . .

. . . and was engulfed in a cloud of two-hundred-degree steam and stinging smoke.

"Holy shit!" he yelled, ducking back to escape being scalded.

"Mitakue Oyasin!" The incomprehensible oath echoed from inside the lodge.

Ray danced back, covering the entrance of the lodge with the shotgun.

"FBI," he shouted clearly. "Everybody out, one at a time, and show us your empty hands as you come."

Coutelle had regained his composure quickly. He stayed to one side, out of Ray's line of fire.

"You heard him," Coutelle shouted. "Out!"

There was a mumble of voices inside the lodge. Then a figure appeared in the thinning smoke and steam. The clouds of vapor parted, revealing a stooped man with the oldest body and the youngest eyes Ray had ever seen.

"It's Grandpa Reaches," one of the Indian officers called out. "Don't shoot him."

Grandpa Reaches stared at Ray for several seconds. The old man was both angry and composed. He was unbothered by the fact that he was stone naked, surrounded by dressed, armed men.

A hand reached out of the steaming lodge and offered the old man a towel. With great dignity, he draped it around his waist and stepped into the evening.

"How many more are in there?" Coutelle demanded.

The old man turned his head and looked at Coutelle blankly, as though he didn't understand or, more likely, chose not to respond.

Coutelle gestured with the muzzle of the riot gun.

The old man moved away and stood by the fire.

"Let's go!" Ray called out. "One at a time."

Slowly, five more men crawled out of the low opening into the evening air. All were naked except for towels. All were drenched with sweat. Several wore the dreamy, detached expressions of men who were a little drunk, but Ray could smell no liquor on them. They were simply intoxicated with heat and smoke and whatever ceremony had been interrupted.

The old man was clearly the leader. The others, who ranged from teenagers to middle-aged, looked to him. He spoke to them in Lakota.

"We'll do the talking," Ray ordered.

The old man stared holes in his chest, then turned and started to walk away. Ray reached out and grabbed the man's bony arm.

"Leave him alone, fed." The commanding voice came from within the lodge.

Ray turned and covered the doorway. So did Coutelle.

"Come on out, Jimmy," Coutelle said. "Buffalo hide is strong medicine, but it can't turn a twelve-gauge."

))) SEVEN

JAMES LOOKS TWICE came through the sweat lodge entrance like an angry badger, his rage coiled in his muscled shoulders and thick legs. He straightened up slowly, glaring at Ray. Looks Twice wasn't stupid; he was careful to keep his hands empty and in plain view.

"What the hell do you think you're doing, fed?" he snarled. Then Looks Twice glanced to the side, saw Coutelle, and said, "Shit. I should have known it would be you."

"How's it going, Jimmy?" Coutelle said. "You're under arrest."

Looks Twice shook his head in disbelief. His long, black hair was bound with a leather thong and decorated with a single white feather. He wiped sweat from his eyes with his right hand.

Ray noticed the feather and circle tattoo on the Indian's forearm.

"This is a religious ceremony you're desecrating," Looks Twice said.

Coutelle moved in close, shotgun at his hip. "Yeah, right, and my hot tub is an altar. Hands up."

Looks Twice raised his hands a few inches, then gestured with his arms, still unconvinced.

"Hey, we're in the middle of an *inipi* ceremony. You don't drag white Baptists out of prayer meeting, do you?"

Coutelle slid the muzzle of his shotgun under the Indian's chin and lifted an inch or two.

"You resisting arrest, Jimmy? 'Cause if you're resist-

61

ing, all this gets real simple, real fast. The report would read: 'Suspect resisted. Suspect died. Case closed.' " Coutelle waited a beat. "Get the picture?"

Looks Twice glared defiantly over the muzzle of the gun but his muscles slowly relaxed. He spoke a few words of Lakota. The other Indians began to disband, heading for the spot where their clothing hung on the branches of a small stand of chokecherry bushes.

Only Grandpa Reaches stayed. He faced Ray, the threadbare old towel clutched with one hand, an odd mixture of anger and sadness in his hundred-year-old eyes.

The black eyes made Ray uneasy. It was as though the old man had seen all the way through him in a way that even Coutelle had not managed. Ray tried to match the intensity of the old man's gaze for a moment but could not.

The realization made Ray angry. It was the first time in his life he had ever been stared down by a barefoot man in a bath towel, much less by someone old enough to be his own great-grandfather. All the FBI's training in command presence and control of fluid situations seemed useless against Grandpa Reaches.

Worse, Grandpa Reaches seemed to know it.

Ray thought about asking the old man what tribe he belonged to; its members didn't need badges and guns to make an impression.

The steel ratchets of Coutelle's handcuffs distracted Ray. Everyone was getting ready to move out, prisoner in tow.

"Go on home, old man," Ray said. "It's over."

The old man just stared.

I wonder if those old eyes saw the last Ghost Dance.

As though Grandpa Reaches had understood, he nodded.

Ray stared, then turned and walked off up the hill behind Coutelle and the prisoner. Five minutes later, they were back in the Diplomat.

James Looks Twice was a sullen prisoner. He never said a word, just sat and stared at the headliner of the car. Ray couldn't decide if the Indian was in a daze or a trance or just didn't give a damn. Coutelle had let him pull on his jeans, and had thrown a shirt over his shoulders, but Looks Twice was still barefoot. If it bothered him, he didn't let on.

Ray read the prisoner the Miranda card, detailing all the rights Looks Twice probably knew as well as anyone in the car. After that, Ray turned away and ignored the man. The usual good-cop, bad-cop ploys wouldn't work on this prisoner. Looks Twice would talk when he wanted to, period.

After ten miles, Looks Twice seemed to come back to the real world. He glanced out the window to orient himself. He realized they were headed away from Rapid City.

"Where you guys taking me?" he asked. His expression changed, as though he was suddenly suspicious. The change seemed to pass through his whole body. His muscles began pumping up again beneath his shirt, as though he was getting ready to fight or flee.

"We just want to take a look around your place," Coutelle said. He turned and glanced at the prisoner, noting the signs of a man under pressure. "Relax, we aren't going to turn you over to Jack Milton. Not yet, anyway."

"Fuck you, Coutelle," Looks Twice said.

Ray was a little disappointed. He had hoped for a more original epithet.

Coutelle turned onto a rough dirt road that ran back toward a sordid block of government housing. The place was set against an old uplift terrace a quarter mile from the main highway. The fields and sparse pastures around the housing were littered with rusting car bodies and discarded appliances. Judging by the body styles, the refuse dated back at least thirty years.

Anger spurted through Ray.

Jesus, don't they know any better? Where is all that respect for the earth I keep hearing about on TV?

Then Ray began to wonder whether the trash had a

meaning deeper than laziness or carelessness. The desecration seemed so complete that it could only be con-
scious, almost as though the inhabitants of the grimy little
settlement were jeering at the world, as though they were
trying to say that a little trash here and there was nothing,
compared to the rest of their dead-end lives.

James Looks Twice had found another way to convey
the message. In front of his battered shack an American
flag flew from a makeshift staff in the hot wind. Stars and
Stripes, red, white, and blue.

Flying upside down.

As Coutelle pulled up in front and shut off the engine,
he shot the prisoner a hard look.

"What's with you, boy?" he asked. "Are you trying
for a record number of flag-desecration charges?"

Looks Twice snorted derisively. "I was decorated in
Nam. I can fly the flag however I want."

Coutelle gave him a hard look. "I was there, too, asshole."

"If you were in the service," Looks Twice shot back,
"you know that an upside-down flag is a distress signal.
Nobody has a better right to use it than an Indian."

Ray opened the back door and dragged the handcuffed
prisoner out.

"Spare us the militant bullshit," he said, checking to
make sure the handcuffs were still tight.

Looks Twice glanced at him, then stared again, seeing
something that he hadn't seen before.

"I'm not a militant," Looks Twice said. "I'm a warrior."

"Yeah, sure you're a warrior."

"Five hundred years of resistance. You can't break that
kind of connection. Follow me? Five-hundred-year-old
voices can't be silenced."

"Try shoving a dirty sock in their mouths. Works every
time."

Ray pointed Looks Twice toward the front door and

gave him a light shove. The man felt like solid wood beneath the shirt, still angry or frightened.

Unpainted wood steps led up to a porch that was all but filled by two discarded refrigerators. Coutelle examined the peeling wood of the front door.

"Where's the key, Jimmy?"

Looks Twice glowered at him and said nothing.

Coutelle shrugged. "Your choice." He turned to Ray. "Agent Levoi, the federal master key, please."

Ray moved Looks Twice to one side and positioned himself in front of the door. He rattled the knob, gauging the thickness of the wood, then lifted his foot to deliver a front snap-kick.

Looks Twice watched until the last possible moment, then decided the agents weren't bluffing.

"Okay, Coutelle, you win," he finally said. "Milton's goddamn goons busted it last Sunday. I'm getting tired of fixing the bastard."

"The key," Coutelle said.

Looks Twice turned and nodded toward a sizable hole in the wall of the house just above the crumbling cinderblock foundation.

"The key's in there," he said.

Coutelle stepped off the decrepit porch and knelt beside the hole. He looked inside but saw nothing in the failing light.

"Inside, in the coffee can," Looks Twice directed.

Coutelle reached into the darkness with one hand but found nothing. He probed further, until his entire arm was in the hole.

Suddenly he screamed, fear and pain, and then a violent rage as he realized what had happened. For an instant, he hung there twitching helplessly, like a man caught in a powerful grinder. Finally he reared back and dragged his arm from the hole.

An enraged forty-pound badlands badger clung to Coutelle's wrist with his teeth, snarling and gnashing, tearing the agent's coat sleeve to shreds with his raking claws.

James Looks Twice waited for the moment of maximum effect before he delivered a snap-kick of his own to Ray's midsection.

Ray sensed the blow coming just in time to turn his body so that most of the kick's force was expended against his flank. But it still had his wind out. He toppled face forward into the dirt of the front yard as the prisoner, still handcuffed, bailed over the tattered railing at the end of the porch and disappeared into the ad hoc salvage yard of dead cars along one edge of the settlement.

"Get that son of a bitch!" Coutelle bellowed.

For a moment Ray couldn't tell whether he meant the badger or Looks Twice.

Coutelle flailed at the air with his injured arm, trying to dislodge the snarling, growling animal. The badger grunted and adjusted his grip and dug deeper into human flesh with its yellowed teeth.

Ray snapped his gun into position.

"Get the fucking prisoner!" Coutelle snarled. "I'll take care of the badger." He reached across his body for his pistol. "Go!"

Ray scrambled up and raced around the corner of the house in the direction Looks Twice had fled. When he caught a fleeting glimpse of one bare foot disappearing behind a rusting Desoto, he snapped the shotgun to his shoulder.

Just as he applied pressure to the trigger, a three-year-old girl carrying a plastic pail in one hand and a black and white cat in the other wandered into the line of fire.

Ray screamed, trying to get the child out of the way. She turned and froze, staring dumbly at him. He lowered the gun and dashed past her.

"Get in the house," he said harshly.

The child ran.

Behind him, Ray heard the muffled report of Coutelle's pistol. A few instants later, there was a second shot. The badger was tougher than most felony suspects.

Ray ran on, reaching the shelter of the Desoto. He stared through its dusty windows, trying to decide which way Looks Twice had fled.

The junkyard seemed silent and empty.

He went around the front of the car, moving more slowly now, shotgun at the ready, hoping to stampede his prey into flight again.

Ray had gone halfway down an alley between two abandoned Rapid City Transit System buses when Looks Twice emerged from the cover of a doorless Chevy. Somehow the Indian had managed to step through his own handcuffed wrists, bringing his hands around to the front of his body. He was holding a sawed-off bolt-action rifle.

Just as the Indian fired, Ray pitched himself toward the shelter of the bus.

The report was heavy and sharp. Ray heard the bullet buzz past his ear and ricochet off the sheet metal side of the vehicle. He surged to his feet again, moving fast, knowing that Looks Twice would be slowed in reloading by the rifle's bolt action.

The Indian was as agile as he was strong. He managed to get off one more shot, driving his pursuer to cover again.

When Ray leaped up for a third charge, Looks Twice was already on the run again. Ray fired once in the direction of the Chevy, more to let Coutelle know where he was than to hit the fugitive. Then he slid between two more wrecks and tried to cut the running man off.

Ray went flat beside a demobilized army four-by-four and tried to catch a glimpse of bare feet in flight. He saw a flicker of movement, marked the spot, then circled another several wrecks and tried to move up. From fifteen feet away, he recognized the waving motion of a single white eagle feather, and knew it must have fallen from Looks Twice's hair.

Kneeling in the shelter of a wreck, holding his breath,

Ray listened. Somewhere behind him, he heard the sound of shouts, Coutelle or the tribal police backup units.

Not good. The junkyard was a nightmare of ambush sites. If more officers stormed in now, they would get chewed up.

Ten yards beyond the feather, Ray spotted a red and white Volkswagen bus. The passenger front door was slightly ajar. As he watched, he sensed as much as saw a tremor of movement, as though someone inside had just shifted position.

Ray lifted the shotgun, fired, then jacked another shell into the chamber and fired again. The Volkswagen's windshield exploded into a shower of glass. Ray fired again. The driver's door popped open but there was no one inside.

Just then a tribal officer stepped into the gap at the other end of the junkyard aisle. Ray moved into the light so the officer could see him, then waved him around to a crossfire position. Together they advanced on the bus, moving carefully, waiting for return fire. Ray found a safe spot and snatched a quick look inside.

The vehicle was empty, except for the sawed-off rifle Looks Twice had used.

Other voices were welling up behind Ray—civilians, innocents, children trying to get closer or, worse, stumbling into the field of fire in their efforts to flee. Ray smelled disaster building. He signaled the tribal officer to stay put, then made one quick run down the last aisle of the junkyard, hoping to flush Looks Twice.

A few seconds later, Ray found himself standing alone and breathless at the edge of the limitless prairie. The only possible hiding place was a clump of stunted elms around an abandoned wellhead.

Ray moved toward the cover, bolder now that Looks Twice was unarmed. When Ray was still ten yards from the elms, he heard a quick, furtive movement. Smoothly the shotgun came up to his shoulder as the sound of drums condensed in his mind, stronger and stronger. The drums stopped. Ray drew a deep breath, ready to shout an order for surrender.

A magnificent eight-point buck exploded from cover and bounded past Ray.

The mule deer was so elegant in its power, so completely unexpected on the ruined landscape, that Ray stood there transfixed. The deer dashed across the open ground, leaped a fence, and disappeared on the other side of the road. Numbly, Ray watched it go. After a minute, he shook himself and walked back through the junkyard, feeling a bit foolish.

Coutelle was braced against a rotting pillar on Looks Twice's porch, holding his bleeding arm between his knees and trying to talk on the radio at the same time.

"That's right, we've got one agent out of commission and an escaped felony fugitive," he said through gritted teeth.

Ray laid the shotgun aside and lifted Coutelle's arm to inspect the damage. Blood welled up brightly from four or five deep gashes. There was bone at the center of one of the cuts.

"No, the agent wasn't shot," Coutelle snarled. "A badger ripped the shit out of his arm is all. No, we don't need an alert on the fucking badger. He's stone-cold dead."

Coutelle looked up at Ray as he added, "That's what the fugitive will be, too, when I catch up with him."

Coutelle dropped the radio on the rotten wood of the porch and glared at Ray. "Lost him, did you, Sal? Looks like we'll have to issue you a weapon you can use—like a bow and arrow."

"You want me to shoot at little girls and shadows?"

"If that's what it takes." Coutelle grimaced. "Help me up and let's roll. There are some bandages in the kit in the trunk."

"You need stitches."

"I need to kick ass and take names. That's what I need."

Ray started to argue, then saw the bleak, black look of rage in Coutelle's eyes.

"Right," Ray said.

He cleared the shotgun as he walked to the car. It was going to be a long night in the badlands.

>>> EIGHT

FOR THE NEXT twenty-four hours, Ray and Coutelle operated on adrenaline. When that wore thin, they added harsh black coffee from a series of all-night diners and truck stops across the southwestern corner of the state. Anger helped to keep both men awake. Cops are most touchy when a prisoner has just made a fool of them.

The agents and raiding parties of tribal officers and Oglala Guardians were like firefighters chasing a wind-blown blaze through dry grass; no matter where they went, the suspect had come and gone.

The raiders followed solid investigative leads, they played hunches, they chased wild guesses on the reservation and in the three surrounding counties. They pushed through doors that were opened too slowly. They kicked in the ones that were locked. They used tear gas on one shack after the occupants refused to come out.

When the two drunken Indian cowhands finally woke up and came staggering out into the early morning light, they were jailed for failing to heed a federal agent.

Along the way, Coutelle's savaged arm was treated by an emergency room doctor in one of the small towns just off the reservation. The physician gave the grim-faced agent a tetanus shot, a bottle of painkillers, and the unwanted advice that he ought to take it easy for a few days.

Coutelle stalked out of the little clinic, still dressed in his bloodstained clothes, and slept for an hour in the passenger seat while Ray drove to another suspected ARM stronghold. But after that hour, Coutelle was back in charge again, as rock-hard and surly as ever and almost as quick with the acid comments.

Sometime after midnight, they were joined by a half-dozen agents from the Rapid City FBI Field Office. The agents were solid, competent professionals who could be polite or tough by turns, whatever got the job done.

Ray found himself falling back into the familiar, almost pagan rhythms of a high-pressure Bureau operation. Kick ass, take names, bust doors, and let the lawyers sort everything out later. Civilians got ruffled, but not roughed up. The federal agents were used to making allowances for noncombatants who happened to be in the wrong place at the wrong time. Even the tribal cops quickly figured out who was simply a frightened, angry homeowner and who was a real hardcase.

Jack Milton's Guardians of the Oglala Nation didn't bother with such fine discriminations. Even worse, the Guardians took over most of the ass-kicking and name-taking as the hours wore on.

Ray first noticed that the short-haired, foul-mouthed Guardians were getting out of hand when they raided a housing compound at the northern end of the reservation. One of the Guardians shot a family pet. The dog's sin was to bark at the intruders when they came into his front yard.

When the homeowner, a long-haired traditional with a withered leg, intervened and threatened the Guardian with his cane, the Guardian slapped him casually with the butt of his shotgun. Ray was bothered because the blow wasn't necessary. Even worse, it was lousy police work because it could have sparked a riot among the rest of the residents of the compound. But when Ray mentioned his misgivings to Coutelle, the senior agent shrugged it off.

"Take it up with the Tribal Council, Sal," Coutelle suggested. "Or, if you want, you can file a 302 with the Civil Rights Division of Main Justice.

"But do it after we find Jimmy. The clock's running on us too fast to be worried about an overeager Guardian."

It had been a long night for everyone, so Ray sat on his

irritation the rest of the morning. It wasn't easy, especially
when he had to watch a squad of Guardians roust the entire
student body of the Bear Creek Indian School onto the
rocky playing field behind the classroom building while
the facility was searched.

The only good part of the whole incident was that it
gave Ray his first close look at the woman whose picture
he had first seen in Coutelle's mug-shot display. Magdalena Eagle Bear was even tougher in person than she had
seemed in the photo. She was clearly the leader of the
Bear Creek faculty, and a focus of attention for both the
school children and the Guardians. The children gathered
behind her like frightened chicks. Several of the Guardians
taunted her when she objected to the raid.

It took Ray about five seconds to decide that Maggie
was a hell of a lot better-looking than she had appeared in
the mug shot. There was a lithe grace about her, a physical
pride that was unusual among the stolid fleshiness of most
reservation women. As Ray watched her move, he wondered if she had been born with that feline smoothness to
her movements, or if she worked out to keep fit.

The question was answered when Maggie started a soft-
ball game among the students to divert them while the
search was being completed. As she played, it became
obvious that keeping up with the students was more than
enough of a workout to keep anyone fit.

As Ray watched Maggie, he saw that some of the Guardians were as physically aware of her as he was. The long-
legged teacher could not have helped but notice the intent
masculine stares. At times she seemed to taunt the sullen
young Guardians with her own freedom and grace.

Ray watched the subtle baiting uneasily. Maggie Eagle
Bear was tough and proud, he thought, but her brand of
female arrogance could get her in real trouble in a rough,
unsophisticated place like the reservation.

In the end, the search of the school house was fruitless,
at least regarding the other ARM leader, James Looks
Twice. So were all the other searches. After a dozen shat-

tered doors, twice that number of potential civil rights complaints, and eighteen hours of nonstop work, Coutelle and Ray were no closer to closing the case than they had been when the badger first sank its fangs into federal flesh.

The only good news was that Ray finally had a car of his own, comandeered from the Rapid City Field Office motor pool. The car was a bulbous Caprice with a pursuit-class V-8, a cellular phone, a radio, and a weapons locker in the trunk.

Ray had gotten one other thing through the long hours— a better physical sense of the badlands. He and Coutelle had logged over two hundred miles on country highways and back roads. Ray began to feel as though he could find his way across the plains like a frontier scout.

What he had not been able to find was a lead on the killer of Leo Fast Elk. When he finally unloaded Coutelle at the Buffalo Butte to sleep, Ray was tired, but too keyed up to slow down. Instead, he pointed the Caprice toward the shooting scene. It wasn't much, but it was all he had; and when a good investigator runs out of leads, he goes back and starts all over again, looking for whatever he missed.

Ray parked the Caprice on the shoulder of the dirt road close to the shooting scene, then sat for a moment and absorbed the reality of the land. He listened to the hot wind rustle through the dry buffalo grass and the sedges. He heard a yellow-headed black bird chortle in a choke-cherry thicket. Somewhere in the distance a meadowlark sang its liquid, piercing song.

Ray recognized each of the bird calls at an unconscious level. He didn't even notice that he was identifying sounds that a city boy rarely heard. If he had noticed, he might have wondered what other forms of unexpected knowledge were hidden in a brain that had once belonged to an Indian child of the Lakota Sioux tribe.

When Ray's eyes had adusted to the colors and rhythms of the natural landscape, it was easy to pick out items that didn't belong. The beer can in the ditch was obvious. The tiny flash of muddy glass shards from broken beer bottles was less obvious.

The hard shine of something alien caught Ray's eye. It was in the distance, off in the direction of the crime scene. He took a pair of FBI field glasses from the glove box. Through the heat waves that rose from the sun-baked slumpstone, he saw a piece of the same mud-caked Triumph 500 motorcycle he had first seen the day before.

Too many investigators can mess up a crime scene.

Ray rolled out of the car and headed off across the cracking gumbo to investigate the investigator.

Walter Crow Horse was on his haunches, duck-walking across the dusty little nose where Leo Fast Elk's body had lain. Every few feet, the big Indian would stop and lay his palm on the ground, as though trying to soak up information by some arcane form of osmosis.

Ray's curiosity turned to irritation. Crow Horse's methods of investigation were likely to smear any residual evidence that might remain. He quickened his pace, approaching Crow Horse from behind. Ray was still ten yards away when Crow Horse spoke without looking up.

"Ray Little Weasel. Federal Bureau of Interpretation. You snuck right up on me, just like a real city Indi'n."

Ray moved around in front of the tribal officer, who was still sitting on his heels.

"You don't listen very well, Crow Horse."

"Watch out, man, you're stepping on sign."

Ray looked down and saw a faint impression in the dust a few inches from the tip of his loafer. Automatically, he took a step back.

Crow Horse bent over and gently blew some floury dust out of the impression.

"Yestiddy," he said, gauging the amount of dust that had infiltrated the print. "Morning, right after the dew, before the ground really dried out."

Ray started to respond, then stopped. He still wasn't sure whether the big Indian was baiting him or not.

"Leo wasn't killed here," Crow Horse continued. "He

was dumped here. From a car. Bald tread on three tires, new recap on the fourth. Muffler held on by baling wire. Found a little twist of it on a rock back there.''

Crow Horse looked up, his expression still hidden behind dark glasses. ''Seventy-two Plymouth, I'd say.''

''Oh, bullshit,'' Ray snorted, convinced he was being kidded.

''I know 'cause that's the car Leo drove. Been looking for it since yesterday, still ain't found it.''

With that, Crow Horse bent back over the tracks again.

''The dude you want''—Crow Horse moved on to another set of marks—''dragged Leo out on his back.''

He gestured toward the faint tracings of blood that marked the spot where Fast Elk's body had been.

''Then he dragged him over there—you can see the tracings from the heels of his boots—and rolled him over, face down, just like you found him.''

Ray looked at the faint marks on the ground as the Indian spoke, half believing and half sure he was being ridiculed.

''He brushed the earth with a lodgepole pine bough to wipe out tracks. Must have brought the branch with him, 'cause there aren't any lodgepole pines within miles of here.''

Crow Horse duck-walked along the trail as he talked, moving with remarkable grace for a big man with a substantial belly.

''He used the same bough to brush out his tracks when he went back to the vehicle. But he was sloppy, missed a bunch of them . . .''

Crow Horse finally straightened up and took off his glasses so Ray could see his eyes.

''Whoever killed Leo walked heel-toe.'' Crow Horse's eyes were steady and serious.

''Plantigrade,'' Ray said, remembering a term from a forensics class. ''That's the scientific name for it.''

Crow Horse shrugged, as though the scientific name for anything was a matter of indifference to him.

"Like a white man," he said, explaining the significance of the tracks for him.

"So?" Ray asked.

"So Jimmy Looks Twice has a serious Indi'n walk. Toe-heel. And he carries about a hundred and fifty pounds. The dude that killed Leo Fast Elk was a big son of a buck. Print depth and pressure releases say he goes two-ten, maybe two-fifteen."

"You gonna tell me how much change he had in his pocket?" Ray scoffed.

Crow Horse looked down at the track. " 'Bout sixty-three cents. Two quarters, a dime, and three pennies."

Ray stared at him for a long moment, trying to see Crow Horse's eyes, but the Indian's head was tilted toward the marks in the dirt. Ray hesitated, intrigued in spite of himself.

Slowly Ray squatted down next to the tribal cop to examine the trail himself.

"You know you don't have jurisdiction on this anymore," Ray said, not looking at Crow Horse.

"Jurisdiction is the only thing you feds have got, seems to me," Crow Horse said, unimpressed. "You sure as shit don't have much of what you call evidence." He looked at Ray. "You gotta listen to the trees, hoss."

The expression in Crow Horse's eyes reminded Ray of Grandpa Reaches, sad and gentle and far-seeing all at the same time.

"You gotta stop and listen to the sand," Crow Horse said. "It'll tell you things, *Kola*. But you gotta listen first."

Ray picked up a pinch of dusty soil and let it trail away between his fingers before he looked back at Crow Horse.

"Listen yourself," Ray said quietly, "I flew in here from a place called the twentieth century. Damn near the twenty-first. The man I work with has more than two decades in the FBI. We don't have to listen to the trees and talk to the sand to get answers."

Crow Horse grimaced and shook his head. "Go back to the medical examiner, then. Take a look inside Leo's

wounds and tell me, with your fancy forensics, how the
red limestone got in there.''

Automatically Ray looked around the immediate area,
trying to spot the place where red limestone might have
come from. Nothing near looked rusty. Nothing far, either.

Crow Horse nodded. "Only one place round here you
find that kind of limestone—the bed of the Little Walking
River. That's where Leo died. Where the river crosses
Maggie Eagle Bear's place. In *Mato Ska.*''

Crow Horse straightened up and walked away without
looking back, as though he was no longer interested in
arguing with Ray. The Indian disappeared among the mud
crags, leaving Ray staring down at the faint trail in the
dry, dusty clay.

With new eyes, Ray examined the ground. He wasn't
surprised to discover that Crow Horse's theory explained
all the physical evidence Ray could now see with his own
eyes.

Suddenly the big Indian popped up from behind a mud
boulder, where he had been working another line of tracks.

"You weigh one-seventy-three, yeah?" Crow Horse
asked.

Ray stared without answering.

Crow Horse came around the boulder. "Not a beer
drinker. You're one of those tofu and pilaf yuppies we see
on the satellite channels.''

Ray said nothing. It didn't matter. Crow Horse had
enough to say for two men.

"You pack your gun under your coat . . . left armpit,
no right hip, just like J. Edgar taught you.'' Crow Horse
smiled. "But you're not all government issue. You've got
another piece, a .32 caliber, maybe a snub .38.''

Ray tried not to show his surprise. He doubted if he
succeeded. Crow Horse had very shrewd eyes.

"You wear the backup piece in an ankle holster. It gives
you a bit of a left foot-drag. You're wearing new shoes,
too. They're a little tight in the instep, but man, they are

cool.'' Crow Foot grinned. ''And that's what's important, ain't it, hoss? Being cool. That's what counts.''

For a few seconds Ray just stared at Crow Horse. Then Ray looked away, out across the badlands toward the western sky. There was an instant when he thought he heard the faint sound of the heartbeat drum. But when he listened, all he heard was the wind. Finally he looked back at Crow Horse.

''Walter,'' he said slowly, ''you are as full of shit as a Christmas goose.''

Crow Horse's laugh cracked across the badlands like thunder. He was still laughing as he walked to his mud-caked motorcycle and threw his leg over the saddle like the bike was a glass-eyed pinto. He kicked the motor into life and rode away into the shimmering afternoon heat.

Ray found the Little Walking River without any problem. The red limestone took longer. He spent more than an hour slogging up and down the streambanks, looking at water that was opaque with suspended clay particles. The water moved so sluggishly that there was a skin of dust on the surface, deposited by the ceaseless wind.

Even after Ray found the spot where the rock of the streambed changed from white sandstone to red, he hunted for another hour before he found anything else. He was almost ready to give up when he noticed a constant stream of horseflies buzzing around a spot on the bank, as though the sand itself was irresistible.

After a few minutes of observation, Ray realized that the flies were stripping free protein from the sand—dark, dried blood. He probed the sand and found signs that it had been used to soak up and conceal a pool of blood large enough to have come from an adult body.

He poked around in the streamside brush for several minutes until he found a switch that had been recently cut, then thrown away. The leaves of the switch were stained with blood, as though they had been used to stir the sand and conceal the evidence. The spot was within a hundred

yards of a little cluster of houses that was known as *Mato
Ska*.

The streambank sign quickly became mixed with the
tracks of children who played in the willows, and adults
who fished the creek or drew water there. Ray opened a
search spiral from the spot, trying to read the confusing
trails and scattered signs like a forensics investigator
would.

Nothing happened. Out of frustration, he tried to mimic
Crow Horse's methods. Intuition or sheer luck led him to
a spot fifty yards from the dried blood. The bank was
clearly visible from the spot. From it, a rifleman might
have gotten a clear shot at a fleeing Leo Fast Elk.

Someone had sanitized the site thoroughly. Ray found
more tracings of a willow brush but no footprints, no shell
casings, nothing that might add to his understanding of
what had happened. Finally, in irritation, he kicked a thick
cottonwood snag that lay nearby. The old, decaying branch
jumped sideways a foot. Sun gleamed off a fresh brass
casing.

At first Ray was suspicious. Perhaps Crow Horse himself had planted the evidence to mislead the agents. But
this casing had been so well concealed that he had found
it only by luck. It must have skipped off a rock when it
was ejected, then lodged under the snag, hidden from the
murderer during the careful clean-up of the site.

Ray smiled. It was nice to know that the crooks had bad
luck, too.

He fished the casing out of the dust with a twig, then
checked its base: .223 caliber, civilian manufacture but
compatible with the fully automatic M-16.

*Take that, Cooch. I don't know who your "doer" is,
but I was right about the weapon the murderer used.*

Ray dropped the casing into a plastic evidence bag and
stuck it in his pocket. An odd feeling of power flowed
through him, like heat coming up from the ancient South
Dakota ground. He didn't have to cast around anymore.
He knew what he was looking for.

He headed up the little bluff to the terrace where the houses stood. Just as he crested the bluff, an old woman came out of the trees on the other side.

The Indian woman saw the strange white man in the white shirt and loosened necktie, with the pistol obvious on his belt. When he moved to get between her and the houses, she quickened her pace. Finally, she broke into a shuffling trot.

She reached the front door of a small house a few seconds before Ray. It was enough. She threw the bolt and refused to answer his knock.

"Ma'am, I'm a federal agent," Ray said loudly when there was no response. "I want to talk to you for a minute."

As he waited, a black van came growling down the dirt road from the highway.

Good. Someone around here must have heard a burst from an automatic weapon. It's not like they use Uzis to hunt rabbits.

The old woman still refused to answer Ray's knock. He stepped out into the yard as the van braked to a halt.

Ray recognized Magdalena Eagle Bear as she stepped out of the vehicle. She looked from Ray's gun to him, and then quickly around the yard.

"What's going on?" Maggie asked tightly. "Where's Grandma?"

"She locked herself in the house. Maybe you could explain to her that I don't want to hurt anyone. I just want to ask a few questions."

The man in the passenger seat, an Indian with a rolled blue bandanna around his head, stuck his head out the window. There were six children in the van behind him.

"Well, well, if it ain't the Washington Redskin," the man in the van said. "No wonder the old woman locked herself up. We seen what you and your friends are doing all over the res."

Ray gave the man a cold look but said nothing. He was more interested in Maggie.

"So you're the Indian FBI," she said, eyeing him skeptically.

Ray nodded.

"What you doing around here? Looking for Jimmy?"

"Have you seen him?" Ray asked.

Maggie nodded slowly as a cool, knowing little smile slid across her face.

"He crossed the highway in front of me back there." She motioned vaguely in the direction from which she had come.

Ray looked back toward the highway. "Where, exactly?"

"About two miles back. He crossed the road just before he flew off toward the butte."

The words were spoken casually. Ray didn't absorb them for a few seconds. Then he looked at her carefully.

"Flew off?"

Maggie nodded nonchalantly. "Yeah. Jimmy can shape-shift, you know."

"Shape-shift," Ray said.

"Yeah, change himself into different animals. You know, deer, elk, badgers. Just now he was a raven. Tomorrow, who knows?"

"Is that some kind of hereditary condition?" Ray replied sarcastically. "Like idiocy?"

Maggie turned her back on the FBI, went to the van, and opened the cargo door. The children filed out, watching Ray curiously as they walked past. After the children were out, the man in the bandanna worked a short hydraulic ramp into position with a lever, then rolled his wheelchair down onto the ground. He wheeled past Ray with a sneer on his face and followed the children inside.

"I know who you are, Miss Eagle Bear," Ray said to Maggie. "I saw you at the school this morning."

"I saw you, too, along with the Guardians," she said.

"I didn't see him, though," Ray said, indicating the man in the wheelchair. "Who is he?"

"Richard Yellow Hawk. He's an aide at the school."

"He live here with you?"

"No." She turned and started to walk away, obviously through answering questions.

"Miss Eagle Bear," Ray said, moving after her, "do you remember where you were day before yesterday, early morning, maybe six-thirty?"

His tone was official, FBI, hard to avoid.

Maggie turned to face him, her eyes angry. "You got a warrant?"

"I don't need a warrant to ask questions. I don't even need a warrant to take you into custody." Ray paused to let the threat sink in. "Now you want to come with me or do you want to tell me where you were at dawn day before yesterday?"

Maggie crossed her arms and glared at him for several seconds, aware that she was now paying for baiting him about shape-shifting.

"I was on my way into Rapid City," she said.

"Why?"

"I had an interview with a network television corre-spondent who's doing a story."

"Who?"

"Reed Claiborne," she said. "He's doing a story on desecration of tribal burial grounds, the sort of thing you FBI agents are supposed to be investigating but never do."

Ray just looked at Maggie.

"The children were with me," she said. "You can ask them if you don't believe me. What is this all about, any-way?"

Ray thought it over, then decided to drop the bomb and see if there were any interesting pieces to be found.

"I have evidence that Leo Fast Elk was killed here," Ray said calmly. "That's why I wanted to talk to your grandmother."

If the revelation had any effect on Maggie, she didn't show it. "That's not my grandmother. Her name is Maisey Blue Legs. But she doesn't want to talk to you. She's afraid of FBIs."

"Maybe you could talk to her, convince her that we're here to serve the community."

"She won't talk to any *wasi'cus,*" Maggie said. "But oh, that's right. You're Indian."

"That's right, I am."

She looked him up and down, not believing it. "What nation?"

"United States."

Wrong answer. Ray tried again. "Sioux."

"Where'd you get your blood from?"

The form of the question puzzled Ray.

"Who was your father?" Maggie asked bluntly.

"I didn't know him," Ray replied.

"That's too bad. Grandma's very traditional. She'll want to know your bloodlines before she talks to you."

Ray turned away, annoyed. "I'm glad she's traditional, because I'm traditional too. So we can sit together on the front porch and she can tell me about tribal burial grounds and shape-shifting and I can tell her all about the big silver bird that carried me here from Washington."

Maggie's face showed anger, but Ray cut off her response.

"Look, I've had a bellyful of this bull," he said coldly. "This is a federal investigation of a murder. Now I know a reservation Indian might not know about obstructing justice, so I'll—"

"You asshole," Maggie snarled. "I'm from Minneapolis. I spent four years at Dartmouth. I know my rights."

"Then you probably know about abetting a material witness, too," Ray retorted. "But the real question is whether you know that the short list of suspects in Leo Fast Elk's murder has your name so close to the top that I could put you in a federal lockup for a few days just to cool you down."

Maggie glared at Ray. He gave the anger right back.

"Think about that for a minute before you shoot off your mouth," he said coldly. "Think about what that might mean to your kids and to that school of yours. Go ahead. Think!"

"I'm already thinking, you bastard. I'm thinking about calling that network correspondent, asking him whether he wants to come out and get some film of a roust taking place.

"And right after that, I think I'll call the National Lawyers' Guild and ask them to send William Kunstler out. He's always been hot to represent us."

Ray made a sound of disgust.

"So you see, Mr. FBI Agent," Maggie continued angrily, "this reservation Indian knows all about your world. You're trespassing on my property."

"Wrong. I'm conducting a murder investigation."

"Do it somewhere else. Grandma's not coming out. She's not going to talk to you without a warrant. So get lost."

Maggie turned and stalked away across the threadbare grass lawn.

As he watched her go, Ray gauged her anger and wondered whether it was deep enough to drive her to murder.

))) NINE

"Christ, I haven't had to handwrite a 302 for ten years," Ray grumbled, filling in the boxes at the top of the field investigation form with a ballpoint.

"That's what comes of being sentenced to Indian Country," Coutelle replied. "Besides, headquarters will have a hell of a time figuring out those chicken scratches of yours."

"Yours are worse."

"Yeah," Coutelle said with satisfaction. "I'm hoping it will add a full day to the time it takes for the damn report to reach the director's desk."

Ray smiled, knowing what Coutelle was driving at.

"But when this baby lands on that desk, Sal, we'd better have this fucking case wrapped up or we're both headed for the field office on the dark side of the moon. Now, where was I?"

Ray shoved a half-eaten chili size out of the way and repositioned the 302 form so he could read it more easily in the dim light of the Buffalo Butt's back booth. He and Coutelle had managed to eat an entire greasy meal without drawing so much as a sideways look from the nightly regulars in the dingy tavern.

Picking up a paper, Ray read back from the partially completed body of the report. "Ess-slash-ays Coutelle and Levoi apprehended defendant Looks Twice at an ARM safe house on the Badlands Reservation but were then—"

"—were then attacked," Coutelle dictated.

"—ambushed," Ray suggested.

Coutelle nodded vigorously and made the change. "—were then ambushed. Ess-slash-ay Coutelle was stabbed in the arm during the ambush. Defendant Looks Twice assaulted Ess-slash-ay Levoi, then committed unlawful flight to avoid prosecution. Ess-slash-ay Coutelle issued all-points bulletin. End of report."

Ray scratched his signature in a box at the bottom of the 302, folded it, and stuffed it in his coat pocket.

Coutelle drained his beer mug, set it down, and used his left hand to massage the stiff, aching muscles above the heavy bandage on his right forearm.

"You find anything more out in the gumbo?" Coutelle asked.

Ray suppressed a grin. "Thought you'd never ask."

He dug the plastic envelope containing the spent brass out of his pocket and tossed it to Coutelle, who caught it left-handed, then opened his palm and inspected the casing. His dark eyebrows rose as he recognized the shell and began to appreciate its importance.

"Two twenty-three," Coutelle said. He smoothed the thin plastic and looked closely at the base of the shell. "Extractor marks look like it was fired full-auto. Where the hell did you come up with this?"

"*Mato Ska,* Maggie Eagle Bear's property, at the edge of the Little Walking River."

Coutelle looked up sharply.

"That's where the shooting went down," Ray explained. "Leo's body was transported, probably in his own car, out to the badlands and dumped."

The expression on Coutelle's face said he was both skeptical and intrigued. "How did you put that together?"

"Fraternizing," Ray said. "I ran into the tribal officer, Crow Horse."

"Don't put too much faith in that dippy bastard," Coutelle warned. "He gets off playing with your head. He's got no jurisdiction out there, anyway."

Ray shrugged. "It happened by the river. I'm sure of it. I found blood trails. Besides, it makes everything else fit, too. The place is an ARM stronghold. Maggie Eagle Bear is part of the central leadership.''

Coutelle picked up the brass again. ''Anybody else know about this? Did you see Maggie?''

''Yeah, she showed up just after I finished the survey, along with an old traditional she called Grandma, six children, and a big, heavy-set guy in a wheelchair.''

''Wheelchair? Must have been Richard Yellow Hawk,'' Coutelle said, summoning the name from his memory bank. ''You interview her?''

Ray nodded.

''Let's hear the tape.''

''I didn't use tape.''

Coutelle slapped his good hand on the Formica tabletop. ''You've got to get tape, Sal. We're building a case here, remember? Tape is what cases are made of.''

The barman mistook Coutelle's gesture for a service call. He came around to the booth and cleared away the half-eaten sandwiches. When Ray waved the two beer mugs off, the barman cleared them and disappeared.

Ray waited until the man was gone. Then he looked around to make sure none of the other locals was eavesdropping.

''Look, I didn't tape her because she started yelling about warrants and lawyers,'' Ray said. ''But I think we can use her, anyway.''

Coutelle looked at him irritably. ''How?''

''Fit her for the bad-jacket. She's one of the heavies, right? But she spent a good ten minutes alone with me. Why don't we just let it slip that she's become a cooperating individual, an informant?''

Coutelle didn't say anything.

''Look,'' Ray said roughly, ''they like fucking with our minds, so why can't we fuck with theirs?''

The other agent examined the idea, looking for flaws. ''She's got media contacts,'' he warned finally.

''So do we. Don't forget, I was sent out here as a media

rep. I could scout up the local cops-and-robbers reporter
and get some stories out. Two sides can play any game.''

Coutelle thought some more, then shook his head reluctantly. "Leave her be, Sal."

"Why? If she's an ARM cadre leader, why should we
back off? What the hell was Leo Fast Elk doing at her
place, anyway?''

"He was councilman from that district. Maybe he was
serving papers, an eviction notice or something. Hell,
maybe he's getting a little ass on the side, I don't know.''

Ray was quiet while Coutelle talked his way through his
own objections. The senior agent shook another painkiller
into his palm and tossed it down without water.

"All I know," he continued, "is that we only have
twenty-four hours to nail Looks Twice. After that, this
won't be an in-and-out case. It will be a career case.''

Coutelle saw the look on Ray's face and nodded slowly.
"Think on it, Sal. How many years you have left until you
pull the pin? However many it is, you'll spend every one
of them eating fry bread and dog soup if you don't come
up with our doer.''

Ray grimaced.

"So, first thing in the morning," Coutelle continued,
"you better start showing your handsome red face around
the res, get the traditionals to talking. They're hiding him.
I know it as sure as I know when payday comes.''

"Red?" Ray touched his own face, then looked point-
edly at Coutelle. "Shit, Cooch, you're darker than I am.
Why don't you go out? You'd pass for Indian quicker than
me.''

Coutelle looked at him sharply. But his words were cut
short as the front window of the tavern exploded inward.
An instant later a one-quart beer bottle with a flaming rag
stuffed in the neck cartwheeled through the opening. The
Molotov cocktail shattered on the end of the pool table
and exploded into a ball of flame as gasoline burned like
a second sunrise in the gloomy bar.

Ray and Coutelle ducked away from the flames and

stayed put, waiting for a second missile. A triumphant, rising war whoop, followed by the sound of squealing tires and a racing engine, told them the attack was over.

The sawdust on the tavern floor burst into guttering flames and the room began to fill with smoke. The barman came out from behind his rank of beer taps, a sawed-off shotgun in one hand and a kitchen-sized fire extinguisher in the other.

"Goddamn prairie niggers!" he bellowed.

When he cut loose with the extinguisher, the stream of carbon dioxide blew burning sawdust in all directions. Locals scrambled out from beneath tables and the shuffleboard machine.

Ray and Coutelle ran out the side door in time to see brake lights flash once before the speeding pickup truck disappeared into the night. Immediately Ray started for the Caprice. Coutelle's shout stopped him.

"Look at this!"

Ray grabbed a flashlight from the car and went to the door of Unit 6. The screen door had been ripped from its flimsy hinges. Ray flashed the light on the solid room door where Coutelle had pointed. Red paint made a crude circle on the warped wood. There was a freehand feather drawn through the red circle.

Coutelle studied the crude ARM symbol. In the darkness, the red paint looked remarkably like coagulating blood.

"Somebody's trying to tell us it's checkout time," he suggested wearily. "You want the first watch, Sal, or the second?"

The Dakotas sat under a dome of high pressure. The clear, dry air magnified the strength of the sun, focusing it like a magnifying glass through the window of the Caprice. Ray drove like a man pursued.

He was.

Four hours of sleep had brought the heartbeat drum back. At first Ray thought it was only the sound of the blood in his own ears. Then he heard it in the slapping trip-hammer rhythm of his tires on the washboard gravel roads as he ranged back and forth across the reservation, seeking leads. It followed him all over, the relentless rhythm of the drum calling to him in a language he was finding harder and harder to deny.

Ray was beginning to feel as though he was suspended in time and place. His worst fear was that Coutelle might be right, that he would spend the rest of his career, the rest of his life, chasing fugitive wraiths and dust devils through the primal currents of heat rising from the plains.

Dog soup and fry bread. The Third World spreading away on all sides, barren and hopeless, spirit-ridden, filled with the beating of a huge, invisible heart.

Why did Maggie ever come back? Why would anyone who got out ever come back? This isn't home. It's hell on earth, hot and smothering, and stronger than any one soul.

The drumbeat quickened, deepened, and Ray's turncoat heart kept time.

Dog soup and fry bread forever. Jesus. Will I have to turn in my credentials to escape the badlands?

For a moment, Ray thought it would be worth the price just to get out. Then he heard his own thought and was shocked. The Bureau was his centering point, his wife, his family, his children, his comrades, his work, and his social life, all wrapped in one tidy package.

How would I ever get by without the order and discipline and purpose that the FBI gives me? What would I do?

The retort came to Ray in Coutelle's derisive tone.

Hell, Sal, you could always become a tribal policeman. You could get Crow Horse to teach you how to touch-track. You could get Maggie to teach you all the telltale signs of shape-shifters. You could take Indian lessons from some reservation medicine man.

Ray heard his partner's jeering tone perfectly with the ear that was in his mind. It managed for a time to drown the throbbing of the heartbeat drum.

Coutelle's bitter humor was a good antidote to the intangible pull of the reservation. Ray wondered if that was why Coutelle turned his humor so often against the Indians. The anger was more complex than the casual racism that overtook so many cops, whether they were federal agents or urban street cops. Professional policemen saw human nature at its worst. They kept sane by slicing back at life with black humor.

But Coutelle's acid-edged jokes were too sharp, too precise, laser-guided ordnance rather than humor. The jokes came in wave after wave, as though the agent felt on the verge of being overwhelmed after nine years of looking at the face of reservation violence.

Too many bowls of dog soup . . .

Ray smiled grimly. He knew as well as Coutelle that aboriginal delicacies such as dog soup didn't exist now and likely never had. It was just that field agents went sour, the same as cops did everywhere.

Coutelle needed some clean white-collar crooks to chase. Maybe even some Colombian dope dealers or Panamanian money launderers. He needed an assignment that would get him off the reservation, away from the oppressive poverty and the subliminal drumbeat of pain and despair that pervaded the badlands.

The red/white, red/white flashing of a dusty lightbar finally caught Ray's eye in the rearview mirror. He blinked and did a double-take, not believing his eyes. A tribal police cruiser wallowed along the dirt road behind him. Walter Crow Horse's massive shoulders and black Stetson filled the driver's corner of the bug-stained cruiser's windshield.

Ray let him eat more dust for a few miles, then gave in. It was obvious that Crow Horse wasn't going to stop short of pulling the FBI over.

The Indian police officer stepped out of his car with a ticket book in his hand. He stopped to make a note of the Caprice's tag number before he approached Ray's window.

"License and registration, please."

"Kiss my ass."

Crow Horse dropped his sunglasses an inch and stared at Ray directly, unsmiling.

"No, fed, you kiss *my* ass. This is *my* jurisdiction and you were doing fifty-nine in a fifty-five."

Ray craned his neck, looking back at the dilapidated cruiser Crow Horse drove.

"You haven't got radar in that pile of shit," Ray said.

"I don't need radar. I can tell."

"Bullshit."

Crow Horse tipped his sunglasses back in place. "I listened to the wind when you went by. It said, 'Fifty-nine, nail his ass.' "

Ray snorted.

The Indian's broad, dark face seemed almost ready to crack a smile as he kept talking. "It said, 'Get him before the traditionals do.' "

The smile came, spread a little—but Crow Horse kept on writing the ticket.

"You need to understand," Crow Horse said without looking up from his work, "that you're just the second coming of the First Cavalry, so far as the traditionals are concerned. They don't want you here, and nobody's going to talk to you."

Ray slumped in the seat, hot, tired, bored, and irritated.

"Nope," Crow Horse went on, "nobody's going to talk to you except the *Wica'sa Wakan,* and I don't know why he'd bother."

Ray sat up, not sure what he had heard. "The what?"

"The man who sent me to find you. Says he has information. He'll only give it to the Indian agent."

Crow Horse savored the play on words, then ripped the ticket off the pad and handed it to Ray.

"You can mail that in or appear in tribal court if you want to contest it. I wouldn't advise contesting it though. We still conduct trial by ordeal round the res." He started back to his cruiser. "Follow me," he said over his shoulder.

* * *

The sun-hammered Airstream trailer crouched like an ancient breadbox with wheels at the edge of the place called White Calf Table. As a place to live, the trailer looked hot, uncomfortable, and lonely way off at the end of the long, washboard dirt road.

But it had the best view of the Dakota landscape Ray had seen in all his quartering of the reservation. Far off to the west the Black Hills loomed darkly behind a silver veil of heat rising from the earth. The badlands lay in front, like a relief map of hell.

Yet the place somehow had a less forbidding aspect now, as though time and proximity had begun to train Ray's eye to appreciate the subtle gradations of color and mood that haunted the land. There was an austere beauty to the landscape that slid past his guard as certainly as the relentless heartbeat rhythms coursing through his blood, through his body, through his mind, becoming so deeply a part of him that he rarely noticed.

Ray parked beside an open-sided brush arbor and stepped out of the Caprice. The sound of insects buzzing in the sage that hung from the rafters of the arbor was oddly peaceful. The astringent fragrance of sage and distance pervaded the whole area, as though time itself had taken up residence here.

"What's this guy's name?" Ray asked, looking around the little compound.

"Grandpa Samuel Reaches," Crow Horse said. "Heavy med'cine. Really heavy."

"He's a medicine man?"

Crow Horse nodded. There was no hint of a smile on his face now. "You bring tobacco?"

Ray looked quizzical.

The Indian cop frowned, tired of dealing with the uninitiated. "When you go see an elder, you always bring some tobacco as a gift."

"I knew that," Ray said in mock defiance. "I learned it in Boy Scouts."

Crow Horse dug a package of cigarettes from the pocket beneath his badge.

"Yeah, right," he said, flipping the pack to Ray.

Crow Horse removed his black Stetson as he mounted the flimsy single step beside the door of the Airstream. A sleeping nest of cats stirred and stared drowsily at him, secure in the knowledge that he would step over them because everyone always did. The tribal officer knocked once before he opened the screen door and stepped into the stifling little trailer.

Inside, the Airstream looked like a disorganized nickel booth at the world's sorriest swap meet. Grandpa Reaches sat in a taped and tucked lawn chair, his alert black eyes moving from side to side, watching TV. The old set was black and white and had a coat hanger for an antenna, but it worked better than the one at the Buffalo Butte Motel. The Rapid City channel played afternoon cartoons, Mr. Magoo. There was no sound.

Grandpa Reaches didn't look up when Crow Horse and Ray came in. Despite the heat, the old man wore a black watch cap pulled down to his ears, a Pendleton wool shirt, and a pair of jeans.

Crow Horse sat down on an old kitchen stool that had a rip in its vinyl seat. He took the cigarettes ceremoniously from Ray and offered them to the old shaman. Grandpa nodded and took the Luckies in both hands, like a priest accepting a chalice. He ran long, gnarled fingers over the top of the package as if he were reading Braille, then glanced at Ray for a second.

Ray remembered the depth of the old man's black, marble-hard eyes from their encounter outside the sweat lodge. But this time Grandpa Reaches seemed to be looking right through his skin and flesh and bones, examining the soul inside. He took Ray's measure in less than a second, nodded, then went back to watching Magoo.

"He a traditional?" Ray asked.

Crow Horse gave him a look of faint disbelief. "No, he's from the fucking Bronx."

Grandpa Reaches glanced sharply at Crow Horse and lectured him in Lakota. Crow Horse nodded, accepting the shaman's rebuke. Then Grandpa began to speak again, amused. He gestured toward Ray several times, then leaned back, waiting for Crow Horse to translate.

"What did he say?" Ray asked.

"He wants to know if you ever watch Mr. Magoo. He says the old dude's not to be trusted. There's something wrong with him. He acts crazy."

Ray glanced at the tiny television screen. At that moment Magoo ran headlong into a wall and saw stars. Grandpa cackled and pointed at the screen, as though Magoo had just proved his point. Crow Horse laughed like a bull and nodded.

"Grandpa says Magoo needs to go up on the mountain, get himself focused."

Ray got the impression the advice was intended for him, but he said nothing.

Grandpa spoke again. The Lakota seemed alien and guttural, but oddly flowing. It was a language that had been spoken for a long time and still was vivid, supple, and alive.

The conversation went back and forth between the two Indians several times, but Ray got the clear feeling he was the subject.

"Grandpa likes to trade," Crow Horse finally said. "No one stops here without getting stuck in the old Indian barter thing. Grandpa says he likes your sunglasses."

Grandpa nodded and smiled toothlessly. He pointed at his own eyes, then at Ray.

Ray shifted unhappily. The Ray-Bans weren't plain, old aviators. They were the model called The General, as in MacArthur. They had amber lenses and gold-plated frames. They had cost him a hundred and a half at a shop in the Tysons Corner Mall.

Grandpa nodded again, drew his fingers across his face, then showed Ray a small stone. It was a river-polished moss agate, pretty enough but not worth fifteen cents, much less the price of the sunglasses.

Trade for trade, the gesture said.

The shaman's smile said he might have something else to offer, too, but not without the trade he had already proposed.

Ray doubted that he could recoup the hundred and a half from Frank Coutelle's informant fund. On the other hand . . .

Slowly, reluctantly, Ray slipped the glasses off and gave them to the sly old shaman, receiving the moss agate in return. The shaman chopped the air with his hand, signaling a done deal.

As soon as the swap was concluded, Crow Horse's laughter filled the little trailer. Grandpa joined in, nodding and pointing at the glasses, then at the stone. Any fool could see who had gotten the better deal.

Ray shoved the rock in his pocket and waited. Grandpa Reaches began speaking. Crow Horse translated almost simultaneously.

"Grandpa says you stopped the *inipi* two days ago."

Ray didn't deny the accusation.

"But he says he's not unhappy with you. He isn't unhappy because he knows you."

"He knows me?"

"He says he saw you in a vision long ago."

Crow Horse hesitated, as though Grandpa's words were a surprise to him, too. The officer tried to ask a question in Lakota but Grandpa cut him off. The alien words tumbled from his tongue so fast that Crow Horse had to scramble to keep up.

And while he spoke, the shaman held Ray's eyes in his clear black gaze, giving Ray the eerie feeling of being able to understand the Lakota words without translation.

"He says you come from a *wasi'cu* city in the East but that your people, way long time ago, are of the Minnicojou Sioux. But you don't know that . . . because you're as far from yourself as a hawk is from the moon. Crazy as Magoo.''

Grandpa became more agitated. He began speaking with gestures as well, sign language that conveyed his meaning more subtly than words. His hands slapped, punctuating sign sentences.

Ray began to feel dazed, as though he were inside a drum, listening to the echoes of his own heartbeat doubled and redoubled, filling the room, the trailer, the world.

"Grandpa says he knew you were coming here. He was told.''

"Who told him?'' Ray asked distantly.

"*Tunkasila*. The spirits. It was their will that you come here. So we will smoke the pipe. Then there can be no lies between us.''

A memory came to Ray like lightning—Carl Vaughn's frightened, furious face at the moment Ray betrayed him in front of Honest Abe's Memorial. Beads of sweat gathered on Ray's forehead. The idea that the old shaman might be able to penetrate all his lies was unsettling. Ray told lots of lies in his work; it was required. He lied every time he went undercover. Lies were one of the tools of his trade.

Lies were necessary to get at the truth, but this old man wanted to strip him of them.

Grandpa Reaches took a long, hand-carved ash stick from a pouch on the counter beside him. He fitted the stick into a carved pipestone bowl that was the color of aged brick. His knobby fingers were deft as he stuffed rough-cut tobacco into the bowl.

Once the bowl was full, he stood up and carefully offered the pipe in each of the four directions, then cradled the heavy stone bowl in his hands.

Crow Horse produced a kitchen match, struck it with his thumbnail, and fired the tobacco in the bowl.

Grandpa drew hard on the pipe, held the smoke in his mouth, then let it trail away. He offered the pipe to Ray. The FBI agent stared at the stone bowl uneasily.

"Go ahead," Crow Horse said. "It ain't Mexican weed or anything. It's just tobacco, an offering. The smoke will carry your prayers up."

Ray inspected the pipe with a cop's cold, unbelieving eye.

"If you don't smoke, he's gonna think you're hiding something," Crow Horse said.

Finally Ray took the pipe, looked at it as though he thought it might bite, then passed it unceremoniously to Crow Horse. The Indian cop looked disappointed. He tried to get Ray to take the pipe again.

"It's important," Crow Horse said. "You've just insulted—"

Grandpa Reaches cut off the words with a gesture. The shaman wasn't insulted. He gave Ray a long, sad, compassionate look. Then the old man's eyelids closed and his head tipped back, as though he had fallen asleep between one heartbeat and the next.

Beneath hooded lids, his eyes moved as though searching for something far, far away. His hands reached into the skin bag he kept beside him. He withdrew an ancient rattle made from the shell of a painted box turtle. Slowly, the rattle turned in his hands. The seeds inside made a soft, unearthly sighing sound.

Hair stirred on Ray's arms.

"Taku wakan," the old shaman intoned.

"Very sacred, he says," Crow Horse translated softly. "Five hundred years old, that turtle shell, passed from four grandfathers. Powerful."

Words came softly from the old man. His eyes moved, searching and finding, seeing something that made him profoundly unhappy, something he could not ignore. Crow Horse translated the vision in soft tones that matched Grandpa's sadness.

"I see a man. *Ieska.* Half Indian. He is in dirty clothes. Bad teeth. Standing near . . . a mission . . . a church . . . no, a school. In a city. He is waiting for someone, someone he loves."

Suddenly Ray couldn't breathe. He had to leave. He reached for the door but couldn't push through it. He stood there against his will, his back to the old shaman, waiting and fearing and knowing it was too late to turn back, too late to flee.

Walter Crow Horse's voice had blended inseparably with the shaman's. Lakota words and English wrapped around one another, reinforcing meanings, making them unmistakable.

Heart breaking, yet still beating, beating, pursuing the truth like a bird of prey.

Striking.

"A boy. Leaves the school. Other *wasi'cu* boys. Playing, just the way boys all do. The boy sees the Indi'n man waiting. But the other boys are laughing, making names, making pain at this Indi'n man.

"And his boy pretends that his eyes do not see him. He runs past him. The Indi'n man stands alone . . . sad."

Ray felt suspended between earth and hell. Slowly he turned around and looked at the shaman.

Grandpa Reaches was old and weak, and he was the most terrifying adversary Ray had ever faced, the ancient rattle in his hand more dangerous than a viper.

Slowly, Grandpa lowered his head until his chin was on his chest. His eyes opened, focused.

Crow Horse handed him the pipe. Grandpa sucked the tobacco in the bowl back into fire again, letting the smoke rise and spread through the air. He passed the pipe to Crow Horse. Then he closed his eyes again.

Yet he was staring directly at Ray. The old shaman's eyes seemed to burn through his own lids with a clear, black flame. The ancient turtleshell came alive. Its sighing sound grew louder, more insistent, more menacing.

Crow Horse translated Grandpa's words almost before they were spoken.

"This Indi'n man with dirty clothes and bad teeth . . . somewhere else now. On a floor? Yes, a cold floor in a cold room in a cold land. He can't breathe. He can't—"

A gasp and a glottal sound burst from the shaman.

Ray jumped as though he had just seen a ghost.

The reaction broke the spell. Grandpa's eyes flew open. He stared at Ray, as though he were as surprised by the vision as anyone else.

Suddenly, Ray was sure it had all been a scam. It had to be. Someone had told them. Someone from the tribe he never knew.

That was the only explanation. It had been like that in the badlands, too. Crow Horse had seen all those things with his eyes—the backup gun, the new shoes that pinched. It was the kind of trick a magician could work, or a carny fortune-teller, the guy who could guess your weight at a glance because you stood on a hidden scale.

Ray's fear turned to anger. He was himself again, an FBI agent, a trained investigator, a rational man; he wasn't an Indian who shared visions and heard the heart beating at the center of all life, beating, beating, beating.

"Knock it off," Ray said coldly. "I came here for some information. Does this old man have something to tell me or not?"

Crow Horse looked at the beads of sweat that rolled down Ray's face. "He gave you all the information he has. And you know it, don't you?"

Ray checked his watch like a man anxious for an excuse, any excuse, to flee. "Ask him, straight out, if he knows anything about Leo's murder or not."

Crow Horse grunted a question in Lakota. He glanced at Ray meaningfully, like he was trying to tell the old shaman that the FBI man was angry.

Grandpa Reaches responded slowly at first, then with increasing intensity. The words came with hand signs again, long, complicated sentences with fingers that pointed and arms that gestured. He worked feverishly, slapping punctuation with palms that cracked like pistol shots in the closed little trailer. Finally, he underlined his words with one solid slap and slumped, wheezing and panting, in his tattered lawn chair.

Ray waited for a translation. None came. "What did he say, damn it?"

Crow Horse stood up and started packing the rattle and pipe back into the skin bag from which they had come.

"He said he knows nothing."

"Shit!"

Ray slammed the tattered screen door of the trailer behind him. Crow Horse followed immediately. He caught up with the agent at the door of his car.

Ray glared angrily. "Don't you people ever get tired of trying to mind-fuck the white Indian?"

"Grandpa Reaches doesn't play games," Crow Horse said evenly.

"Then what was that last bit?" Ray demanded. "He went on for five minutes like he was reciting the Gettysburg Address and all you can translate is no. Bullshit. Tell me exactly what the crazy old bastard said."

Crow Horse studied Ray uneasily, not sure whether to tell him the truth. Or how much of the truth.

"Grandpa saw an owl," he finally said. "Last week."

"So?"

"The owl is a messenger. You see one, it means someone is going to die." Crow Horse looked around, as though he was telling a well-guarded secret. "The owl told Grandpa about Leo."

"Are you saying that he had prior knowledge of the killing?"

Crow Horse shook his head quickly. "Not unless you call a premonition prior knowledge."

"It didn't take the old man all afternoon to tell you about the owl," Ray accused.

"The owl also said, 'Listen to the water.' "

"Listen to the water? *Listen to the water?* Jesus, Crow Horse, get a life. I suppose the owl was the same one that told Grandpa to look out for Mr. Magoo!"

Ray climbed into the Caprice, slamming the door behind him. He started the engine and snapped the shifter into reverse, but Crow Horse stopped him by bending down and looking into the window. His expression was earnest.

"I'd better tell you the rest, even if you think it's a crock of shit," the Indian said unhappily. "Grandpa said you're chasing the wrong man. Jimmy didn't do it."

Crow Horse reached in with one hand and gently touched the breast pocket of Ray's white shirt with a crooked forefinger.

"Grandpa said you have a good heart but you have to learn to follow it."

The gentle understanding in Crow Horse's eyes only made Ray angrier. He showed Crow Horse an extended middle finger, the only sign language he knew.

"Tell him, 'Follow this,' " Ray snapped.

"No sense in that," Crow Horse said without anger. 'Grandpa's been eighty-seven years a holy man. He talks to the earth. He can read you like last year's Sears catalogue."

Without waiting for an answer, Crow Horse turned and walked to his battered cruiser. He left in a cloud of dust.

For a moment Ray sat confused and pursued, listening to the heartbeat he didn't want to hear. Then he let his foot off the brake of the Caprice and drove off. As he passed the trailer, he caught one more glimpse of Grandpa Reaches. The old shaman sat in his chair, staring contentedly at the silent Mr. Magoo.

Staring through a very expensive pair of sunglasses. Ray's glasses.

Scammed again.

TEN

FOR A TIME, Ray simply drove, letting the highway carry him along, trying to find his balance after the unnerving encounter with the two Indians.

Medicine men or ministers, shamans or hustlers, they're all alike. They all played their own little mind tricks, trying to get behind your guard.

He had never found it difficult to see through the sidewalk preachers, the Hare Krishna chanters, and the black faith healers in Washington. But Crow Horse and Grandpa Reaches were different. He didn't know why. He just knew it was true. For just a second, he had come close to buying their act. It must have been the heat in the trailer. Or the isolation.

Maybe the spell of the Great Plains and the badlands is nothing more than sensory deprivation.

Ray looked almost desperately out the windshield. There was nothing to look at, nothing to break the landscape, nothing to distract him. He wished he were back in the city, with pretty girls on the sidewalks and chauffeured limousines and the familiar bullpen in the Washington Field Office. He knew what to expect from those things. He knew how to control them.

And right now he needed them to define the boundaries of his world.

That old man couldn't have seen what he saw. He couldn't have been hearing heartbeat.

And neither could I.

Ray drove west at eighty miles per hour, looking for

landmark, looking for anything that might orient him in a world that was increasingly alien. It was a long time before he felt the butt of his gun digging into his ribs. He took the .357 Magnum out of its belt holster and put it on the seat beside him. The heft of the gun was familiar, a reminder.

Automatically he tapped the leather badge holder in his shirt pocket, a gesture he repeated a dozen times a day, like a priest crossing himself. The Bureau gun and the credentials. They were what defined an agent. The Bureau handed them to you your first day on the job, and stripped them from you the last day. In between, they were your responsibility. Protect them with your life.

Lose your gun or your badge and you're fired.

There was a story that every agent swore was true about a poor son of a bitch who was on his way to the field office one morning when a civilian brushed passed him on the New York subway platform. Suspicious of pickpockets, the agent tapped his breast pocket. Sure enough, his credentials were gone.

The agent yelled and sprinted after the thief, who was running for an uptown train. The thief made it just as the doors started to close. The agent caught the thief's arm and tried to pull him off the departing train. The doors clamped shut on the thief's arm. The desperate agent hung on.

Something had to give. It was the thief's arm. The agent felt the bone snap just before he let go.

There might have been a certain pleasure in vengeance, but it didn't recover the agent's credentials. As soon as he got to the office, he summoned the members of his squad and told them what had happened. Putting their detecting skills to work, they began checking every hospital emergency room in Manhattan, because any man with a compound fracture of the arm was going to need help, and fast.

The manhunt had just begun when the agent's phone rang. It was his wife. "Guess what you left on the bureau

this morning, dear,'' she asked. ''You're always so worried about losing your credentials, I thought I'd let you
know they were safe.''

Only an FBI agent would laugh at the story, because
only an agent could understand the tribal importance of
the piece and the badge. Ray still had the icons of his
office, but he felt as though the rest of it had somehow
disappeared, leaving him one man alone in an empty landscape that was infused with heat and the beating of a drum
only he and a crazy old shaman could hear.

Ray stopped on a small rise and got out to shake the
tension from his body. He stood beside the road, letting
his eyes adjust to the immense scale of the landscape. Off
toward the north, the plains rolled away forever. The once-
glaciated ground was broken here and there by tables and
terraces, interruptions in the otherwise level surface that
gave definition to the land.

Each of these spots held its own mysteries, its own ex-
planations; but Ray felt as though he would never begin
to decipher the code. He was doomed to stand forever on
the outside of a desolate landscape, listening to the wind.
For a man whose pride lay in uncovering secrets, the sensation was immensely frustrating.

He squinted off into the west, beyond the badlands, toward the Black Hills a hundred miles away. He was not
used to places where you had to look so far to see anything. The glare of reflected sunlight reminded him of the
sunglasses he had traded for a simple river agate. Now the
heat haze of the Dakotas obscured everything.

And when you did penetrate the haze, there was nothing
to see except more of what you had already seen.

*What a fucked-up piece of country. No wonder they gave
it to the losers in the war.*

Ray stood there for a long time, trying to see through
the sinuous currents of heat. He saw nothing but more
waves, more haze, more endless, wind-scoured land. He
squinted harder, trying to focus his eyes. Nothing new
appeared in his field of vision.

I need a new pair of sunglasses.

Farther down the road he found a sign saying, REDPATH GENERAL STORE. Almost as an afterthought, someone had added: SUPPLIES, SPORTING GOODS & SUNDRIES.

The sign needed new paint. So did the general store. On the other hand, it was the only store in twenty miles.

The storekeeper was a heavy-set Anglo with a curly red beard and a wind-burned red face. He looked up from a stack of carbon-copy charge-account books and nodded pleasantly.

"Afternoon," Ray said.

He looked around the store. It was crowded with an ill-organized mixture of tools and fishing rods, work clothes and groceries. Ray supposed there was an order to it all, but that order escaped him. The feeling of missing clues was beginning to irritate him.

"You have any sunglasses?" he asked sharply.

"A few," the storekeeper said, nodding toward a display case. "Help yourself. I've got these damn accounts to straighten out."

There were no Ray-Bans in the case, which was no surprise. But there were several other types of sunglasses. They were popular items on the plains. Ray found an off-brand pair that had glass instead of plastic lenses. He cleaned the dust off with his handkerchief and laid the sunglasses on the counter.

The storekeeper looked up from his accounts. "You must be that federal agent."

His tone was amiable enough, but Ray immediately felt his back hair rise.

"What gave you that idea?"

The storekeeper let his eye trail down the silk four-in-hand tie, over the white oxford-cloth shirt, to the sturdy leather belt and the empty clip-on holster.

"Just a hunch," he said dryly. "Maybe it was the shoes."

Ray glanced at his leather loafers. Crow Horse had been right; they looked better than they felt. Except that now, after several days in the dust and several hours in the riverbank mud, the expensive loafers had begun to lose their looks.

So had the wool trousers that he wore. The seam that held the left cuff had torn open. His holdout gun showed through the gap in the fabric.

When in Rome . . .

"How about some jeans?" Ray asked.

"Coming right up. We've been outfitting people round here since 1890."

The storekeeper went to a shelf and hunted through a stack of Levi's.

"I thought this was reservation land," Ray said as he waited. "You don't look like an Indian."

"I'm a quarter Sioux, and the rest Scots," came the muffled answer. "That's where the name comes from."

"Quite a mix."

"Not as much as you'd think. My Scots ancestors were just as wild and unruly as the Sioux ever thought of being. They were transported to Canada in 1745 and just kind of migrated west and south until they ended up here."

He turned around, grinning broadly beneath his ginger-colored beard. "My people have been on the losing side of battles for about five centuries, from Culloden to Wounded Knee."

"Five centuries. Must be hardheaded folks."

"Yeah. And piss-poor politicians. Good outlaws, though. Comes of not believing in anything bigger than your clan. They fit right in with the Lakotas. Same kind of way of looking at the world. A warrior's way."

"I've got some Scots-Irish blood in my ancestry," Ray said. Then he added dryly. "It doesn't seem to be in as much demand as the Sioux blood at the moment."

Redpath gave a crack of laughter and went back to sorting through jeans.

"Someday people will figure out that the Sioux tribe is as noble, and as corrupt, as any other social organization," Redpath said after a moment. "Institutions make rules to suit themselves. There are always some people in every clan or tribe that are good at making those rules sit up and do tricks. Others are only good at rebelling against eating stone soup year after year.''

Only half of Ray's attention was on Redpath's monologue. The rest of it was on the stack of account pads on the counter. They kept track of monthly charges the old-fashioned way, listing purchases by individuals and families. No credit card, no monthly statement, just a good deal of trust on both sides. The customers bought what they needed, when they needed it. The storekeeper recorded each purchase in the customer's account book. Once a month, or whenever the debtor had money, the account was settled.

Many of the names were the same as the ones on Coutelle's intelligence reports listing traditionals and ARM sympathizers.

The storekeeper handed a pair of Levi's to Ray. "Try these.''

Ray went in to the closet-sized changing room with the sheet for a door, stripped off his slacks, and pulled on the jeans. To his surprise, they fit. He pulled the cuff of the jeans down over his hideout gun and emerged from the changing room. The storekeeper examined him and nodded, then glanced at his loafers.

"They still give you away. Try boots. Or maybe Nikes. Lot of them around the res. Cheaper than boots and a lot more comfortable in the heat.''

Ray remembered the hideout gun and opted for boots. The storekeeper dug out a pair of low-heeled Red Wings with tops wide enough to cover the .38. Surprisingly, the boots pinched less than the loafers had.

Redpath wrapped the loafers and slacks in a piece of butcher paper, then toted up the sale. It came to seventy-three dollars, including twelve dollars for the sunglasses. Redpath gave him a handwritten receipt, the parcel, and two dollars' change.

"Whatever you do,'' the storekeeper warned, "don't

try to pass yourself off as a representative of the tribal government. To some of the traditionals, that's damn near worse than being from Washington.''

"I picked up on that," Ray said, "but I haven't figured out why."

"Stick around. You'll figure it out real quick."

Ray parked the Caprice in a little cottonwood grove far enough from Maggie Eagle Bear's house that she wouldn't have to explain a second federal visit, if she didn't want to. When he approached the house on foot, he caught a flicker of movement in some scrap lumber piled against the foundation.

Very carefully Ray went to investigate, having developed a certain wariness about creatures that lived in the crawlspaces beneath reservation houses. He spotted the movement again. This time he was close enough to see it was nothing but a young rabbit cowering in a blind corner formed by two heavy timbers.

At first Ray thought the rabbit was caught on a nail. As he moved closer to free the shivering creature, he almost stepped on the coiled body of a diamondback rattlesnake.

The snake had trapped the little rabbit against the scrap lumber and was preparing to strike. When the snake sensed the human intruder, it went into defensive posture, coiled and shaking its tail, making its rattle sing a death song. The gaping mouth exposed pale fangs whose hollow, razor-tipped length was meant to pump poison into the victim's nervous system.

With the smooth speed of a man who has done it a thousand times, Ray snapped the Smith & Wesson from its holster and fired. Before the sound of the shot exploded against the side of the house like a thunderclap, he fired again.

The first shot hit the snake in the body. The second shattered its head and flung the body aside like a bloody rag. The sound of the shots echoed away across the prairie and faded.

Ray stood locked in the shooting stance until he was sure the snake was dead. Only then did he realize his hands were shaking and his body was drenched with sweat. The frightened cries of children seeped through the wall beside him.

He stepped back from the tattered rattlesnake and started to holster his weapon; then instinct warned him he was no longer alone. He spun around and found himself looking into the black eyes of a double-barreled shotgun.

Maggie Eagle Bear's equally black eyes stared at him from just over the bead sight of the shotgun.

"What are you doing here?" she asked in a low, cold voice.

Ray still had his gun in his right hand, but he spread his arms and pointed the muzzle skyward to demonstrate his peaceful intent.

"It's okay," he said. "There was a rattlesnake hanging around the lumber. I had to shoot. Sorry. I didn't mean to frighten the children."

Slowly, Maggie lifted her cheek from the stock of the shotgun. But she kept the weapon at her shoulder. She studied Ray for a few seconds, trying to decide whether to believe him.

The decision was too long in coming for Ray's comfort. He had visions of a shootout on the steps of a cabin in the great dead heart of South Dakota. He wondered how his service record would read: *Killed snake but was killed by mistake.*

Then Grandma Maisey Blue Legs shuffled out onto the porch and craned her neck to see who was doing all the shooting. She stood behind Maggie and studied the federal agent. Ray half expected her to turn and run again, but she didn't. Instead she whispered something in Lakota to Maggie.

Maggie glanced at the old woman, listening, but she kept the gun trained on Ray. Grandma spoke again, more insistent this time. Finally Maggie lowered the gun. Grandma spoke again. When Maggie didn't respond,

Grandma picked at the sleeve of her flannel shirt, pushing her. Maggie hesitated, as though she were being forced to do something she found distasteful. Finally, she faced Ray.

"Grandma wants to know if you want a cup of *waka-lapi.*"

Ray lowered his hands slowly. He had been tricked and taunted by traditionals once too often. When Grandma waved her hand, repeating the invitation, he nodded.

"Sure," he said. "But what the hell is it?"

"Coffee."

The interior of the house was as neat and culturally eclectic as Maggie herself. There were Native American weavings and wall hangings, braided rag rugs that looked as though they had come from an Anglo pioneer household, a Georgia O'Keeffe print side by side with an Ansel Adams photograph and an R. C. Gorman lithograph. Some of the art was Indian, some Anglo, and some that indefinable mix that Ray had always dismissed as "hippie-dippie," but which looked oddly peaceful in Maggie's house.

The coffee was distinctly South Dakota, though—boiled and gritty with unfiltered grounds, like the campfire coffee Ray had been forced to drink in the army. Grandma and Maggie sat at the table in the kitchen with him, drinking their own cups while they tied ceremonial tobacco into small cloth bundles.

Grandma said something in Lakota without looking up from her task. Maggie hesitated, still reluctant to aid and abet Grandma's unexpected friendliness with the FBI agent. Grudgingly Maggie began to translate.

"Grandma says you were asking about gunshots yesterday."

Ray swallowed the rough, harsh coffee and nodded. "I need to know whether she heard any gunshots from an automatic weapon. Rapid fire, like a machine gun."

Grandma understood well enough to reply in halting English. "I hear."

"When?"

"Every night," Grandma replied matter-of-factly. "I just stay in chair and pray. *Tunkasila* help us. Big danger. So I stay with this girl."

Ray looked confused.

Grandma slid a plate of what looked like unleavened bread toward him in an hospitable gesture, then glanced at Maggie.

"She has a lot of land out there in Hubbel," Maggie said, gesturing off toward the north. "They moved her off it so they could lease it to white ranchers."

A small surge of excitement rippled through Ray. "Was it Leo Fast Elk who moved Grandma off her land?"

Maggie replied when Grandma was slow to answer. "Jack Milton." She spat the name like an epithet. "The Goons. Tribal government. They can lease the traditionals' land whether we like it or not."

Grandma Maisey spoke up now. "The ARM is to protect us, but it's the water, see . . . the childrens get so sick."

Grandma glanced toward the front room where a half dozen children, two of them Maggie's, played with battered trucks and toys on the floor.

"What's wrong with the water?" Ray asked.

Maggie shrugged. "It's contaminated."

"Sewage?"

"Chemicals of some kind." Before Ray could ask her any more, she said impatiently, "That's all I know, fed. The water is bad. We bring drinking water in from outside. But it's hot and the children don't understand, so they drink it anyway."

Ray shifted to Grandma again. "When was the last time you saw Leo Fast Elk?"

Before the woman could answer, Ray felt a pair of eyes on the back of his head. He turned to see a small boy, about seven, in the doorway. The boy had a GI Joe doll in one hand but he looked unhappy.

"I'm thirsty," the boy said. He looked from Maggie, his mother, to Ray, then to Grandma.

"Come here, Hobert." Maggie held out her arm.

Hobert came forward slowly, watching Ray carefully. The big man who looked like an Anglo was more interesting than GI Joe.

Grandma Maisey touched the boy's face gently and spoke in Lakota to him. Then she got up and went to the back of the tiny house.

Hobert stared at Ray from the protection of his mother's knee. Then, after a moment, he solemnly offered Ray the doll. Ray wasn't comfortable with children, but he knew a peace overture when he saw one. He took the doll.

"He's quite a guy," Ray said.

"His name's Joe," Hobert said.

Maggie looked uneasy. She tried to distract her son. "Did you find that kitten yet?"

Hobert shook his head. "Still looking. What's your name, mister?"

"Ray."

"Are you a soldier? Like Joe?"

Ray was saved from having to explain by Maisey's return. She carried a glass full of clear water from her own bottled supply. She offered it to Hobert, who reached for it the way another child might reach for a soda.

Maggie glanced sharply at Ray and spoke in a voice too low for the others to overhear.

"Why don't you just leave her alone?" Maggie said. "She doesn't know anything. She didn't see anything."

"Why don't you let me do my job?" Ray replied.

Without another word Maggie got up and walked across the kitchen, turning her back on the FBI agent.

Ray noticed the shape of Maggie's body again. She was an attractive woman, in her own fierce and independent way. But there was an anger in her that made him wonder what she might do, if pushed.

While he watched, Maggie gathered up an armload of file folders from a counter that seemed to serve as a workplace. She strode back across the room and handed the folders to him.

"Okay, Mr. FBI Agent. Do your job, then, if that's what you're really here for."

Ray took the folders and looked at them blankly. "What do you mean?"

"Sixty-one traditionals and ARM supporters killed," Maggie said savagely. "Not one of their deaths ever investigated. So start investigating, fed."

She grabbed the first file and snapped it open angrily.

"On second thought, you don't want this one," she said. "It was a suicide. Somehow he managed to shoot himself in the back of the head. Twice."

Ray looked at Maggie's angry face.

"And while you're at it," she continued, "why don't you find out what happens to the tribal funds Jack Milton handles. Find out what he's done—hasn't done is more like it—for our schools and our health programs and for the members of the tribe who don't kiss his ass."

Before Ray could say anything, Maggie leaned forward and gave him a look of contempt that went right to the bone.

"Stop pretending you don't know what's going on, *fed,*" Maggie said. "It makes me want to puke all over your fancy tie."

Ray tossed the files on the table and stood up. "I already know what's going on, lady. You graduated from Dartmouth with honors. Came back here and organized local control of the schools. You're the co-founder of the Oglala Shelter for Battered Women. You did that after you were raped."

Maggie's expression hardened even more.

"You've contributed to an anthology on the Wounded Knee occupation," Ray continued relentlessly, "and you've kept steady contact with the media since then."

Maggie shrugged.

"The last time you saw Hobert's daddy was eighteen months ago, when his parole was denied."

"You really get off peeping through windows, don't you? Sure you're name isn't Tom?" she asked coldly.

"I'm not interested in your private life. I think you're very brave. You've done good work for your people."

Ray paused, wanting to be sure he had Maggie's attention. "If you want to keep on doing it, you'd better stay out of the way of federal agents. I'm a nice guy. Frank Coutelle isn't. You give him the kind of shit you've given me and he will make your life hell."

Grandma Maisey turned away from Hobert, took something from the cupboard, and went to Ray. Hobert followed, his dark eyes wide with curiosity and unease. Grandma began speaking rapidly in Lakota. Maggie didn't translate. Grandma said something in a sharp tone.

"This is something she made," Maggie said angrily. "It's a medicine wheel."

Grandma held it out for Ray.

"She wants you to have it," Maggie said. "She said Grandpa Reaches told her you come from brave people."

Maggie's voice said she didn't believe a word of it.

An odd feeling spread through Ray when he took to the quill wheel and studied it. The beadwork was a spiral pattern of blues, whites and reds; looking into it was like falling and soaring at the same time, flying without fear because your wings were as wide as the sky and your heartbeat was the center of the world.

Ray shook his head and forced himself to concentrate on the tangible reality of the medicine wheel. It was cool to the touch, smooth-textured, surprisingly heavy for its size. Each quill was carefully selected and mounted. Each bead was a bright bit of hope. It was a handsome gift, if rather hypnotic.

"Tell her thank you," he said. "It's . . . very beautiful."

When Maggie didn't translate immediately, Ray looked up from the compelling pattern of the medicine wheel. Her dark eyes had lost their anger. They were startled, luminous, hopeful, the eyes of a woman who had just seen something she had been certain didn't exist.

Ray felt a surprising wave of reciprocal emotion, as

though he had discovered the source of Maggie's rage in the tenderness that she kept so carefully hidden.

"Maggie. . . ?" he whispered.

Before she could answer, a fusillade of bullets smashed through the flimsy walls of the old house.

Maggie screamed even as Ray shoved her beneath the table with one arm. With the other, he grabbed the old woman and the child, pulled them to the floor, and covered them with his own body.

A second volley of shots rang out.

))) ELEVEN

THE SCREAMS OF the children were lost in the trip-hammer racket of an automatic weapon. Bullets tore plaster from interior walls. Glass windows and wooden casements exploded into shards. The thundrous blasts of a shotgun underlined the machine-gun fire. Heavy lead shot battered the house like savage hail.

The trained portion of Ray's brain analyzed the attack, categorized the weapons, and established the direction of the threat. He caught Maggie's wrist and dragged her toward him, away from the window that seemed the primary target. He rolled toward the door to the living room, checking the rest of the children. Everyone frightened, no one hit.

Ray checked the loads in his pistol and ached for the riot shotgun in the trunk of the Caprice. He had counted at least three weapons in the attack, and more likely four. If they rushed the house, he wouldn't be able to take them all.

The shots kept coming, but it was Maggie's scream that chilled Ray. He looked up in time to see Hobert stand, a determined expression on his face, and his eyes fixed on the GI Joe doll that Ray had left on the table.

"Hobert! Get down! *Get down!*"

Ray lunged, but Hobert was out of reach. There was a hesitation in the gunfire. For an instant, it seemed Hobert would make it unhurt. But just as he grabbed the doll, another volley rang out.

A hail of slugs opened a hole in the wall. Hobert

screamed in pain. He stared in confused horror and shock at his own small forearm which had been shattered by a bullet.

Ray snagged the boy around the waist and dragged him to the floor.

The ringing, deafening silence that followed unexpected gunfire was shattered by the roar of an accelerating motor. Ray snatched a look through the smashed kitchen window in time to see a pickup with two armed men in the bed and two in the cab. They were waving their weapons triumphantly as the truck fishtailed down the dirt road in the direction of the highway.

Maggie reached her son, sobbing his name. Her face was a mask of rage and fear and anguish. Very gently she cradled Hobert. His dark eyes were round and full of pain. His skin was pale, cool. Blood flowed down his hand and dripped on the floor like heavy water.

Ray took a single look at the boy, then abandoned the idea of pursuing the gunmen. He grabbed a dish towel from the table and wrapped it around Hobert's wound. Then he jerked open the Windsor knot on his tie and fashioned a slip knot around Hobert's upper arm to restrict the blood flow.

"Where's the nearest hospital?" Ray asked.

Maggie just stared at him.

"Hospital," he snapped. "Quick!"

"There's a clinic. Main village."

Ray gathered Hobert in his arms and burst out the kitchen door, his pistol still ready in his right hand. His white shirt was already stained bright red with the boy's blood.

Maggie issued rapid orders before she followed. "Grandma, get the children across the river. Go to Looking Elk's place. Go!"

Ray was halfway to the Caprice when Maggie caught up. She opened the car door, took Hobert, and braced both of them for the ride.

The car made a sweeping broadside slide from the dirt

road onto the potholed pavement of the reservation highway. Ray kicked the big engine down into passing gear
and held it there. The needle touched one hundred and
stayed put.

"They'll pay," Maggie said softly, cradling Hobert,
soothing him.

"Who'll pay?" Ray said without taking his eyes from
the road.

"You know who it was. You saw the blue pickup, same
as I did."

Ray didn't reply. He had recognized the dark blue signature color of a tribal corporation vehicle, but he was
more cautious in his conclusions.

"I'll get a task force in here, if I have to," Ray vowed,
"but whoever it was, we'll get them."

"Bullshit, fed," she snapped. "Bull*shit.*"

Maggie's disdain for the FBI was obvious. For the first
time in his career, Ray couldn't argue. Milton and his men
had gotten out of hand. They had to be reined in and
reined in hard, no matter what it meant for Coutelle's case.

Dog soup and fry bread.

Ray snatched the radio microphone from its dashboard
bracket, keyed it, and got a response from the network
operator in Rapid City.

"This is Levoi. There's been a shooting in Mato Ska.
I'm en route to the reservation health clinic with one
wounded child. Tell Coutelle I want him there. Now."

Ray flattened the accelerator and put the big sedan in
the middle of the narrow highway. Let the rest of the world
look out. He was tired of being the public relations man.

The Caprice had a siren and a set of emergency lights
hidden in the grille. Ray found the switch about the time
they hit the main village. The yelper and lights scattered
pedestrians and civilian traffic like sheep.

Maggie cradled her son in her arms and directed Ray.
Her voice was like her face, quiet and cold, the face of
someone who no longer took prisoners in this private, un-
declared war.

Ray braked to a hard stop at the front door of the non-descript little bunker that served as a clinic. He was out of the car instantly, easing Hobert from Maggie's arms. The boy was slipping in and out of consciousness, no longer even crying.

Ray kicked in the front door of the clinic as though he were on a dope raid. The nurse at the shabby front desk, a hippie holdover with long, stringy hair and a madras print smock, gaped at the bloodstained white man and the unconscious Indian child for an instant. Then training took over.

"Doctor!" she yelled. "Front! Trauma case! Now!"

She pushed open the door to the back of the clinic and stood aside.

"What happened?" she asked as Ray brushed past her.

"He's been shot," Maggie said.

The examination room was already occupied by an old Indian woman who lay prone on a table, waiting. A white doctor with a ponytail and a stethoscope burst in from somewhere in the rear of the clinic. He took one look at the amount of blood on Ray's shirt and on the towel and began moving.

"Get another table, quick," Ray snapped.

"We don't have one," the doctor said.

Ray went to a desk that was piled with books and supplies. He cleared the desk top with one swipe of his arm, then placed the boy on it. Immediately the doctor was at his side, unwrapping the bloody towel to examine Hobert's arm.

"Trauma cart," the doctor ordered. "And get an IV started, Amy. Now!"

Ray stepped back to give the doctor room to work. He looked around the little room, appalled at the makeshift equipment and the unsanitary conditions. For an instant, he considered piling Hobert back into the car.

But as Ray watched, he saw that the doctor was competent. He went to a window, making room for Maggie to be close to her son. She stood at the head of the makeshift table, stroking her son's dark hair and trying to comfort him. The doctor did something that brought a small, whimpering groan from Hobert.

Ray flinched and wished there were something he could do. Now that the emergency was abating, he felt useless and a little ill. He hadn't guessed how difficult it would be to witness a small child's pain. He stared out through the window, trying to control his emotions.

A dark blue pickup pulled into the vacant lot adjacent to the clinic. There were two men in the cab of the truck and two in the bed. All four wore the baseball caps that were the uniforms of the Guardians of the Oglala Nation.

The pickup was the one that had attacked Maggie's house.

Ray went through the front door of the clinic like a bloody avenging angel, .357 in his right hand. He was on the men in the pickup before they could react. He jerked open the driver's door and covered them with his cocked pistol.

"FBI! Keep your hands where I can see them and get out. Do it slow and cool, you chickenshit Goons, or I'll kill you where you sit."

None of the men doubted it. In ten seconds, all of them were face down in the dust, spreadeagled and frozen.

Ray glanced inside the cab of the truck. It looked like the weapons locker of a SWAT team—two assault shotguns, two automatic weapons, and three high-powered pistols.

"What's the matter?" Ray asked the three men contemptuously. "Afraid you'll meet someone that will shoot back? Is that why you go after kids and old women? You bastards are under federal arrest."

One of them started to roll over and complain.

"What you mean, man," the Goon snarled. "We're on—"

The words stopped abruptly when Ray rapped the man between his eyes with the blade sight of the Magnum.

"Roll over and shut up."

The man rolled over and shut up.

Tires barked on the pavement behind Ray. He kept his gun on the suspects but glanced over quickly.

Coutelle's sedan jerked to a stop. The senior agent piled out, shotgun drawn, just as two more blue tribal corporation pickups pulled into the clinic's small parking lot. A half dozen Guardians piled out of the trucks and followed Coutelle.

One of the men was Jack Milton.

"Glad to see you, boss," Ray said, keeping his pistol trained on the four prisoners. "I was beginning to feel like Custer at the Little Big Horn."

Coutelle stiff-armed Ray, throwing him against the open door of the blue pickup. The sudden attack caught Ray completely by surprise. He whirled on Coutelle in shock, then realized his gun was aimed at his partner's midsection. Ray lowered the gun and stared.

"Have you lost your mind?" Coutelle shouted. "I told you Eagle Bear is the key. You just fucked the whole thing up. You've got the ARM people thinking she's talking to the feds."

"ARM didn't attack her house," Ray shouted back. "It was Milton's Goons!"

At the moment, Jack Milton was helping the last of his men to his feet. Milton glared at Coutelle.

"You'd better put a leash on this boy," Milton said, jerking a thumb at Ray.

Ray took a step toward the tribal chairman. "You're the one who needs a leash. You and your goddamn thugs. Those three men are under arrest!"

He took another step forward, but Coutelle shouldered him aside.

"Get yourself together, Sal. These guys are on our team. You'll set off a powder keg here, if you don't watch out. I told you to stay away from that bitch. What the hell is the matter with you? Are you letting your cock do your thinking?"

"Hey!" Ray shouted as Milton hustled the four prisoners to the truck. "Those assholes are under federal arrest!"

Ray tried to fight past Coutelle, only to find himself in a come-along hold, with his finger bent back. The pain was bearable as long as he didn't move.

Abruptly Ray realized he was fighting the man who should be his partner. He took a deep breath and stopped struggling. Coutelle stepped back, releasing him.

"That's better," Coutelle said. "Now listen up, white boy. I don't give two farts what went on with Dawes in some office back in D.C. This is my case and we'll run it my way. Got it?"

In a smoldering silence that throbbed with drums only he could hear, Ray watched another truckload of Milton's men drive up. Coutelle dragged Ray toward the Caprice, opened the door on the driver's side, and pushed Ray in.

"Watch your head, Sal, or you'll lose it, sure as shit." Then, as though nothing else had happened, Coutelle said, "We just got a lab report on the eagle feather you took off of Jimmy. It's a deadbang genetic match to the one we found by Leo's body."

Like a drunk just sobering up, Ray looked at Coutelle, trying to hear something besides the insistent beat of drums.

Coutelle clapped him on the shoulder again, closed the door, and leaned in through the open window.

"Just stick to the assignment and you'll be okay," Coutelle said. "Remember, this is a sensitive operation. You can't trust everything you see."

For a few seconds, Coutelle's words and the drums fought for Ray's mind. Then Ray's eyes slowly focused on Coutelle.

"I'm all right," Ray said.

"Good. Now let's just catch our Tonto and get the hell off the reservation."

Ray nodded.

"Now," Coutelle continued quickly, as though afraid he would lose Ray if he stopped talking, "you said something this morning about going out to talk to that old Indian, Samuel Reaches.''

"It was a blind alley," Ray said, ignoring the subtle thunder of drums rippling through his blood. "The old man's crazy."

Coutelle brushed the dust of the clinic's lot from his pants. "He's crazy like a fox. That old shaman is the spiritual leader of ARM."

Startled, Ray stared at Coutelle.

Coutelle sensed Ray's disbelief and explained, "They all go to Grandpa, get their pieces blessed or something. I want you to stake his residence out. You know the layout and you know what the subject looks like. Nail his red ass."

"It's a waste of time. He's just a harmless old man whose head isn't screwed on real tight."

"You know that and I know that, but Jimmy doesn't. The heat is coming down on Jimmy, and when things get hot, Jimmy gets holy."

Coutelle glanced at Ray's bloodstained shirt, then at his blue jeans and boots. The senior agent didn't much like what he saw.

"Go get cleaned up and then get over to Grandpa Reaches's trailer," he said briskly. "Take one of the surveillance units from the motel. It'll go real good with your new outfit."

With that, Coutelle turned and walked back to his own car.

After a minute, Ray got out of the car, stripped off his ruined white shirt, and dug a fresh one out of his kit in the trunk. As he dressed, he looked back at the clinic.

From inside, he heard a long pained wail—Hobert, in agony. The boy's screams rose and fell in time with the beating of hidden drums.

Ray slammed back into the Caprice and drove off, trying to flee the drums whose beat became more insistent with every instant he spent in the badlands.

* * *

The Ford pickup was a decade old and covered with clay dust, but it still stuck out in the impromptu junkyard adjacent to Grandpa Reaches's property. Ray tried to melt into a narrow slot between two rusting wrecks. He killed the engine and settled in.

After half an hour, the hot wind from the badlands and the subliminal beating of drums drugged Ray. He felt his mind go numb, dragging him toward sleep . . . or something else. Something less understandable.

Something he had spent a lifetime fighting.

Almost desperately, Ray rummaged in the bag beside him, which held supplies for the long lay-in. One loaf of Wonder bread, a shrink-wrapped stack of sliced bologna, two canned Cokes, and the closest thing to health food he had been able to find in the reservation grocery store—a package of Fig Newtons.

The bread was like Styrofoam, the bologna had already started to turn green around the edges, and the Cokes were flat. Ray broke into the cookies and ate them one at a time, whole. He longed for some fresh fruit, an apple, a peach, anything, but as near as he could tell, there wasn't any fresh fruit within a hundred miles of the badlands.

Grandpa Reaches was eating too. Ray could see him at the rickety old table under the brush arbor. The old man had some kind of sandwich. Apparently he didn't like Wonder bread, either. He ate part of the sandwich, then set it aside. He broke into a small bag of potato chips.

After a while, the old man gathered the remnants of his meal on his paper plate, shuffled over to the edge of a patch of sage, and stood, head bowed. A minute later he straightened his back as best he could, looked up, and offered the remnants of his meal to the sky. Then he set the plate down on the ground, turned, and shuffled back to the brush arbor.

Ray sat among the junked cars, watching the old man make his offering, and felt reality slipping away. The heartbeat drum throbbed just beneath the threshold of hearing. Wind buffeted the pickup ceaselessly, shaking it.

Uneasily Ray shifted. The hair on his neck prickled in a primal signal of danger.

He was being watched.

A whimper came in the pause between bursts of wind. The sound was low and thready, as weak as the pulse of an injured child. The whimper came again, a low, animal sound from just beyond the truck's door.

Ray looked out. A black and white reservation dog sat patiently on its haunches, watching him with something that was neither fear nor hope. When Ray's eyes met the dog's, it looked away as though to deny any begging.

When the animal shifted position nervously, Ray noticed the dog was male, had only three legs, and was as thin as a shadow.

"Get out of here," Ray said softly.

The dog wagged his tail, but didn't otherwise move. He licked his chops and drooled ropes of saliva. There was an old scar over one of his eyes.

Ray knew he should never have opened the package of bologna.

"Go on," he said again in a low voice.

He didn't dare raise his voice any more for fear of alerting Grandpa.

The dog barked once, short and soft, almost as though he read Ray's mind and was threatening to blow his cover. Then the animal sat and wagged, guileless and expectant.

Ray fished a slice of the warm lunch meat out of the bag and held it out the window. The dog drooled like a leaky faucet.

"Is that you, Jimmy?" Ray muttered. "If it is, I have a warrant for your arrest. Shape-shift for me and I'll give you the whole package of bologna."

The dog tilted his head and drooled.

Laughing, Ray flipped the slice of bologna into the air like a Frisbee. The dog leaped, caught, swallowed in one gulp. Then he sat, ready to play the game again.

Ray quickly counted the slices of meat in their plastic wrap and tried to estimate how long he could keep the animal quiet. He glanced back toward the trailer, just in time to see the old shaman pick up a bucket and shuffle off toward a stand of tall cattails. The reeds marked the spot where a narrow little rivulet of clay-colored water cut the edge of the bluff and spilled down its face.

Grandpa moved slowly, unsteadily, the gait of a man who should be using a cane or a walker. When he reached the rushes, he parted them and stooped down with great difficulty, scooping up half a bucket of muddy water from the narrow stream.

Even half full, the bucket was almost too heavy. Grandpa staggered as he climbed the muddy little bank. On top, he stopped to rest for a moment, setting the bucket down and panting from exertion.

After a minute of puffing and blowing, the old man picked up the burden again, shuffled six steps, then put the bucket down and rested. He repeated the process, now carrying the bucket with his left hand. This time he had to rest after four steps. When he lifted the bucket again, he carried it with both hands, spilling a little of the precious water against his shins with each step.

Ray watched the old Indian's progress and estimated that his water would evaporate just about the time he reached the trailer.

Finally, Ray could watch no more. He stepped out of the truck, slammed the door irritably, and jogged across the open space to where Grandpa Reaches panted.

The old man was about to lift the bucket again when Ray walked up briskly. Without a word, the FBI agent snatched the bucket from the ground. Walking quickly, as though he wanted to be done before he changed his mind, Ray carried the bucket back to the stream, filled it to within an inch of the top, and headed back toward the trailer.

Grandpa Reaches watched. When Ray passed, the old man's crinkled, weathered face split with a delighted grin. Ray had the clear feeling that the old shaman had finally seen Mr. Magoo do something right.

Grandpa fell in beside Ray and shuffled along, moving

so easily now that Ray suspected he had been scammed again. He set the bucket on the stoop beside the trailer door and turned to go, for the sound of drumming had become unbearable.

Still smiling, Grandpa watched him. When Ray glanced over his shoulder, the shaman said something in Lakota, a single word that Ray took to be a kind of thanks. The old man gestured, waving Ray back to the trailer. Ray went, not really wanting to but not able to stop himself.

From a separate surveillance post in the brush, Walter Crow Horse watched, holding his breath, knowing that much depended on the next moment.

Grandpa gestured again, his eyes bright and alert. Ray took a few more steps in the direction of the trailer. Behind him, the three-legged dog sat in the dirt and smiled his openmouthed smile.

When Ray was only a step away, the old shaman reached for a paper bag on the stoop. He took out a fresh pear, its skin greenish-yellow and vibrant. Saliva welled up in Ray's mouth. The old man held out the fruit. Ray took it, tasting it before he set his teeth to the tart skin.

The sweetness of the pear exploded in Ray's mouth, sweeping through him, becoming part of him. He shivered with pleasure and tension; the pear tasted better than an earthly thing should. Warm, sweet, complex, perfect. He took half the fruit in a single bite, ate it in a trance of pleasure, and nodded to the old man.

The shaman smiled.

Ray turned and headed back toward the truck, taking most of the rest of the pear in a quick, single bite, seeds and all. He was ready to pop the last morsel into his mouth when Grandpa called after him.

Ray turned.

"Hieh." The old man gestured toward the ground.

Ray looked down to see the remnants of the shaman's own meal set out for unknown gods.

Under the watchful eye of the old man, the FBI agent knelt and dropped the last chunk of pear into the middle of the offering. Grandpa nodded approvingly, then chuckled as Ray straightened up and went back to the pickup.

The three-legged dog was gone.

When Ray got back inside the pickup, the paper bag was empty in the footwell. The bread was gone, the bologna was gone, and the package of cookies had been thoroughly licked. Ray closed his eyes and sighed. When he opened them, the dog was sitting on the passenger side, waving his ragged plume of a tail.

"Did that half-rotten bologna taste as good to you as the pear did to me?"

The dog grinned.

Ray jerked the door open. "Yeah, I thought so. Well, no more free lunches. Out."

The dog stared at him with eyes as clear and bottomless as the night. Drums rippled like distant thunder. The sound had become such a part of Ray that he no more noticed it than he did the sound of his own breathing, his own pulse, his own heartbeat.

"Out," Ray repeated.

The dog laughed at him, pink tongue lolling.

"You don't listen any better than Jimmy Looks Twice, do you?"

Just as Ray reached for the mutt, he heard the sound of Walter Crow Horse's motorcycle. The Indian officer broke from a clump of sage and bounced across the rough ground toward Grandpa's trailer. Grandpa came out of the trailer as though he had been expecting Crow Horse. This time the old man was wearing his big black Stetson.

Crow Horse gunned up to the trailer, waited while Grandpa climbed on the saddle seat, then gunned down the little rise toward Ray's vantage point.

As the motorcycle passed, picking up speed, Crow Horse took his hand off the crown of his cowboy hat long enough to extend his middle finger in the metaphorical sign of greeting.

Watch this, buck, the man's grin said.

"Damn!" Ray muttered. "Hang on, Jimmy. It's going to be a rough ride."

He fired up the truck and pulled out after the Triumph. The three-legged dog watched intently through the windshield as the truck bounced across the grasslands to the dirt road racing after the disappearing motorcycle.

))) TWELVE

WALTER CROW HORSE drove the reservation back roads and country lanes like they were a motocross course. By pushing the old pickup hard enough to draw a couple of nervous glances from the dog, Ray managed to keep the motorcycle in sight, but only barely.

After a while, the mindlessness of the pursuit began to take over. Ray settled in, all decisions made. He let Crow Horse tow him along without worrying about what would happen next.

The spare, dry landscape of the plains and the badlands unreeled past Ray in familiar shapes and colors, their rhythms as predictable as his own heartbeat. He was no longer concerned about getting lost on the tangle of narrow gravel roads and twisting highways.

He had learned that all roads led eventually to the same place. The difference was in the amount of time the journey took.

Just when Ray began to weary of the chase, Crow Horse bounced off the blacktop onto a dirt track that took off over a rise. Ray closed with the Triumph, then had to brake hard when he crested the rise and almost ran headlong into a lithe young brave wearing a breechcloth, fierce face and body paint, and a headdress of feathers and quills.

Ray wondered what century he had driven into.

The brave scowled angrily, then stepped out of the way. As Ray drove past, the brave spoke.

"Slow down, man, there's lots of kids playing round here."

Ray didn't argue. There was no need to hurry any longer. Crow Horse and Grandpa Reaches had disappeared into a crowd of Indians gathered beneath a long canvas banner that announced the Twenty-first Annual Rosebud Powwow.

After Ray dodged several more dancers in traditional costumes, he found a parking spot among half a hundred pickups, vans, cars, and recreational vehicles. Most of the cars had the rusty, dusty, and battered look of reservation vehicles.

The throb of a great drum filled the air, similar and yet different from the heartbeat sounds that haunted him. The powwow drum was quick and light, almost joyful.

Two hundred Indians in modern clothing were scattered across the hillside, watching twenty or thirty costumed dancers stomp-step and jig around a drum that was the size of a small trampoline. A ring of singers joined in a keening call as the dancers broke into circling patterns that reminded Ray of the aerial patterns of red-tailed hawks.

Ray stayed in the truck, watching, for several minutes. Nobody paid much attention to him except a few Oglala teenagers in modern dress who lounged, bored, on the hoods of cars, smoking cigarettes and trying to look sophisticated. A sullen boy of fifteen wore the first fade haircut Ray had seen since Washington. The boy sensed Ray's glance and glared back at him defiantly.

"Nice racing stripes," Ray said.

Crow Horse settled Grandpa Reaches into a lawn chair in the shade of an arbor with a half dozen other elders in the group, old men who chatted amiably in Lakota and nodded pleasantly at the new arrivals. The tribal officer turned and went back to where the federal agent sat in the truck. The Indian officer approached with a sour expression, like he was about to issue another traffic ticket.

"I wanted you to see this, *Kola.* " he said.

Ray looked out at the swirling dancers and singers. Beyond them, in the outer circle, he watched what appeared to be a security formation—members of ARM; young,

tough-looking, long-haired, some with headbands or ribbon shirts, as many women as men.

"What's going on?" Ray asked.

"Powwow," Crow Horse said. His face relaxed into a
grin. "Take a look around, hoss. We're still alive. We're
still here."

The drumbeat grew louder, as though to underline the
big Indian's words. Ray felt the pounding rhythms. They
were surprisingly natural, although he had not heard them
since he left the reservation.

Crow Horse leaned into the truck window. "Did you
find anything at Maggie Eagle Bear's?"

"A print."

"Jimmy's?"

Ray hesitated, then shook his head.

Crow Horse nodded, satisfied. "I'll bet the eagle feather
you found gave you a little chub, though."

Ray glanced at him but didn't answer.

"We all have feathers from the same eagle." Crow
Horse chuckled. "We share everything on the reservation." His grin broadened as he pushed the sunglasses up
on his nose.

Ray did a double-take. "Those are my glasses," he said.

Crow Horse shook his head. "I traded Grandpa for
them," he said.

Ray shook his head in frustration and amusement.

"You got nothing on Jimmy, do you?" Crow Horse
said.

Ray got out of the truck and leaned on the open door,
his eyes following the ARM members automatically.
"Jimmy's an enemy of the United States," Ray said.

The drumming stopped abruptly and the dancers walked
back to the shade. Crow Horse picked up his hat and re-
settled it on his head. Then he looked at Ray, a mixture
of unhappiness and irritation on his face.

"You know, Ray, when we were kids, and we used to
play cowboys and Indians, I always wanted to be Gary
Cooper."

Then he turned and walked slowly back toward the shade where Grandpa sat. Ray fell into step beside him.

"I didn't want to be Indian," Crow Horse went on. "The government boarding school made sure of that. They cut off my hair. If I spoke Lakota, they washed my mouth out with soap." He spat reflexively, clearing a foul, old taste from his mouth.

"When the ARM warriors came out here, it was like an awakening," Crow Horse said. "They got Indian people proud of their heritage again. Their elders. Their language.

"ARM is waking people up, Ray. Waking 'em up to their roots. Their rights. You call them enemies. Dissenters. You chase them off the reservation. Well you just keep doing that, 'cause tomorrow morning I'll have the real doer in the Bear Creek tribal jail and to hell with your jurisdiction."

Crow Horse broke away and walked back into the crowd that was gathering around the communal fires and stew pots. Ray followed, passing the gathering traditional people who lined up with their own bowls and plates to collect their meals. He saw Maggie bring two bowls to old grandmothers in their lawn chairs. Between them, Ray caught a glimpse of Hobert sitting with them, his arm heavily bandaged.

Maggie seemed to sense Ray's eyes. She looked up and met his gaze for a moment. Then someone moved between them and faced Ray.

An ARM warrior. Richard Yellow Hawk. The big Indian in the wheelchair rolled in front of Ray and stared up at him through sweat-filmed bifocals. He pointed a finger at Ray in recognition.

"Hey . . ."

"Yeah, the Washington Redskin," Ray said, beating him to it. "How you doing, Yellow Hawk." He brushed past the wheelchair and continued after Crow Horse.

"Watch yourself," Yellow Hawk called after him. "I'm FBI, too. Full-Blooded Indian."

A coterie of ARM warriors had gathered behind Yellow Hawk. Several of them followed Ray's every move. But they kept their distance as Ray caught up with Crow Horse and pulled him aside.

"Listen, Crow Horse, if you're withholding information, you're going to find yourself in deep pemmican."

Before the officer could respond, a soft voice called out in Lakota. The two men looked. It was Grandpa, who sat alone in the shade. He looked at Ray and gestured, pointing to his own wrist.

"He wants to trade," Crow Horse said. "He likes your watch."

Ray shook his head without hesitation. "No way."

"Ray, Grandpa wants—"

"I said forget it."

Grandpa produced a bent cigarette from his shirt pocket and held it out, gesturing again, as though he didn't understand.

Crow Horse explained Ray's response in Lakota. Ray caught one word in the middle of the explanation: "Rolex."

Grandpa spoke again and Crow Horse translated. "He said you need to go on Indian time. White-man time will give you stomach cancer."

Ray pretended he hadn't heard and tried to return to the subject of the investigation. "I don't know whose prints those were by the river," he said, "but I don't think I'm looking for a white man anymore."

"Good," Crow Horse said, " 'cause neither am I. It's an old Lakota belief that if a dead man is turned face down, his spirit is trapped inside his body. It won't come back.

"That's a Sioux thing a white man wouldn't understand."

"Then who did shoot Leo?"

Crow Horse shook his head. "I won't know until tonight," he said. "They're coming to Grandpa's."

"Who is?"

"They are."

"Who are you talking about?" Ray demanded.

Crow Horse thought for a moment, as though searching for something. Finally he shrugged. "Informants," he said. "Yeah, Grandpa's informants. They'll be there tonight. You go chase Jimmy." He turned his back on Ray and joined the line that had formed in front of the stew pots. Ray stood there, watching, shut out. After a moment, he felt eyes boring into his back. He turned and met Grandpa's gaze. The old man nodded slowly, as though agreeing with Ray's unspoken thoughts.

The battered, sun-struck aluminum side of Grandpa Reaches's Airstream caught and reflected the flickering light of the small campfire. Seven old men in sweat-stained baseball caps and battered Stetsons sat in a circle on the ground, drumming and singing a dissonant song that was older than any of them, older than their grandfathers, as old as the land itself.

The song was the land. It was the land's rhythms, its austerity, an openness so great it hid the creation of the world. Listening, Ray knew he hadn't mastered the rhythms yet, but he had begun to recognize their importance.

The song and the drum faded away into the darkness. Grandpa Reaches rose from the circle of elders. He waved Ray and Crow Horse forward. The two younger men stood where the shaman positioned them while he went to the fire with a long twist of sweetgrass. He dipped the grass brand into the flames until one end caught fire. Then he fanned the brand with an eagle feather and let the fragrant smoke wash over each of the two policemen.

Watching, Ray felt an odd sense of dislocation that increased with each breath, each heartbeat. He should have seized the old man's eagle feather and sent it off to the FBI laboratory for a genetic match. It would have been good procedure, what he had been trained for, what he had been sent here to do.

But he wasn't going to do it.

His investigation had already turned up too many facts, too much information. What he needed now was insight, not more meaningless details.

He breathed deeply, taking in the sweet smoke, feeling his heartbeat change, deepen, keeping rhythm with a drum he had heard the first time as a child; and as a child he had feared it.

He was no longer a child.

Grandpa intoned a Lakota prayer. The words burned in Ray's mind, just on the edge of understanding. But not yet. Not quite.

"He's talking about a place back behind Red Deer Table," Crow Horse translated, "out where the Elk people used to live. He says there's all kinds of strange beings there, beings from another world who eat the stones and the dirt."

Crow Horse hesitated, as though even he was confused by Grandpa's words. The shaman clapped his hands. Crow Horse translated without pausing again.

"He says the beings will kill anyone who crosses that place. This is what the spirits say."

Grandpa's monologue went on.

"He says the spirits saw you, going back into that land behind Red Deer Table. I was with you."

The two investigators traded uneasy glances in the firelight.

"That's all the spirits say, so he doesn't know if you were killed or not. He thinks you probably were, but he says it was a good day to die."

No one else thought it was funny, either.

An eagle call keened up into the night. It seemed to come from the fire itself. The eerie whistling sound divided and became the voices of elders singing in Lakota.

Uneasiness washed through Ray. He felt as if he were being pulled apart. He knew what the elders were saying, *yet he could not know.*

"The elders speak as one," Crow Horse said. "You

should go to the land where the Elk people used to live.
That's where you'll find the answers. But you must go as
two."

Memory surged in Ray, demanding his attention, called
by the hiss of fire and the eagle's cry, the Lakota words
that were promise and warning, indivisible. He had heard
the words before, heard the song before. As he stared at
the fire, he felt himself grow as drowsy as a child. Strong
arms were holding him, protecting him, spreading peace
through his body. He was secure for the last time in his
life.

Then he heard a woman's voice, his mother's voice.

"Raymond!"

The world shifted, condensing out of a shimmering heat
mist.

*An Indian man sitting in the dark in front of a fireplace.
The man had a crewcut. He wore a T-shirt with one sleeve
rolled up over a pack of cigarettes. His teeth were bad.*

*He sang the song of the elders. He sang it fervently, and
as he sang, he rocked a small boy in his lap, holding him
tight.*

"Raymond! Get away from him! He's drunk!"

*The boy responded slowly. Until his mother spoke, he
had not been afraid. He tried to sit up.*

*The man gripped him tighter and sang louder, rocking
and watching the fire, trying to pass some part of himself
to his son.*

Ray, the boy.

The man, Ray's father.

*The ancient song droned on, sung to spirits that had
gathered at the summons. In the fire.*

In the air.

*Everywhere nowhere inescapable, life pouring between
father and son.*

"Let go. Let my son go!"

*The mother's fear was infectious. The boy was torn be-
tween two loyalties, two lives, two times, two pasts, two
futures.*

He was being torn apart.

"Let go. Let me GO!"

Ray exploded out of the circle, sweat-drenched, disoriented. He fled across the camp, Crow Horse right behind him.

"Where you going, Ray?"

"Home."

"You are home, hoss."

Ray said nothing.

"Red Deer Table," Crow Horse said. "We have to go there. Together. That's Grandpa's vision. That's what the elders all say."

"You go."

"A man can't mess with the visions. That's heavy shit."

Ray ripped the Indian's hand from his arm.

"Look," he snarled, "I went along with this crap for one reason—because somebody was supposed to talk."

"They did."

"Bullshit!"

"No, you're the bullshit," Crow Horse shot back, angry again. "You're scared."

An odd expression spread across the big Indian's broad, dark face, as though he was hearing his own words and understanding for the first time what was beneath Ray's cool facade.

"You really are scared, aren't you?" Crow Horse said.

Ray whirled on the Indian, ready to fight. "Do you have some problem with staying out of my face?"

"Use your heart, you dumb bastard. Just once. All you have to do is listen and—"

"Knock it off!"

The authority in the voice was clear. Ray spun around and came face to face with a furious Grandpa Reaches. The old shaman stood on the stoop beside the door of the trailer, holding on to the porch railing.

"You heard me," the old man said. "Knock this shit off. I'm sick of you both."

His English was clear and touched with a slight, flat

accent that made him sound like a cowhand from the Northern Plains.

Ray looked at Crow Horse. "He speaks English. The old fraud speaks English!"

"Only when he's really pissed off."

The old shaman glared at the two of them for a long moment. Finally he turned and opened the screen door.

"Come inside. Let's watch some television, get straight."

The screen door slapped shut behind Grandpa Reaches.

Ray stared, stunned. Crow Horse threw his head back and laughed at the moon in joyful appreciation of the surrealistic logic of his badlands.

Ray fled down the little dirt road to his truck, accompanied by a three-legged dog and pursued by the unsettling suspicion that he might never understand the living Indians around him, much less the dead ones in his past.

))) THIRTEEN

Low in the east, the moon was the bright yellow of summer squash glowing through the ground haze left over from the day's heat. The hills and gullies cast inky shadows, but the moonlight made them seem less threatening. Light and dark were only steps on the same continuum. That truth was easier to grasp at night.

Ray drove with the window down, letting the cool, silky air strip away the unsettling memories of campfire and sweet smoke and time turning back on itself. On him.

He could not remember ever having so much as dreamed about his father. Now he was living a kind of half dream, half hallucination that was disturbing, even frightening.

Ray had no idea what the dreams meant or when they might strike again. He had always regarded himself as a well-integrated man, fully in control of himself and capable of dominating his surroundings. Now he was no longer so sure of himself and his abilities.

He was damned grateful Coutelle hadn't been part of the campfire circle. The FBI was a very cautious organization. It didn't give badges and guns to mental cases.

That was the root of Ray's unease. He believed along with the FBI that the world was rational, that it could be understood and explained by the force of human reason. But the killing of Leo Fast Elk had drawn Ray into a world that did not bow to reason. The deeper he went into the case, the more the killing seemed part of a swirling dust-devil of motives and forces too elusive to be named, much less untangled.

Even a confirmed hardhead like Frank Coutelle was stumped . . . and had been for a decade, Ray suspected. A lot of killings and no arrests.

Ray was beginning to believe that the truth would continue to elude the FBI. Jimmy Looks Twice wasn't some Mafia don leaving paper trails. He wasn't even a bank robber. He was a half-baked Indian revolutionary with few supporters in a poverty-stricken rural community. Yet Coutelle—an FBI legend, the smartest lawman in eleven Western states, a modern descendant of the Hat Squad— had failed to close the case.

That was all that would save Ray's career. They couldn't drop the hammer on him without dropping it on Coutelle.

Ray let out a long breath and began to relax a little. Now, if he could just keep Walter Crow Horse and his goofy grandfather at bay, things might return to normal.

The three-legged dog woke and growled low in his throat. Ray looked at the dog, wondering what was wrong. The dog stared out through the windshield. So did Ray, but he saw nothing except the moon-softened landscape of the badlands.

There was a spectral beauty to the night. The realization both surprised and reassured Ray. He began to understand why someone might leave the pleasures of the city for the very different pleasures of the wild land.

The dog threw back his head and howled, responding to the moon in his own way.

Then the spell of the moon was shattered by a bright spotlight that snapped on beside the road ahead. Ray felt like a jacklighted mule deer. He stabbed the brakes and simultaneously unsnapped the keeper on his holster.

A Guardian in a blue windbreaker and baseball cap stepped into the headlights and waved him down.

Milton's irregulars no longer were operating their road-blocks from behind a line of vehicles. Now they stood in a row on the highway, a dozen strong. A single glance told Ray why the men felt more secure; every one of them carried a factory-new, matte-black Bullpup assault rifle fitted with a starlight night scope.

Suddenly Ray's short-barreled .357 seemed like a child's toy.

A Guardian approached the pickup in an exaggerated combat stance, one hand on his pistol. Cursing under his breath, Ray sat with his hands in plain sight on the wheel, not wanting to give the ill-trained, overarmed Indian an excuse to overreact.

"Oh, it's the red fed," the Guardian sneered when he recognized Ray.

"At least I've got a badge to back up my armament," Ray said evenly. "What's going on?"

A second Guardian approached, covering Ray with his assault gun. The gesture was not only unnecessary, it was dangerous. Ray's hands tightened on the wheel. He looked hard at the second man.

"Somebody declare war?" Ray asked coolly.

"Just routine, fed. Go on."

Ray put the truck in gear and rolled forward, trading hard stares with the Guardians in the picket line beside the road.

No wonder the traditionals call them Goons. They're as badge-heavy as the worst street cop I ever met. They're just sweating to use all their shiny new toys.

Christ. This reservation is heading for bad trouble.

The memory of Leo Fast Elk face down in the clay came back vividly to Ray. Horseflies feeding on blood. The burst from an automatic weapon that had brought down a man whose crime was to believe in the past rather than the future.

The three-legged dog leaped back onto the seat from his hiding place in the footwell. Slowly the dog's ruff settled back into place. He turned around three times and lay down, sighing deeply. Eyes the color of the night watched the man who drove the truck.

When Ray turned into the parking lot in front of the shabby motel, it was jammed with shiny federal government cars. Whip antennas and pigtail cellular antennas bristled from every vehicle. Two local field agents were huddled over an open car trunk, shoving Magnum loads into twelve-gauge pump shotguns. Two Treasury agents in green ATF jumpsuits walked German shepherds on long leashes.

Ray's headlights flashed across an olive-drab tractor-trailer parked in the deep shadows behind the tavern. A pair of South Dakota National Guard soldiers were un-chaining the tracks of an armored personnel carrier.

A full-scale invasion force to chase after one skinny Indian with an eagle feather in his hair?

Christ, has the whole world gone crazy?

The three-legged dog hit the floor and stayed there, concealed by shadows. Ray parked, slammed the door, and went angrily to Unit 6, wondering what the hell had happened.

The operations center in the motel room had been activated. Three local field agents were crowded into the kitchen, one working the computer, one on a cellular-phone connection with headquarters, and the third putting together a briefing board which already contained the mug shots of all known ARM activists.

Coutelle lounged on one bed, talking on the motel phone. He put his hand over the receiver when he saw Ray.

"How'd it go with the old man?" Coutelle asked.

Ray shook his head.

"Too bad." Then Coutelle grinned and pointed at a tattered canvas gun cover on the next bed. "We hit gold," he said gleefully. "Go ahead, check it out. We've already dusted it for prints."

Coutelle took his hand off the receiver and went back to his phone conversation while Ray unzipped the canvas case and pulled out an M-16 rifle. The gun had been hard-used. Its matte-black plastic stock was worn and scuffed. Three letters had been carved deeply into the cheek piece.

ARM.

"Yeah, that's right, hon," Coutelle said. "Maybe tomorrow night, for sure the next day. Things are finally beginning to break loose around here."

Ray snapped the rifle's action open. It was coated with old oil, field dirt, and half-burned gunpowder, as though it hadn't been cleaned in months.

"It's Jimmy's personal piece," Coutelle whispered over the mouthpiece. "I've got the invoice for it."

The senior agent grinned like a kid with a new baseball mitt. Then he spoke into the phone. "I've got to go, hon. I'll call you after we close this thing down. Yeah, me too."

Ray waited impatiently until Coutelle hung up.

"What the hell is going on?" Ray demanded, gesturing at the operations center and the troops outside.

"Field support from Rapid. We're setting up, this time for the kill." Coutelle slammed his fist into his hand. "I had him. Honest to Christ, I had him."

"Jimmy? Where?"

"We hit a traditionals safe house in Red Crow. He must have got out just before we closed the circle." Coutelle pointed at the gun. "But he left that behind."

"You've already done ballistics, a pin test?"

"No, somebody's going to run it into Rapid City and put it on the night plane to Washington. But that's the animal, I know it is, and I can tie Jimmy's ass to it with a bill of sale and a serial number."

"Great, Cooch. Hell of a job."

"You too, kid. Good work."

"Not mine."

Coutelle grinned. "Your name's on the 302, just like mine."

Ray shrugged and wished he could feel better about wrapping up the case.

But he didn't. The heartbeat drum that had subsided beneath the moon was beating more heavily now in the motel room, riding him relentlessly, telling him . . . something.

Jimmy Looks Twice hadn't been anywhere near the Red Crow safe house. Ray was as certain of that as if he had had Looks Twice in custody himself. But there was no way to explain that to Coutelle. There were just the drums, beating, beating, beating, driving him out of the room and into the night.

Coutelle looked at Ray closely. Then he looked at the other agents, who were too busy to see the strain on Ray's face.

"Come on," Coutelle said quietly. "Let's grab a soda."

He pulled Ray out of the room and into the darkness. The gravel of the parking lot rattled dryly as they walked toward the wheezing Coke cooler.

Coutelle examined Ray's face closely again. "You okay?"

Ray shrugged. He had nothing to say that Coutelle would understand.

"You look like you saw a ghost or something," Coutelle said.

Ray flinched inwardly. The senior agent was too damn perceptive.

"Yeah, well, I almost hit something out on the road, a deer maybe, or maybe a man. I couldn't tell for sure," Ray said, trying to sound casual. "It rattled me."

Coutelle became very still, then sighed. "Yeah, this place will do that to you."

The older agent shoved two quarters in the machine. Nothing happened.

"I expected you to boot me off the case, after our little dustup at the clinic," Ray said quietly.

Coutelle smacked the machine hard with the heel of his hand, just above the coin slot. Nothing. No soda. No change.

"Nobody likes seeing a kid shot," Coutelle said. "First time?"

"Yeah."

Coutelle nodded. "Thought so. Let me tell you, though. It doesn't get any easier the second time."

He smacked the machine again. Still no action.

"I got stopped on the way in," Ray said. "Goon road-block."

"Yeah," Coutelle said, as though he already knew.

"I didn't like what I saw," Ray said bluntly. "They're armed like some kind of assault team. All they're missing are fancy hats. And training."

"Relax, it'll all work out."

"I don't think so."

Coutelle slapped the machine again and looked at Ray.

"We have a fugitive alert going," Coutelle said flatly. "We've got primary evidence and we've got corroborative evidence. Rock-solid motive. Jimmy's bought and paid for. We're just one live body away from a conviction."

"Or a dead one?"

Coutelle shrugged. "Like I said. He's bought and paid for."

Ray shoved his hands into the pockets of his jeans, trying to stay nonchalant. But his hands became fists and his voice was as sharp as broken glass.

"We're coming at this from different directions, Cooch. I'm worried about the so-called Guardians going nuts and shooting kids. All you seem worried about is Jimmy."

"That's all I have jurisdiction over," Coutelle said. "If they'd been able to catch Jimmy, the FBI would still be on the outside looking in."

"More people have died than Leo Fast Elk."

Coutelle's fist connected with the side of the Coke machine, rocking it on its rusty bottom.

"Look, I don't like what's happening any better than you do," Coutelle said flatly, "but nobody asked me to. This is their reservation. What they do on it is their business."

"But—"

"No," Coutelle interrupted. "No buts about it. The FBI is here to take down a murderer. If the Goons and the traditionals want to have a guerrilla civil war, then they will."

Ray tried to relax his hands. Finally he succeeded.

"This guy Milton," Ray said. "Does he really check out? I'm hearing some very bad things about him out there on the reservation."

"Maybe you've been spending too much time there and not enough on the case."

There was nothing Ray could say to that. Coutelle was right. The case had been made while Ray was out wandering around talking to medicine men and listening to his father's ghost chant with the heartbeat drums.

Meanwhile Coutelle had acted like the professional investigator he was, putting together the classic elements of a murder case—motive, opportunity, and means.

Ray should have been helping him.

"Sorry, Cooch. I was out of line."

Coutelle gripped Ray's shoulder and squeezed the tense, knotted muscles. The gesture was spontaneous, man-to-man, compassionate. It made Ray feel worse than ever.

"It's a mess out here," Coutelle admitted. "Hard to understand. When I was a kid and we played cowboys and Indians . . . Well, I always wanted to be the Indian, just like you're doing now."

Coutelle laughed wearily. In the flickering light of the soda machine, his face looked ancient, a longer, leaner version of Grandpa Reaches's withered, weathered visage.

"I've been studying this field for nine years," Coutelle said quietly. "I know more about the law and the history of this reservation than the people know themselves. Let me tell you, I feel for them. The Sioux are a proud people."

A lighter rasped and burned with a bright, clear flame as Coutelle lit a cigarette. He blew out a soft stream of smoke that reminded Ray of the campfire and the burning brand of South Dakota grass.

"But they're a conquered people," Coutelle said simply. "It means their history isn't their own, anymore. It means their future is dictated by the nation that conquered

them. That's the way things have always worked. That's
the way they're working here.''

He shoved his hands into his pockets and stood quietly,
studying the ground at his feet while smoke curled up from
the cigarette in his lips. Slowly his expression went from
regret to determination. The tip of the cigarette burned
suddenly, fiercely.

"In nine years, I've seen some bad things happen out
here," Coutelle said. "I've seen some field agents break
some rules. I've seen screwups and just plain shoddy police work.

"But I've also seen two of my brother agents, whose
kids played with my kids, lying belly up in the sweetgrass
with their brains blown out. They were killed with less
fuss than you'd kill a coyote. Seeing that . . ." Coutelle
shrugged. "Seeing that changes a man."

For a moment, he was silent, seeing again the blood
and the brains and the Dakota sweetgrass.

Ray compared the vision of two dead agents to his own,
the vision of his father and the fire. He heard once more
Grandpa Reaches's words, that first day in the hot trailer.

Only this time, Ray understood the Lakota words. Then
he saw the vision that Grandpa had described. Two men
walking into a land from which no man returned un-
changed.

"Dreams," Ray said softly, unsure whether anything
was real.

Coutelle glanced at him and smiled wearily. "Yeah,
dreams. We've all had them. 'To protect the integrity of
the American Dream . . .' Did I write that in my entrance
essay. Or did you?" He pulled hard on his cigarette. "Or
was it one of those two dead agents, lying there in the
sweetgrass?"

Far off in the night Ray heard an owl hooting gently.
The hair stood up on the back of his neck, but he said
nothing.

Coutelle blew smoke and studied Ray with an expression on his dark, handsome face that was more complex

than regret, and more sad. He dropped his cigarette on the cracked cement and ground it to darkness. When he looked at Ray again, there was no expression on his face.

"James Looks Twice is an enemy of the people—his and ours," Coutelle said. "That's all there is to it. Either you believe that or you don't. If you don't, turn in your badge and gun and get out."

Ray wanted to argue that nothing was that black and white. But he knew that Coutelle was right, at least from the FBI's perspective.

"I guess that's what the director meant when he called this a sensitive operation," Ray finally said.

Coutelle waited, then asked, "You right with this or not?"

What he was really asking was: *Are you with us or against us?*

The question made Ray understand how far he had come in three days. He knew he wasn't as right with it all as he had been in Washington. He wasn't wrong with it all, either. He had doubts. Hell, everybody had doubts, even Coutelle. Doubts were natural.

But an agent couldn't act on doubts. As long as he had no better idea, he went with the senior agent in charge. That was the Bureau's way.

That was the way of the world.

"I'm right with it," Ray said quietly.

Coutelle grinned and clapped Ray on the shoulder again, harder.

"Glad to hear it, Sal. Get your vest. Get your game face on. We're going to clean it up tonight and go home heroes."

Ray walked back to his car to get his bulletproof vest. When he opened the door, the three-legged dog was gone.

Coutelle gave Ray the supreme vote of confidence. He made Ray the point man, the tip of the spear, the cutting edge of the knife. Ray liked it that way. He was never so alive as when he was on the point, waiting for it all to go down. The adrenaline of being on point banished all thoughts, all questions, all doubts, leaving only a training so deep it worked at the level of reflex. You lived every instant as it came. No past. No future. Just the breaking edge of *now*.

Moonlight gave a surreal beauty to the landscape of the tabletop mesa. Even Grandpa Reaches's trailer looked magical, its rounded shape like a sod-covered winter lodge or a brush-covered wigwam. The medicine wheel glowed in a patch of moonlight on the truck seat.

It was the shadows Ray watched, rather than the light. He was waiting for the flicker of movement that would signal Jimmy's arrival. An FBI radio lay on the seat. The volume was so low Ray had to strain to hear the occasional terse reports from Coutelle or one of the other agents who lay in wait farther back from the trailer.

The net was spread, the trap was laid, and the hunters waited for the quarry to trip the wire.

Far off in the badlands, a coyote howled. The sad, restless sound died away, then was echoed from another direction. A pack of the prairie wolves took up the cry, yowling and crying and laughing all at once, as though the antics of the men around them were confusing but endlessly entertaining.

Softly came the stirring of the Ghost Dance.

At first Ray thought the faint, anguished cry rising and drifting across the night had come from a coyote. Then the rhythmic call of the heartbeat drum rippled out over the land like an invisible tide, rising higher and higher.

The odd cry became a distant, plaintive song—lonely supplicants calling to powers that had fled, frightened souls seeking peace in a world that had none.

The tide swirled around Ray in the potent spiral of the medicine wheel, burning with a cold white light, holding him in a net of light, calling to him . . .

He could not hear the singers' words, but their voices rose and fell as his father's had. This time there was no mother calling warnings in the background. This time he was no longer a child.

This time the song didn't frighten him.

The sound thinned, then dissolved into silence, leaving the night to the coyotes and the waiting men once more. Ray leaned back into the seat, settling in for a long wait.

He came fully awake to the sound of the Ghost Dance calling to him in an old shaman's voice. Ray stared toward the trailer, wondering if he had fallen asleep and was dreaming. He saw a flicker of movement beside Grandpa's trailer.

Adrenaline flashed into Ray's bloodstream. He sat up in the seat and reached for the radio.

A figure stepped out of the shadows, a bent old man who shuffled across the dirt yard and stood at the edge of the mesa, his arms flung wide as he sang. Grandpa Reaches, sleepwalking or merely performing his matins.

Ray put the radio back and watched.

The old shaman walked until he was on a small rise, silhouetted against the moon. Then he began chanting the ancient song.

For a moment, Ray chanted along in his mind, echoing the sounds, amazed that he still remembered them from his childhood.

The rough Kevlar fabric of the ballistic vest rasped across the seat cover as Ray shifted his weight. He wondered if Grandpa Reaches felt as protected by his chants as Ray did by Kevlar.

A man does what he can.

The words came to Ray, carried on the tide of the heart-beat drum.

A man uses the tools he is given.

But to what end? Each day lived, but to what end?

The shaman finished his song and turned away from the moonlight and shadow sea that was the badlands at night.

Slowly Grandpa Reaches shuffled back across the dirt to the trailer. He picked up the plastic bucket from beside the stoop and walked slowly toward the rush-choked, gleaming river.

Uneasily Ray remembered Maggie's warning about the pollution in the streams. He wondered if Grandpa Reaches knew.

Someone ought to tell the old man to stick to bottled water.

Ray hesitated, his fingers on the door handle. With a silent curse, he opened the door and slid out of the truck.

CRAAACK!!!

The windshield glass turned into a spider web of lines that radiated from a bull's-eye hole in the center. A heavy rifle slug ripped into the seat where Ray had been an instant before. The slug passed through the seat and slapped hard against the heavy steel at the back of the cab.

Ray dove for the grass. A second shot smacked the windshield and rang against the back of the cab. Ray belly-crawled ten yards, took cover behind a discarded truck axle, and held his breath, listening.

The Ghost Dance song was gone. The crickets and the coyotes were silent. It was as though the night itself was holding its breath, waiting.

Moonlight sparked off shattered glass. Ray stared at it, wondering why the old shaman had chosen that exact moment to draw water from a poisoned stream.

Ten seconds went by. Fifteen. Twenty.

Grandpa Reaches was still on his knees on the marshy bank of the stream, his hands clamped hard over his ears, as though the rifle shots had caused him enormous pain.

The FBI radio on the truck seat came alive. Men shouted orders and countermanded them, sending teams right and left, calling for reserves and the armored personnel carrier and air support. The only voice Ray recognized was Frank Coutelle.

"Move up! Move up! We've got that Indian son of a bitch now!"

))) FOURTEEN

THE INVASION WAS a complete success. FBI forces and tribal rangers stormed the heights in the moments just before dawn. By the time the sun rose, the position was secure. The defenders—actually the single defender, an old man named Samuel Reaches—were in custody. A methodical search of the trailer and grounds had been conducted.

Unfortunately, no fugitive was found.

Not Jimmy Looks Twice. Not whoever had shattered the windshield of the FBI surveillance vehicle, narrowly missing S/A Raymond Levoi. ASAC Frank Coutelle stalked around on the campsite, furiously seeking evidence in the slanting early morning light.

"Son of a *bitch*," he snarled, hacking a deep gouge in the dirt with the toe of his assault boot. "It's Jimmy. I know it is. He's playing Crazy Horse with us."

Ray had watched the raid with surprising detachment, calm despite nearly being killed. He didn't feel quite real, as though the shots had transformed him from agent into crime victim.

Other agents quartered the area, each with an assigned task. There was nothing for Ray to do but feel the adrenaline coursing through his veins, telling him he was still breathing, still alive. He felt as though he were floating a few inches above the ground, as immaterial and unstoppable as the heartbeat drum singing across the centuries.

A Rapid City field agent walked through the brush at

one corner of the trailer until he found Grandpa's sweat lodge.

"Bunker over here!" he called out. "Get a dog in to check it for explosives."

Ray thought about correcting the field agent but was distracted by the deafening low pass of an incoming Hughes 500 helicopter. The bird's blue and white FBI paint job glistened in the early morning sunlight. The chopper settled into the cleared area fifty yards from the trailer.

Grandpa Reaches stood in the swirling dust a few yards away, watching the helicopter with a child's happy smile on his seamed face.

Walter Crow Horse was on a little ridge a hundred yards away, hunkered down on the ground, as though he were feel-tracking.

Ray started in that direction. Coutelle joined him. Crow Horse straightened up as the two agents approached. He watched the two of them carefully, his eyes shielded behind dark glasses that glinted in the sun.

"Don't give me that lawman look," Crow Horse said. "At this range, I wouldn't have missed."

Coutelle met the Indian's stare for a moment, saying nothing. Neither did anyone else. Finally Coutelle turned and went toward the crime scene, searching for evidence the way he had been trained to do.

Crow Horse waited until the senior agent was out of earshot before he spoke quietly to Ray.

"You think you were sent out here because you're a Heinz 57 Indi'n, supposed to make us all feel better? Or maybe because you're a good government agent, sent to straighten things out?"

"I don't know."

"Well, here's another idea for you to gnaw on. You ever think that the feds need one good reason to go in and wipe out this entire reservation? And what better reason than another FBI agent getting killed out here?"

Ray's eyes narrowed. His whole body stiffened.

"A no-name agent set out on the res like a staked goat,

just sitting dumb and happy, waiting for a bullet right here.'' Crow Horse tapped Ray sharply on the forehead. ''You don't wear no Kevlar there, hoss, and that's where the bullets would have caught you.''

The same thought had occurred to Ray as regularly as his own heartbeat ever since the windshield had exploded in his face.

Coutelle called out. ''We missed the bastard. Let's take a drive, Sal. We've got work to do.''

If Ray felt Crow Horse's eyes watching him, he gave no sign as he turned and walked toward Coutelle.

The FBI sedan raced across the desolate surface of the land. Coutelle sat behind the wheel, staring coldly at the road. The dark stubble of his beard was a mask. His face looked haggard, as though he hadn't slept since he picked up his new partner in Rapid City.

Ray sat without moving. He felt like a raptor rising into the sky on a column of warm air. Suspended above everything, untouched, untouchable, he watched and waited, letting his eyes play restlessly around the car. Again and again his glance returned to Coutelle's NATO-green Remington sniper's rifle. It lay, bolt open, on the back seat.

''Jimmy's losing his grip,'' Coutelle said. ''He knows better than to take a shot at a federal agent. He kills one of us and he can kiss his red ass goodbye.''

Ray said nothing.

Coutelle shook his head, following his own thoughts. ''Good thing he missed, or we'd have been drawn into the middle of the reservation war.''

Ray smiled slowly.

''I say something funny?'' Coutelle asked.

''No. It's just that I heard almost the same thing from Crow Horse, back at the trailer, all about staked goats and federal wars.''

''What the hell does that—'' began Coutelle.

''Stop!'' Ray said urgently. ''Look. In the slough.''

Automatically Coutelle jabbed the brakes. He followed

Ray's gaze down the short dirt road that ended near a slough fed by the milky waters of the Little Walking River. Normally the banks of the slough were a wall of dark green cattails, but something had flattened the rushes.

The slough wasn't quite deep enough to cover the battered, rusted roof of an old car.

"See it?" Ray asked.

"Yeah. Son of a bitch," Coutelle said, recognizing the color of the paint, if not the line of the roof. "Will you look at that?"

"Yeah," Ray said quietly. "I'll bet the muffler is held on with baling wire, too."

It took an hour to get a wrecker from a towing company off the reservation. In the meantime, field agents arrived and thrashed through the reeds beside the water, searching for evidence that might have washed out of the car.

The tow-truck operator was a salvage expert. He waded out into the water, slapped a hook on the bumper of Leo Fast Elk's beat-up 1972 Plymouth, and towed it from the slough in less than ten minutes.

Ray brushed the mud from the back tires. They were bald.

He untangled a ball of reeds that had become hooked on the muffler assembly. The bracket had indeed broken a long time ago, but Crow Horse had been off the mark about the baling wire. Leo had done his repairs with a half-dozen turns of the kind of braided wire that is used to hang picture frames.

"It's Leo's, all right," Coutelle announced, after checking the vehicle identification numbers against the muddy registration certificate he had recovered from the glove box.

"Never doubted it," Ray said.

He took the key from the ignition and opened the trunk. It was still half full of murky water. He felt around in the water and found a spare tire so used up that the steel belts had popped through the tread.

His fingers touched fabric that was too soft to belong to a tire. He pulled out a rumpled ball of wet clothing.

Coutelle appeared at his elbow. "Got something?"

Ray carefully shook out a man's plaid shirt with phony pearl buttons and white piping, a wash-and-wear cowboy special, the kind that half the population of South Dakota wore. The front of the shirt was stained with a dark crusty substance.

"Blood," Ray said, not needing a lab test.

Coutelle squinted at the shirt's label. "J. C. Penney's, Extra Large."

"Leo was a medium."

"Might fit your pal Crow Horse," Coutelle suggested.

Ray went through the contents of the shirt's single breast pocket. A package of Winstons, hard-pack. The eight or ten cigarettes inside had dissolved into a mess of loose filters and shredded tobacco. Ray closed the pack and turned it over.

A piece of red paper had been slipped between the cellophane wrapper and the box. Carefully, Ray eased the paper out.

"What is it?" Coutelle asked.

"A raffle ticket."

Actually it was only one-half of a raffle ticket, the half that proved purchase. The lettering on the ticket was smeared but still legible. So was the logo of the organization that sponsored the raffle.

The logo was an eagle feather inside a circle and the initials ARM.

Coutelle read the ticket over Ray's shoulder: "Benefit concert for Oglala Civil Rights. Sponsored by ARM. First prize—one live buffalo." He snorted. "Wonder who the big winner was?"

"It wasn't Leo," Ray said as he slipped the raffle ticket into a plastic evidence envelope and wrote his initials on it.

One of the field agents scrambled up the little bank,

muddy to the knees. He looked at the dripping car, then out at the slick-covered surface of the rancid little slough.

"Only a cigar-store Injun would forget that water evaporates," he said. "Really dumbshit. Makes our job easier, though."

The badlands sun bore down like a search light. Sweat popped out on Ray's face and along the length of his spine as he made the turn onto the dirt road that led to Maggie Eagle Bear's house. For the hundredth time he glanced in the rearview mirror. No one in sight.

He had lived in the Caprice's rearview mirror since leaving Buffalo Butte. Even though the highway had stayed empty, he couldn't shake the feeling that Coutelle was back there somewhere, watching over his shoulder, second-guessing, jealously guarding a case that was coming apart in front of them.

Ray didn't like the prospect of punching holes in another agent's case, particularly the case of a senior agent like Coutelle.

But he would if he had to.

In whose interests? Who will benefit?

The words were from his training, but they were spoken in the voice of the heartbeat drum that had become a part of him.

In the past, he had always accepted that the interests of the Bureau and the interests of justice were identical. He still believed that, but he had begun to question whether the interests of the Bureau and the interests of one Frank Coutelle in closing the case successfully were the same.

It wasn't that Ray didn't trust Coutelle; he simply didn't share the senior agent's certainty that Jimmy Looks Twice had shot Leo Fast Elk.

As Ray pulled into the yard in front of Maggie's house, he saw her coming up the path from the river, across the muddy flats, carrying a bottle of cloudy water.

Holding a plain envelope in his hand, Ray climbed out of the Caprice. He leaned against the fender of the car, watching Maggie approach. Once she spotted the envelope, she didn't look away from it.

"If that's a warrant for Grandma, you're too late. I sent her and the children away, where they'll be safe."

Ray took off his sunglasses. "Are you sure they're safe?"

Maggie nodded, then looked away. They had not spoken since Ray left her in the clinic. For a moment neither knew what to say.

"How's Hobert?" Ray asked finally. "I saw him at the powwow. He looked okay, except for the cast."

Maggie's smile was almost shy. "He's already healing." She took a deep breath and met Ray's eyes. "Thank you. The doctor said Hobert would have bled to death if you hadn't gotten us to the clinic so quickly."

"No thanks needed. I just wish to hell it never happened."

For a moment the silence hung between them again. A huge horsefly buzzed curiously around the bottle that Maggie held. Ray nodded at it and raised an eyebrow questioningly.

"I was just taking some samples for testing. More people have been getting sick," Maggie said. "Everybody uses the same water, so maybe that's the cause."

Ray nodded. Tests and laboratories were the kinds of proof he could understand . . . which reminded him of the envelope in his hand. He drew a deep breath.

"Maggie, I don't think Jimmy killed anybody," Ray said quickly. "When they take him out of this reservation, they'll do it because he was a warrior, not a murderer."

Maggie met Ray's eyes with a level gaze. Her look said she had already reached that conclusion, but was surprised he had.

Ray held up the envelope. "I've got some evidence. It might blow our case against Jimmy straight to hell and gone."

Maggie looked at the envelope suspiciously, as though she thought this might all be a trap.

"What do you mean?" she asked.

"You organized a benefit concert a couple of months ago," Ray said. "There was a raffle, for a buffalo. I need to know who bought a particular ticket."

Maggie's rejection was instant and emphatic. "No. I can't do that."

"Do you want to help Jimmy? Do you want to get Leo Fast Elk's murderer?"

"Of course, but that—"

"No, listen to me," Ray interrupted. "I'm an investigator. I can help Jimmy and catch the real murderer. But I need evidence. Evidence will give me the power to—"

"Evidence," Maggie interrupted scornfully. "Facts! Facts aren't power, not even when they're enforced by machine guns."

"Maggie," he said, but she kept on talking.

"Power is what a rainstorm is. Power is that river over there. And that's what I protect. Not the white law, not evidence, not *facts* enforced by machine guns."

"Machine guns can kill you."

"But they can't kill our spirit because our spirit is part of this earth. It's part of this river. That's what real power is, and it will outlast them and you, too. That's the Indian way. My way."

Maggie turned and looked out across the dry, rolling plains, out to where the shimmering waves of heat turned the hills into a mirage.

"Is it the Indian way to let Jimmy go down?" Ray asked.

She turned on him, furious. "You wouldn't understand the Indian way. You're not Indian. That was just some crap dreamed up by the FBI so that—"

Ray cut her short with a sharp gesture. "My father was Indian."

"You didn't even know your father."

"I knew him."

"Then why all the lies?"

Ray hesitated.

Maggie waited, not making it any easier.

Finally, he said simply, "I was ashamed."

Maggie still waited, her face a mask.

"I was ashamed of the way people looked at us when we'd go into the grocery store," Ray said. "I was ashamed of the way he drank, the way he walked through town yelling and chanting."

Ray closed his eyes, remembering all the things he had spent a lifetime forgetting.

"When the school bus passed him, the kids would shout at him, call him Tonto or buck or Indian, like he didn't have a real name. I wanted a real name, Maggie."

Ray opened his eyes. Maggie was no longer staring angrily at him. She was watching the far horizon with a mixture of emotions on her face that were too complex to name. He looked from her to the prairie . . . and felt it looking back at him, embracing him, power flowing up from the soles of his feet.

"I remember him," Ray said. "I remember his songs. I remember the Indian name he gave me on my fifth birthday: *Wa-shee*. I buried the songs along with the name and my Indian memories and I swore never to be a part of the shame that came of being Indian."

"When did you remember?" Maggie whispered.

"When an old shaman blew sweetgrass smoke over me."

Ray took a few steps toward the river, toward the limitless horizon. His face was hidden from Maggie as he stood for long minutes, as motionless as the trunk of a cottonwood and as powerful as the land beneath his feet.

Then he threw back his head and laughed, alive and whole and free as he hadn't been since he had been dragged screaming from a drunken shaman's arms.

Turning to Maggie, Ray smiled and walked back to his car, stopping only long enough to slip the envelope containing the raffle ticket under the windshield wiper of her truck.

"Whoever bought that ticket killed Leo Fast Elk," he said.

Maggie lowered her eyes, unable to speak, unwilling to tell him what he wanted to know. She went over and opened the front door of her truck.

"I'm getting out of here," she said.

"Where are you going?"

"To the source. You'll have to do the same, sooner or later."

Maggie held out a string of tiny tobacco offerings. Ray took them and turned them over in his hand, trying to read their message.

And hers.

She climbed into the truck and closed the door. The engine turned over several times before it finally caught. She shifted into gear, then seemed to remember something. She stuck her head out of the window and gave Ray a smile that was gentle and amused, but still had teeth in it.

"Wa-shee. It's like a . . . a dumpling. Tallow we put in stew. I think your father was calling you Chubby Boy."

The smiled changed as she looked at Ray's lean, hard length. "It was a long time ago, wasn't it?"

She let the clutch out and pulled away, leaving Ray standing in the badlands dust and the sun, wondering if medicine men learned anything useful when it came to dealing with women.

))) FIFTEEN

As RAY WATCHED Maggie disappear, he prayed that he hadn't just thrown away a case, a career, and perhaps a life. Even if she decided to help him rather than cut his throat, there was no guarantee she would make up her mind in time to help Jimmy Looks Twice.

Ray felt the euphoria and power leave him as suddenly as it had come. He felt drained from fighting for so long on so many fronts—fighting himself, fighting Coutelle, fighting Crow Horse and Grandpa Reaches. He had made a religion out of never asking for help.

Now that he had, he doubted he would get it.

Blankly he stared at the string of small tobacco ties, wishing that he had learned to pray in English or Lakota. At the moment, prayer made as much sense as anything else. He twisted the strings of the offerings idly around in his fingers for a time.

Then he got back into the Caprice, intending to drive away. As he slid into the seat, a sense of lassitude spread through him. The sun beat through the windshield and the hot prairie wind drained all will from him. All the sleep he had missed in the past three days sat like lead on his eyelids.

Exhausted, he lay his head back and closed his eyes. He drew a deep breath. As he let it out, he felt weightless, free, spinning in a medicine spiral, riding the thunder of the heartbeat drum.

He had never heard it so forcefully.

He tried to open his eyes, wanting to see where the

drum was. It wasn't necessary. Like Grandpa Reaches, he could see through his eyelids.

Shimmering heat waves distorted the prairie landscape, but not enough to deceive a shaman's eye. Ray saw figures dancing slowly on the opposite riverbank, keeping the stately measure of the heartbeat drum. Their faint song came to him through the heat of midday, the song of Grandpa Reaches, the song of his dead father . . .

The Ghost Dance song, ancient and untamed, sad and serene, a plea and an exhortation to absent spirits, a song created by people who followed the rhythms of the earth rather than trying to make the earth dance to their own pleasure.

He could almost understand the individual words. Almost . . . if only they would sing louder, come closer. He had to hear . . . *he had to understand.*

The wind came, blowing the song away. Ray sat upright and knuckled his eyes impatiently, trying to clear his vision. The windshield was blinding, each mote of dust shimmering and reflecting the sun.

He couldn't see the dancers. He stepped out of the car, half expecting them to disappear at his intrusion. When they didn't, he took a step toward the river, then another, pulled toward the silent dancers.

He was a river being pulled to the sea, all his strength useless. He had never felt more helpless.

Or more free.

The dancers drew him toward the spot on the riverbank where Leo Fast Elk had died. Ray walked slowly, thinking at first that he might have missed something, some crucial piece of evidence, that the dancers wanted him to see.

But each time he took his eyes from the dancers, the sound of the heartbeat drum and the Ghost Dance song faded.

The dancers drew him past the crime scene, down into the river itself and across. He splashed through the shallows, unaware of the water. He climbed the low bank on the far side and looked out across the plains.

There was a small, unkempt cemetery on a rise a few hundred yards away. Before, the cemetery had been hidden in the folds of the land, but now he could see a single large stone marker surrounded by smaller wooden crosses.

He set off through the undulating, heat-struck land, walking toward the tall gravestone. As he walked, the heartbeat drum grew louder, as though it had always emanated from the cemetery.

Then Ray was standing at the fence, looking at the prayer flags and tobacco bundles tied to the wooden crosses. Smaller stone markers were scattered among the crosses and at the base of the large stone spire. The weather had rounded the edges of the gravestones and pitted their polished surfaces.

There was lettering on the markers but he couldn't read it. He touched the metal gate in the fence, ready to go inside.

Muffled thunder came off to the north.

He turned and saw a horseman on a distant bluff. The man was half naked. He carried a long gun and sat astride his horse as though born there. The horse spun on its hocks and plunged down the rise toward the cemetery, heading right for Ray.

The horseman gave a cry like a voice from the dead. His hair was dark. His face was hidden. He dug his heels into the horse's flanks. The animal flattened out into a hard gallop, covering the ground in longer and longer bounds, charging like a horse that had been bred and trained for war.

The horseman was still a hundred yards away when he threw the long gun to his shoulder and aimed it right at Ray.

Automatically Ray reached for his own gun. The holster on his belt was empty. He turned and ran back toward the river, back toward the car, back toward his weapon.

Over the beat of the drum, Ray heard the thunder of approaching hooves. His boots slipped in the red dirt. He snatched one quick look over his shoulder.

The attacker was still there, still coming on at a dead run, his gun still aimed at Ray's back.

Ray ran and knew how Fast Elk must have felt just before the bullets cut him down.

Suddenly Ray wasn't running alone any more. A woman appeared beside him, running just as hard as he was, an Indian woman in winter rags and a dirty, old-fashioned shawl. She clutched a baby to her breast. She was crying, screaming, praying.

The drumbeats mixed with the sound of their running feet, the horse's hooves, all sounds the same, beating, beating, beating.

Two more women ran past Ray. One fell, screaming. Three children scattered in different directions, like a frightened covey of quail. Ray's arms and legs flailed but he got nowhere. His body wasn't responding. The harder he pushed himself, the slower he ran.

Panting with fear and exertion, he looked for the river, for the road where he had left his car. The empty plains spread away in all directions, mocking him, asking him if he wanted to claim them as his home now. He tried to answer but no words came.

Hooves thundered behind him. As he turned, the horseman raised his rifle and pulled the trigger. This time he couldn't miss. Ray tensed against the stunning shock of a bullet . . .

The shot made an odd, hollow sound, like that of the bullet striking the surveillance truck the night before.

"Hey, Ray, wake up."

Crow Horse smacked his palm hard against the windshield of the Caprice again, duplicating the sound of the faceless rider's shot.

Ray stared at the tribal policeman, trying to shake off the panic of the nightmare. His heart beat like a trip hammer against his ribs. He was drenched in sweat. He felt as though he couldn't breathe.

"I'm awake," Ray managed finally.

And prayed that this time he really was.

" 'Bout time, man. Jimmy's at Grandpa's. He wants to see you."

The sun had baked the mesa top to brick hardness. The Airstream was an oven in the breathless heat. Ray parked a little distance off and got out, cautious and still disoriented.

As he crossed the dirt yard, the three-legged reservation dog got up from the shade of the brush arbor and walked alongside.

The door to the trailer was closed. Sheet plastic covered the windows. Ray hesitated, then knocked. After a moment, Grandpa opened the door and looked out at him.

"What's going on?" Ray said.

The old man stared at him with smooth onyx eyes.

"I know you speak English," Ray said. "What's going on?"

Grandpa nodded slowly and began to speak.

In Lakota.

Ray's temper flashed. He started to slam his palm against the aluminum side of the trailer, but Grandpa opened the door. The dog shot through. Ray waited until his eyes adjusted to the dim interior before he followed.

Jimmy Looks Twice had grown in stature. He seemed to fill one end of the tiny trailer. But he had the look of a man on the run. His faded jeans and a tattered shirt were coated with badlands dust. His scuffed boots were mended with hand-stitched strips of leather and wrapped with duct tape. He looked exhausted.

And he was holding a short-barreled M-1 carbine with a banana clip. The barrel was upright, pointed at the ceiling. That could change in a heartbeat. Both men knew it.

Grandpa spoke again in Lakota.

Slowly, reluctantly, Looks Twice laid the rifle aside.

Grandpa sat down in his lawn chair and resumed the job at hand, which was cutting the sprouts and rot from a bag of old potatoes.

"Grandpa told me about you," Looks Twice said finally. "I know who you are."

"I could say the same about you."

Looks Twice smiled oddly. "Maybe. Maybe not."

The trailer was silent for a moment. Grandpa dropped a potato chunk into a coffee can on the floor at his feet. The chunk made a hollow, tinny sound. Outside, off in the distance, thunder rolled. The storm was still some distance away.

Ray waited, trying not to crowd the trapped man. Looks Twice was almost finished or he would never have sought Ray out. But the fugitive was still wary as a deer.

The heat inside the trailer was overwhelming. Only Grandpa was comfortable. The younger men had already sweated through their clothing.

Looks Twice kept his eyes on Ray's right hand, the one closest to the butt of the Magnum. Each time the hand moved, Looks Twice tightened, ready to fight or flee.

"What was Leo coming to tell my sister?" Looks Twice asked after a moment. "What was he coming to tell us when they wasted him?"

The question stunned Ray. He absorbed it, tried to digest it, shifted his eyes to the old man who sat, still peeling potatoes quietly.

Thunder rolled again, closer this time. Then it became a wet, sharp *slap-slap-slap* that came closer with every instant.

Ray and Looks Twice recognized the approaching helicopter at the same instant.

Looks Twice snarled and snatched his rifle. "You treacherous son of a bitch. I shoulda known better than to trust a white Indi'n."

The door of the trailer exploded inward. Instinctively, Ray pulled his gun and turned to face the attack. He found himself face to face with a regional field agent in dark blue jumpsuit. The agent sprang into the doorway in perfect Quantico shooting-house form, assault shotgun covering the entire room at once.

The attacker came from full, hard sunlight into a world of shadows. He hesitated, giving Ray the only opening he was likely to get.

Ray whirled and threw himself directly at Looks Twice, catching the barrel of the M-1 in one hand and using the other to sweep the fugitive out of the way.

"I've got him," Ray yelled. "He's down!" Then, under his breath, he added, "Stay put or you'll die, Jimmy. They're just looking for an excuse to waste you."

A second agent came in hard on the heels of the first. He saw Grandpa Reaches turning to face him with a short-bladed paring knife in one hand.

"Drop it, drop it or die!"

Grandpa sat frozen in the tattered lawn chair. Ray could see the attack agent's finger squeeze down on the trigger.

"Drop it, Grandpa," Ray said urgently.

Confused, the old shaman turned and looked at Ray. The knife fell and clattered on the floor.

A second later, the back door of the trailer burst open. A third agent leaped in, followed immediately by Coutelle. The tiny space was filled with orders and shouts. Grandpa's television was knocked off its shelf and shattered on the floor.

One of the agents snatched Looks Twice from Ray's grasp, threw the fugitive roughly to the floor, and cuffed him. Coutelle came over and stood above Looks Twice, shaking his head.

"Thought you were a real warrior, Jimmy. Thought you'd make a better showing for yourself. Now here you are, one more Indian headed for the joint with nothing to show for it but a lot of empty brags. Just like a traditional. All hot air and memories."

Coutelle turned and looked at Ray with dark eyes.

"Way to go, Sal. Good collar."

Ray said nothing, not trusting himself.

One of the agents grabbed Grandpa's arm. "Come on, old man, outside. Move it, move it."

"Take it easy with him," Ray said sharply. "He's not a suspect."

The other agent didn't listen. Grandpa was hustled outside, followed by Looks Twice. Coutelle moved past Ray to follow. Ray stopped him with a stiff arm.

"What is this shit?" Ray asked evenly. "You have a tail on me or what?"

Coutelle stared coldly for a long moment before he shrugged.

"I'd stake you out like a piece of meat, if that's what it took," Coutelle said. "You'd do the same to me. What matters is the collar, right?"

For a moment there was silence. Then Ray said, "Yeah. Right."

But it was a long five-count before Ray dropped his arm, letting the senior agent past.

Federal cars and Guardian trucks were scattered like junked vehicles across the mesa top. The FBI helicopter was just coming down in the open space. Two agents squinted into the prop wash as they waited, prepared to hustle Looks Twice through the aircraft's open door at the first possible moment.

Ray stood on the stoop, shaken by the extent to which Coutelle had used and betrayed him.

A staked goat. Crow Horse was right.

Something cold spread out from Ray's gut. It crept through him as completely as the heartbeat drum, changing everything.

He looked around the mesa with eyes the color of night.

The Guardians and several of the agents hooted derisively at Looks Twice. One of the Guardians put his hands to his throat and danced crazily, mimicking the death throes of a man on the end of a hangman's rope. Off to one side, an agent stood guard over Grandpa Reaches and lectured him at the same time. The shaman stood like a disjointed scarecrow, his back bowed but his expression distant.

"Harboring a fugitive, huh? Sam, looks like you finally got yourself into real trouble," the agent said.

He had already turned the pockets of the old man's trousers inside out. Now he patted the rest of the bony old body down for weapons. His hands found something in a shirt pocket and dug it out. It was the ancient turtleshell rattle. He stuck it in Grandpa's face.

"What's this, Sam? Maybe you want to do a little rain dance for us, get rid of this drought?"

Ray came down the trailer's steps and went to the agent.

"Give it back to him," Ray ordered.

The agent ignored the interruption. He shook the rattle beneath the old shaman's nose.

"How about it, Sam?" he baited. "Can this get Jimmy out of federal slam? Can it?"

"The old man doesn't understand English," Ray said. "He doesn't know what's going on. Leave him alone."

Coutelle appeared. "Let him go, Mackey."

Mackey looked disappointed but stepped back, still holding the rattle.

Grandpa kept his eyes on the sacred rattle. When he reached for the shell, Mackey dropped it. As Grandpa bent over slowly, the agent brought the toe of his heavy boot down, crushing the old shell.

Ray grabbed Mackey and slammed him against the side of the trailer. Coutelle intervened instantly, forcing his way between the two angry men, trying to break them up. He couldn't. Ray had his fingers around Mackey's throat. The local agent's face turned red from anger and exertion as he tried to break Ray's grip.

Finally, Coutelle got Ray in a headlock and wrestled him away.

"Calm down, damn it," Coutelle snarled. "We've got him now. It's all over."

Ray was facing Mackey, panting, ready to go again at the slightest provocation, when the helicopter lifted off, distracting everyone. The dust was still dying down when Jack Milton walked up. The tribal president carried a new

Browning pump shotgun. He was flanked on either side by Guardians carrying assault weapons. Coutelle clapped Milton on the shoulder.

"I told you he'd show up here, Jack," Coutelle said. "Ray made the collar. I'm going to see that he's recommended for a special commendation."

"Special Agent Levoi, huh? Guess you were worth something after all." Milton smiled. "Now that the ARM is handcuffed, it'll be peaceful around here again. No more agitators making trouble. Ain't that right, Special Agent Levoi?"

Ray said nothing.

"I'm real happy things worked out," Milton added. "I'm so happy I might even write a letter to Senator Horton, my old friend. You know Senator Horton, don't you, Special Agent Levoi? He's chairman of the Senate Justice Committee. That's the one that tells the Bureau what to do and when to do it."

The tribal president paused. "The senator's always looking for bright men of Native American blood. He might be able to find a spot for such a man on the committee staff."

The silence hung heavily in the air between. All Ray had to do was nod, accept what had been done, and all would be forgiven. He knew it. All he had to do was nod . . .

Drums beat in Ray's head, making him feel like he would explode. Without a word he turned his back on Milton and walked away.

"Hey, guys, it's Miller time," Coutelle called out. "Free beers at the Buffalo Butt, courtesy of the Denver Field Office informant fund. That's an order."

He caught up with Ray a moment later, grabbed his arm, and turned him around. "C'mon, Sal. With any luck we can both get shitfaced and still make the eight o'clock out of Rapid City. Let's go."

He gave Ray a good-natured shove in the direction of the Caprice before he turned away to round up the rest of the agents.

Ray watched his fellow agents start to come down from their adrenaline jags. The beery decompression was as much a part of the ritual of being a cop as kicking in doors and snapping handcuffs on struggling suspects. Ray had done it many times in the past. He had expected to spend the rest of his life doing it.

He waited while agents and Guardians drove off from the scene. Then he walked back to the spot where Mackey had crushed the ancient talisman with his boot.

Ray knelt in the dust and salvaged as many pieces of shattered shell as he could, feeling a little like a priest trying to salvage the shattered fragments of a chalice. Whether or not he believed as Grandpa Reaches didn't matter. A man didn't have to be a true believer to respect the beliefs of others.

Ray carried the handful of shell fragments toward the dirty, battered Caprice. He opened the door and slid in, only to realize that the passenger seat was occupied.

Grandpa Reaches stared straight ahead, his cowboy hat pulled down firmly on his gray head. In no way did he acknowledge Ray's presence.

"Are you all right?" Ray asked.

Grandpa said nothing.

"Look, I'm sorry about . . . everything," Ray said, looking at the pieces in his palm. "I guess you're pretty pissed off but there's nothing I could do. I didn't know Coutelle was using me."

The old man stared out over the prairie, ignoring Ray's apology.

Ray looked at the sacred fragments in his hands and didn't blame the old shaman for his anger.

"Out that way is a place called Wounded Knee," Grandpa said in his clear, flat English. "I was one year old when our people were shot down because they were Ghost Dancing."

Slowly Ray turned to face the old shaman.

"The Sioux," Grandpa said softly, "believed this dance

would stop the white man from coming and would bring back the buffalo.''

Grandpa drew a deep breath that came out like a sigh, remembering a time long past.

"The soldiers shot three hundred of us, but my mother hid me in the snow in a blanket. One of those who died was a holy man named Wakiyan Cante—Thunderheart. They killed him while he was running for the Stronghold.''

The old man raised a quaking hand and pointed his bony index finger toward a distant ridge. Then he turned and his black eyes bore relentlessly into Ray's.

"It is the blood of that holy man in your veins," Grandpa said, "the same blood that spilled on the grass and snow at Wounded Knee. It runs through your heart like a buffalo. Can't you hear it drumming?"

Ray looked away, not wanting to face the old man and the even older truth he was speaking.

"Look at me, Thunderheart," the old shaman commanded.

"My name is Raymond Levoi."

"It is Thunderheart."

Grandpa jabbed his long finger at Ray, nodding with conviction.

"Yes," Grandpa said, his voice sliding into the rhythms of a sacred chant. "Thunderheart has come again, bright as the sun, strong as the buffalo, he comes to his troubled people. That is what I am told.''

The drumming in Ray's mind increased, ripping through his objections, smashing the truths that he had always known.

"My name is Raymond Levoi!"

Ray's shout rang in the closed car.

Grandpa Reaches sighed and lowered his gnarled hands to his lap.

"Maybe you're right and I am mistaken," the old man said in his frail voice, dry like autumn sweetgrass stirred by a wind. "Your mind is young, mine is old. If my mind is wrong, so be it. *Ho Hecetu Yelo.* I will speak no more."

Ray sat paralyzed. His mind rejected the old man's words, even as he had rejected Coutelle's words a few moments earlier.

It was one thing to turn his back on the Bureau. It was quite another to believe an old shaman's ghostly voice.

Grandpa had closed his eyes. He began to move his head slightly, listening to a drumbeat somewhere inside his head. Then he began to mumble a Lakota song under his breath. Slowly, his voice got louder. He chanted to himself, like a madman. Then he broke into an anguished cry.

"Run, Thunderheart, run for the Stronghold. Run. The soldiers are coming. Run!"

The old man's eyes snapped open. He groped for the door handle but couldn't find it.

Uneasily Ray reached across the shaman and opened the door for him. Grandpa stepped out stiffly into the shimmering heat. He looked back at Ray with the sad, confused eyes of a child.

"They broke my TV," Grandpa said.

He turned and walked away, ignoring the trailer, heading straight into the shimmering vortex of the badlands.

Ray followed the old man with his eyes, knowing what he must do. As he put the car in gear and gunned away, a sheet of blue heat lightning burned across the sky. In its wake came the immense beating of drums, shaking the earth.

))) SIXTEEN

THE GRAVEL PARKING lot of the Buffalo Butte was jammed with celebrating federal lawmen and tribal rangers. Two dozen men, all of them heavily armed, stood around drinking beer from cans. The crew of the armored personnel carrier were showing off their rig, letting it climb into and out of the deep ditches along the road at crazy angles.

Ray parked and immediately started for his room. He had seen these kinds of powwows turn sour. The mixture of adrenaline and testosterone was volatile enough; add a liberal dose of ethyl alcohol and there would be trouble. Somebody would roll the steel pig over on its top or a macho gunfighter like Mackey would decide to see whether his .44 Mag could penetrate the engine block of a Bureau pickup.

Ray didn't want any part of it.

Just inside the door to Unit 5 there was an envelope with his name on it. He noticed it the moment he opened the door, but he slipped inside and closed the door behind him before he picked up the letter. He didn't recognize the handwriting, but he could feel the thin outline of a plastic evidence envelope through the paper.

His hands shook a little as he held the envelope. He was pleased that he had read Maggie correctly, but he had no illusions about what would happen if anyone but Jimmy Looks Twice had purchased the raffle ticket. Coutelle had too much invested in the case against Looks Twice. He

178

would have to fight anything or anyone who suggested the
case was cockeyed.

But would Coutelle argue with physical evidence?

Ray pulled out his pocket knife and slit the envelope.
There were two slips of red cardboard inside the evidence
envelope: one was the ticket that Ray had found in the
cigarette package in Leo's car; the other was its mate, the
stub that would have gone into the raffle barrel. The front
of the raffle stub bore the familiar ARM eagle-feather logo.
Ray turned it over and read the name of the purchaser on
the back.

Richard Yellow Hawk.

A mental image of the sullen, crippled Yellow Hawk
flashed through Ray's mind. He tried to build a scenario
in which this piece of evidence fit.

He couldn't find one.

*Did Maggie make a mistake? Or did she take the ticket
and turn it into some trick to protect Jimmy by putting
suspicion on someone else?*

*Christ, Maggie. At least you could have picked a guy
that could walk and leave tracks, plantigrade or not.*

Abruptly the increasingly familiar sensation of turning
and floating on a medicine spiral claimed Ray. The world
shifted beneath his feet, melting away and then flowing
back into a new configuration.

Slowly Ray turned the raffle ticket over again, as though
he expected the name would change. But when he looked
again, the truth remained.

Yellow Hawk.

Queasiness roiled in Ray, a gut-deep rebellion over what
he was being forced to discover. For a long time he stood
without moving in the stifling little motel room, taking the
evidence apart and reassembling it again in his mind,
looking for a credible alternative explanation.

He could think of none.

He was sure he was right.

But he needed more proof. He needed lead-lined cor-
roboration. Absolute certainty.

Ray put the envelope containing the raffle tickets into his shirt pocket, then slipped out of Unit 5 and into the noonday heat. He didn't notice it. The sound of drums filled him to bursting.

The party in the parking lot had progressed. Two agents were shooting at beer bottles, trying to snap the caps off without shattering the glass necks. No one paid any attention to Ray. He paid attention to no one.

The door to Unit 6 was unlocked. The makeshift operations center was deserted, although the computer screen still glowed with data from the last briefing. There were four cardboard file boxes stacked in one corner of the kitchenette. Coutelle's handwriting identified them all as part of the Operation Powwow archives.

Ray pulled the first box down, dropped it on the bed, and rummaged through it like a desperate thief. The folders inside were all old and out of date. Some of them went back twenty years, as far as the Wounded Knee shootout.

The second box was filled with duplicate 302s, every federal case involving ARM members or sympathizers in the past five years. Ray slapped the lid back on without looking further. Any clue there would be buried in the landslide of trivia that was the hallmark of any extended investigation.

There were manila envelopes in the third box, some sealed and some open—mug shots, intelligence photos taken at Red Power demonstrations, and surveillance photos of suspected ARM safe houses and sympathizers. Ray sped through the envelopes until his eyes fell on one marked "Richard Yellow Hawk."

The thin envelope was sealed. Ray ran his finger under the flap and ripped the tough paper open. Inside he found two blow-ups of prison identification photos. Each featured the bulky Indian with his thick glasses and tangled jailhouse tattoos on his arms. One mug shot was marked "Leavenworth Federal Prison." The other was stamped "Sioux Falls State Penitentiary."

The envelope contained a smaller envelope as well, this

one similarly sealed but stamped with the warning: **"Do Not File."**

Ray broke the seal without hesitation. Inside there was a third mug shot of Yellow Hawk. On the back, someone in the Sioux Falls penitentiary had stamped the enigmatic notation, "Special Parole."

Ray went cold. He jammed the photo back in the envelope and stuffed it in his shirt pocket behind the raffle ticket. Then he stacked the file boxes as he had found them and quietly let himself out of the operations center.

None of the other agents paid much attention as the white Indian climbed into the Caprice and headed for the reservation.

The government housing unit was a scattered collection of dilapidated prefab houses and storm-battered trailers. Half-naked children played in puddles of milky, muddy water, the runoff from irrigation channels in nearby fields.

Ray parked and made his way to Richard Yellow Hawk's trailer. Before he knocked on the door, Ray unfastened the holster that held his pistol at his side. He removed the pistol, put it in the small of his back, and pulled the tails of his shirt out to cover it. Then he smacked the thin, aluminum siding with his fist.

"Open up, Yellow Hawk. This is the FBI."

The door opened a crack, enough for Ray to see a dark eye peer back at him through the smeared lens of a pair of glasses.

"Open up," Ray repeated. "Come on. It's hot out here."

The door swung open. Yellow Hawk sat in his wheelchair, a string of tiny tobacco bundles in his lap.

"The Washington Redskin," he said. "Thought you'd be gone by now."

He turned his chair and rolled out of the way so Ray could enter.

The trailer smelled as though it hadn't been cleaned in a year. Dirty dishes stood in the sink, and sour, grimy clothes lay on every piece of furniture except the small-screen television set.

Yellow Hawk spun the wheels of the chair smartly and swung around to face Ray.

"What do you want?"

Ray looked around the cramped trailer. "Must be a bitch getting around in that chair. How long you been at it?"

Yellow Hawk poked a fat finger at the bridge of his nose, shoving up the purple-tinted glasses. He shrugged, as though he didn't really remember the date he had gone from two legs to two wheels.

"Ever since I got an iron pipe across my knees," he said. "It was a fight with three *wasi'cus.*" Yellow Hawk sneered, as though he regarded Ray as white, regardless of his heritage.

"Was that at the pen in Sioux Falls?" Ray asked.

Yellow Hawk shook his head. "No. Leavenworth."

He pointed to a scar that ran from just below his right ear to the corner of his mouth. "That one was Sioux Falls." His hand dropped. "What do you want, fed?"

"Leavenworth's a tough joint," Ray said, letting his eyes rove the room, as though he were measuring the boundaries of Yellow Hawk's cramped life.

The Indian nodded, con-proud of having done time in the worst joint in the United States.

"Leavenworth makes Marion look like Disneyland," he said. "You ever heard of O-Wing? Control Unit?"

Ray smiled without moving a muscle. Yellow Hawk was no brighter than Carl the bond thief, and Ray had done Carl in five minutes flat.

"Listen," Ray said, as though getting down to business. "Do you know why I'm here?"

"D.C. sent you," Yellow Hawk replied.

Ray let a cold, knowing smile spread across his face. "Yes, D.C. sent me. They sent me because this whole thing has gone from sugar to shit. Know what I mean?"

Yellow Hawk shook his head, then poked at the bridge

of his glasses again, nervous. The gesture left one more grimy smudge across the lenses.

"There was an arrangement," Ray said coolly, "an arrangement between you . . . and us. Do you remember the terms of the arrangement?"

Yellow Hawk stabbed at the purple glasses again. He looked away, unable to meet Ray's stare. He shrugged but still said nothing.

Ray let the silence hang like an accusation. It was all he could do without revealing his own ignorance.

Silence is the most effective interrogation technique short of wiring a man's pecker to a twelve-volt battery. Silence had worked on less nervous men than Yellow Hawk.

Ray prayed it would work this time.

"Hey, look, man," Yellow Horse whined. "I'm here, ain't I?"

Silently, Ray let Yellow Horse dangle for the space of two long breaths. Then Ray stabbed an accusing finger at the frightened ex-con.

"You won't be here for long. Your special parole had conditions. You had to live up to those conditions or go back."

Yellow Hawk poked at his glasses to hide his agitation. "I did live up to those conditions. You guys know I did."

Ray swept some dirty clothes off a broken chair, turned it around, and sat down on it. He reached down nonchalantly and pulled the .38 out of his ankle holster. He made a show of popping the cylinder, checking the load, then snapping the cylinder back in place with one hand. The barrel came to rest pointing at Yellow Hawk's groin.

"Get out of the wheelchair."

Yellow Hawk looked like he had just seen his own ghost. "What's with you people?" he yelped.

Ray gestured negligently with the gun. "Get out of that chair and walk toward the back door. *Do it.*"

"Why, man?"

Ray smiled. "I've always wanted to see a miracle."

Yellow Hawk rolled the chair backward until it jammed against the corner of an unmade bed. He held up his hands, as though to ward off the blow he expected to come.

"I get thrown in the Control Unit until I don't know my own fucking name, and then—"

"Stand up," Ray snarled.

"—you people tell me I can beat twenty years if I help you. Well, shit, I helped you. I helped you, damn it! The ARM is gone! What more do you want? What more—"

The sharp snap of the cocking hammer hit Yellow Hawk like an open-handed slap.

"Get up."

Yellow Hawk stood slowly, like a power-lifter trying to press a million pounds. Slowly he kicked the footrests of the chair out of the way. He took a short, labored step forward, then another. He limped painfully. Each step was awkward, heels first, then toes. He had an odd, rolling, bowlegged gait.

But he walked.

Ray kept his gun trained on the Indian's legs, watching his feet with fascination, remembering the tracks on the cracked badlands gumbo.

Yellow Hawk continued to hobble for a few feet, then turned and stood there, his hands at his sides, the jailhouse tattoos ugly and purple on his forearms.

"They told me if I cooperated in the pen, I'd never see FBI again, and now I'm living with you scum," he said, his voice broken by a strangled sob. "What is it you want now?"

"The usual."

"What else can I do, man? You say if I don't rat on the ARM, it's back to the pen, so I tell you about the ARM. You say if I don't get the boys to make trouble, it's back to the pen, so I stir up trouble."

Yellow Hawk jabbed so hard at his glasses that he nearly lost his balance.

"What's a con supposed to do?" he asked. "It's always

your word against my word. The FBI against an Indian con's word. I really got a chance, man, right?''

"You violate parole, you go back to the joint," Ray said. "That's the way it is."

Tears ran down behind the purple glasses. "What do you people want? I done everything you asked. I blew Leo away with the rifle you gave me just like you told me to. You can't send me back to O-Wing, man. I ain't going back!"

Horror welled up in Ray as his worst fears were confirmed by this desperate man. Cold sweat slicked his body and his stomach tried to climb up his throat. For a second he was certain he was going to puke. He wiped the sweat away from his forehead with the back of his gun hand and then stared at the weapon as though it were a snake coiled to strike.

Yellow Hawk sobbed softly, leaning against the wall, imprisoned by his own guilt at what he had done.

"You people tol' me I could beat twenty years if I helped you. Well, I helped you!"

Ray swallowed hard several times before he could speak. All that remained was to find the traitor who had turned Yellow Hawk into an instrument of injustice—a man who would shoot another in the back.

"The men who came to see you in Leavenworth. The ones who made the arrangement," Ray said hoarsely. "Maybe I can reason with them. Who were they?"

"Just one. Coutelle." The name came out like a strangled curse. "Ask Coutelle. He's the one that set it all up."

Ray felt his heart stop. "Cooch? I don't believe you!"

Ray's tone was wrong, too shocked, too astonished. Too honest. Yellow Hawk went still and then turned his head slowly, sniffing the air like a feral reservation dog.

"What is this shit?" the Indian asked raggedly. "You work with Coutelle, you must know all that he knows." He stared at Ray, suddenly understanding that he might have been scammed. "Where's Coutelle? I want to talk to him. Now, man. Right now!"

Ray pointed the .38 right at the bridge of Yellow Hawk's purple glasses. "You talk only to me. From now on, I'm the only law that matters to you."

Yellow Hawk stared unhappily into the bore of the gun. This was more like what he expected from a cop in a suit. This Yellow Hawk could understand. Threat and obedience, a beating and then a bargain struck and kept.

More or less.

"Look, suit," Yellow Hawk whined. "I'm tired of all this shit. Take me out of the game or take me back to the pen. Either way. Just do it. I can't take no more of this."

Yellow Hawk wavered on his feet and grabbed for a counter as a crutch. He slumped against it, then slid down to the floor and stayed there, staring blankly at his feet.

"Aw, man," Yellow Hawk said, "I don't even know who I am no more."

"That makes two of us."

Ray lowered the gun, uncocked it, and put it into the holster.

The FBI radio was silent except for the sharp pop of static each time heat lightning flared across the summer sky. Ray kept the channel open as long as he could, as though he hoped to hear something that would change the world back to what it had been before he talked to Yellow Hawk.

After a time, Ray turned the radio off. There would be no headquarters directive clarifying the situation, no advisory from the special agent in charge, no guidelines from the attorney general, no legal opinion from an assistant United States attorney.

Ray was alone, dragged screaming from everything that had given him comfort.

His hands shook when he realized how easy it would have been to shut this can of worms once and for all and go back to the fold.

A cold weapon. A well-placed bullet. Another Indian face down.

No big deal.

Killing Yellow Hawk would have been intelligent and pragmatic. In political terms, it would have been brilliant. It's what Coutelle would have done, had he been in Ray's place.

It's what any shrewd organizational politician would have done. In politics, survival is the only rule that counts.

The Bureau was a political organization from its clipped hair to its wing-tip shoes; a bureaucracy; a corporation of sorts whose first goal was survival. It was interested in justice, sure. But it was more interested in survival.

Jack Milton had already made Ray one offer. Ray wondered what kind of a deal he could cut now that he understood the stakes of the game. But he could never go home again. He would never again be able to give his allegiance to a Bureau that was better than he was, more able.

More honest.

He would never be able to believe, not in the way he had.

Grimly Ray kept the Caprice pointed toward the thunderheads that boiled up in the darkening western sky. Twilight had begun to fall as he slowed for a curve in the rough old highway. Something familiar about the scene made him glance around. There was a bluff beside the road, and a cemetery.

He braked hard, astonished. He had seen this in his dream, where the warrior on horseback had tried to run him down.

Ray backed up, pulled off the road, and got out. Off in the west, the thunderheads were being pulled apart by an invisible wind. The descending sun dropped through the clouds and sent lances of unearthly golden light across the graveyard.

The ten-foot-tall stone marker at the center shone as though newly washed by rain. A freshening breeze whispered over the prayer flags and medicine bundles on the smaller stones and the wooden crosses.

The little gate hung crookedly on its hinges. Carefully Ray opened it and stepped through. He walked quietly among the graves, letting the rhythms of distant drums guide his feet. Soon he found himself standing in front of the tall stone monument.

The grave wasn't well-kept but in the sweet sunset light, even the weeds that grew in the rocky ground between the markers were suffused with a primal beauty. The tall stone marker was hung with tobacco bundles, eagle-bone whistles and dried hawk talons. Name after name had been chiseled in the gray stone. Ray read them slowly, letting their music sink into him, blending with the drums that had become a part of his unknown soul.

Chief Standing Bear
Mr. High Hawk
Afraid of the Bear

Stillness pervaded the cemetery as surely as light. Ray had the unshakable feeling that the spirits of the dead were reading the list with him, waiting for him as the drums were waiting, waiting, waiting . . .

Tall sheaves of rye grass and wild western wheat had grown up around the base of the marker, obscuring some of the names. Ray went to one knee and pushed aside the plants.

Pretty Hawk
Blue American
Sherman Horn Cloud
Strong Fox

There were more names. There had to be. He knew it as surely as he knew the drums. Ray ripped the weeds away, clearing the face of the stone, bending low and reading fiercely.

Thunderheart

Exhilaration speared Ray, shaking him. From the clouds overhead came the wild keening of an eagle. Beneath it, in steady counterpoint, was the throbbing of the heartbeat drum.

It was coming from him.

The world turned beneath his feet. He shifted with the grace of an eagle and the certainty of thunder, meeting the new world. He knew now what had to be done, and by whom, and for whom, and why.

But above all else, he knew his own name.

))) SEVENTEEN

WALTER CROW HORSE inspected the silent radio set with professional interest, then looked to see what kind of glorious investigative gimmicks a real FBI cruiser might have hidden in its glove box.

"I thought you guys had a little crime lab behind the dashboard," Crow Horse said after a minute of futile rummaging. "I'm really disappointed."

He kicked back in the spacious front seat of the Caprice, hung his big black Stetson on his knee, and enjoyed the ride.

"Where we headed, hoss," he said, "or should I ask?"

Ray watched the dark road ahead, looking for the glowing eyes of range cattle or the flickering wings of night owls hunting in the ditches.

"Red Deer Table," he replied.

Crow Horse's face split with a delighted grin. "No shit? Red Deer Table, huh. Grandpa will be pleased. I know you thought he was just some old poverty-done crazy man, talking myths and bullshit. A lot of people around here think the same thing. They think he's dried up, like the river. But let me tell you, hoss, his visions are strong."

Ray nodded, still watching the road. Then he asked, "Do they come in dreams, these visions?"

Crow Horse turned the Stetson on his knee. "Sometimes. Sometimes they come during sickness. Vision quest. Sweat lodge. You never know when."

Ray hesitated, sure of what had happened to him but not sure how to talk about it.

190

"Just before we caught Jimmy, I . . ." Ray's voice faded, then returned. "I had a dream that I was being hunted down. I was running with other people. Indian people. I was shot. In the back."

Crow Horse said nothing.

Ray finally looked over and saw the tribal cop staring at him. Ray glanced back at the road, then at Crow Horse. The Indian was still staring at him, amazed.

"Then, tonight, I drove past the place where it all happened. I saw it," Ray added.

"Saw what?"

"Wounded Knee Memorial."

Crow Horse shook his head. "The Knee, huh? You were running with the old ones at the Knee? Heavy duty, man. *Heavy* duty."

"Well, it was just a dream," Ray said, not knowing how else to meet the awe and envy in Crow Horse's voice.

"Just a dream," Crow Horse retorted. "Just a dream! Hey, white Indi'n, who the hell are you, anyway?"

Crow Horse sounded angry. Ray looked at him.

"What do you mean?" Ray asked. "You know who I am. What's wrong?"

Crow Horse stared out the side window into the darkness, averting his face.

"Nothing," he said bitterly. "Forget it."

For a few minutes there was no sound but that of tires and wind rushing over the road. Then Crow Horse sighed heavily and looked back at Ray.

"Sorry, man," Crow Horse said. "It's just that . . ."

"What?"

He groped for words, then shrugged. "You had yourself a vision, whether you know it or not. A man waits a long time for a vision. Might go his whole life and never get one."

Ray waited, but Crow Horse said nothing more.

"So?" Ray asked.

"So I never had one and then along comes some instant

Indi'n with a MasterCard and new shoes that hurt his feet and that son of a bitch has an honest-to-God vision.''

Ray didn't know what to say. "I didn't ask for it."

"I'm a full-blood Oglala, for Christ's sake," Crow Horse replied, still bitter. "Who the hell are you to have a vision and not me?"

After an uncomfortable silence, Ray changed the subject. "What's the best way to get to this place Grandpa said we should go?"

But Crow Horse wouldn't let the subject drop.

"Maybe it was just a dream," he said hopefully. "You know, one of them . . . what do you call 'em, fever dreams?"

"Yeah, fever dreams," Ray said, agreeing on the name if not on the diagnosis.

Crow Horse stared out the window, seeing only his own reflection colored very red by the dashboard lights. He compared his face with Ray's and nodded, as though agreeing with himself that he was much more Indian than Ray.

Then he sighed and turned back to look at the man rather than the reflection.

"Bullshit, man," Crow Horse said heavily, "you had a vision."

"Well, what do you want me to do, apologize? Great. I apologize. I'm sorry as hell."

Crow Horse gestured ahead, irritably. "Turn right up here. It's the back road up onto the table. The road ain't much, but if the res cars can make it, this federal rust bucket ought to be able to."

The moon rose slowly, fuller and brighter than it had been the previous night, making everything clearer. Or perhaps it was that Ray had become more accustomed to the night and its darkness. He drove quickly, without headlights, guiding the Caprice through loose sand and rough gravel as though it had four-wheel drive.

The sacred monolith of the mesa dominated the land-

scape of the badlands the way a cathedral dominates a
European city. From its top, Ray could see the lights of
reservation settlements and Anglo ranches scattered all the
way to the horizon. Just beyond the curve of the earth, a
hundred miles away, he could see the glow of Rapid City's
lights.

Finally the two tracks of the rough road faded into rock
and weeds. Ray turned to Crow Horse.

"That's it, hoss. We walk from here," Crow Horse said.

Ray shut off the engine and they both got out. The night
air was quiet except for the restless wind, but Ray no longer had the sense of peacefulness that had come over him
at the memorial. This mesa top might have been sacred,
but it had the scent and feel of a church that had been
defiled in some subtle, hidden way.

The cold torrent of moonlight pushed shadows out of
everything. The two men walked together, the dry grass
rasping against the rough cloth of their jeans and snapping
quietly under their feet.

Suddenly, a shape exploded silently at Ray's feet. He
reached for his pistol in the instant before he recognized
the quick wingbeats of a bird.

"Burrowing owl," Crow Horse said softly. "They're
all over the place."

The two men looked at each other. Both of them remembered the dire predictions in Grandpa Reaches's vision. But neither of them said anything. After a moment
both men moved on, coming closer and closer to the center of the sacred mesa.

Crow Horse stopped and knelt to examine some tracks.
With a low grunt of satisfaction, he dug in his pocket and
produced a tobacco offering, which he laid on the ground,
appeasing whatever spirits guided him in his own touch-
tracking.

Ray walked past. Ahead, something fluttered in the
black, transparent wind.

A ribbon danced in the wind. By day the ribbon would
be scarlet. By night it was another, lighter shade of black,

shiny in the moonlight, attached to a bright new pinewood
stake that had been hammered into the ground.

Ray looked beyond the stake and saw another, then another, and another, a whole line of stakes marching down
a little slope to the banks of a small stream, then on up
the far side until they blended indivisibly with the night.

Slowly Ray followed the line of the stakes, splashing
through the shallows and up the bank on the other side to
the flat mesa top. By the time he had counted off thirty
yards, he began to understand the dimensions of the gigantic construction grid that had been laid out atop Red
Deer Table's sacred ground.

Suddenly the ground gave way beneath Ray's feet, sending him falling into the heart of something dark and hor-
rible, a nightmare come true. Helplessly he sank to his
knees in a noxious blue-black slime that welled up all
around him. The putrid mud drew him deeper, up to his
hips, sucking him inside like a snake swallowing a mouse.

Ray tried to break free of the mud's grip, but could not.
Silently he fought and silently he lost, until a powerful
hand grabbed his shoulder.

"Here," Crow Horse said. "Grab on to me."

Ray twisted around and grasped the other man's wrist.
With a grunt and a heave, the powerful Indian broke the
mud's hold and dragged Ray onto solid ground. Then Crow
Horse took another step and slipped into the same kind of
hole. This time, Ray had the better footing. He heaved
and yanked until both of them were free.

"What the hell is this stuff?" Ray muttered.

He wiped his hand down the leg of his jeans and came
up with a sample of the blue-black sludge that had trapped
them.

Crow Horse sniffed the mud and rubbed it between his
fingers. Then he inspected the hole they had fallen into.
Slowly he looked around the sacred mesa. There were at
least twenty more such holes. All had been drilled in a
symmetrical pattern within the area marked off by the construction stakes.

"Oil?" Ray guessed.

Crow Horse shook his head with disgust and said flatly, "Uranium. The Oglala have been voting against this shit for years."

"Who owns the land?" Ray demanded. "The tribal corporation? Milton?"

Crow Horse shook his head. "He'd like to, but he doesn't. Probably gets a kickback from the lease, though."

Ray took a few steps back from the hole. He tried to brush the ugly mud from himself. All he succeeded in doing was smearing it around.

So much blood. So many lives. For something as mundane as this.

Hell. Uranium isn't even a rare commodity. It doesn't make sense. There must be something more to it, something right under my nose that I'm not seeing.

Slowly a suspicion condensed in Ray's mind. Coutelle. Dark-eyed, cold-blooded, strong, accomplished in deceit and manipulation.

"How could they keep it a secret?" Ray asked. "How could no one find out? This is your sacred place, for Chrissake!"

"Your government pushed our people off here years ago. The Goons have been making sure nobody comes back."

Ray frowned. Possible, but not enough. He bent down and wiped his hands on dry grass, trying to scrape off the last of the muck, thinking fast and hard.

"Leo Fast Elk was trying to get to ARM to blow the whistle," Ray said. "That's what he was doing at Maggie's. So they zapped him and pinned it on Jimmy. To destroy the movement."

Crow Horse knelt beside Ray, touching the ground with his own hands, trying to read the rest of the sign the Guardians had left behind them. A sudden realization dawned in his face.

"The source," he said urgently. "It starts here."

"What?"

"The Little Walking River." Pain swept over Crow

Horse's dark features in a wave of understanding. "It starts here, in the springs. The test drilling gets uranium into the springs. That's what contaminated the water. Those bastards are strip mining this. The whole reservation is going to be a dead zone."

Crow Horse scrambled to his feet, fearful. "Let's go, hoss. We've to get the people off the res."

Ray grabbed his arm. "We've got to get Yellow Hawk safe, first."

"What the hell does he have to—"

Crow Horse's words broke off. He and Ray looked around in the night, suddenly alarmed.

They were surrounded by ghostly lights. Glowing eyes. Coyotes, watching them from the dark like hungry jackals.

Crow Horse stared at the glowing, his atavistic soul touched by their menace. Ray watched, too, until he began to make out the coyotes' shadowy forms in the moonlight. The wild dogs danced and circled, unafraid.

Ray pulled his pistol and fired a single shot in the air. The heavy report of the .357 Magnum echoed through the night. The coyotes scattered, ran a few strides, then stopped. They circled back quickly, still reluctant to be driven away.

"Crow Horse?"

"Keep 'em back, man. I got sign to read."

Ray watched the coyotes while Crow Horse knelt and ran his hands over the ground like a blind man.

"Fresh truck tracks," Crow Horse said. "Somebody's been up here. In the last few hours, maybe." He bent down until his face was nearly in the grass. "Goons. I recognize their smell." He scrambled to his feet. "I got a bad feeling, hoss."

Ray and Crow Horse followed the truck tracks toward the scattered pack of coyotes. The animals gave ground but lingered, held by something stronger than their fear of the two men. The tracks continued for fifty yards, to the edge of another sludge pit filled with drilling mud.

Something lay in the dry grass at the edge of the pit,

left where it had been dragged from the sludge by the coyotes. Something horribly familiar.

A body. Dark hair, blue denim jacket, jeans, and soft-soled moccasins.

Ray knelt beside the body, his hands shaking. Even before he touched the body to roll it over, he knew. He gritted his teeth, making himself do something that he wanted to avoid like death itself. He took hold of one shoulder and rolled the body over.

Maggie's face was streaked with blue-black muck. Behind him, Ray heard Crow Horse groan like a man who had just been knifed. Silence followed the groan.

Then Crow Horse began to chant a soft, dissonant crying song of death. Slowly Ray brushed away the mire that blurred the lines of Maggie's face. Her eyes were open. Even in death they seemed filled with fury, a woman warrior denied the vengeance she rightly sought.

Ray's hand moved over Maggie's cold face. When he lifted his fingers, her eyes were closed. So were his. After a few moments he began to chant, his voice rising and falling in a death song for the woman who was his spiritual sister.

The two men struck in the first light of dawn, like avenging angels. They moved silently through the government housing unit, guns drawn, eyes bleak with a warrior's knowledge of death.

The people in the housing unit were still asleep. The early morning birds were still. The only sound was the discordant metallic squeak of the windvane on an old, rusted windmill.

Silently Crow Horse opened the screen door of Yellow Hawk's trailer. When he nodded, Ray slammed his boot against the solid door. The lock gave instantly and the door swung open. Richard Yellow Hawk was lying face down on the floor, the top of his head blown off by the shotgun that lay at his side.

Too late. Too fucking late. Always too late.

Despair settled on Ray like a vulture. Yellow Hawk had been the key. Without him, the mystery of the sacred mesa was unsolvable, unprovable, because everything became deniable.

Coutelle could deny it. Milton could deny it. The Bureau could deny it too, and would, whether innocent or not.

The Bureau would be at least as interested in burying the truth as Coutelle or anyone else, regardless of what initial role the organization had played. A renegade agent was worse than a corrupt one, more frightening to congressmen and the President, more intriguing to the press and the public. In dealing with a renegade agent the Bureau had only one rule: shoot, shovel, and shut up.

But at least he knew, now.

Ray stood and stared down at the cooling remains of his hope of purifying the mesa. Without thinking, he cleared his mouth and spat, trying to banish the sour taste of death and despair.

"Just another dead Indian, laying face down in the dust. Right, Walter?"

Crow Horse stared at the dead man for a moment. Then his head whipped up and he looked at Ray.

Ray nodded.

A sardonic smile curved across the mask of Crow Horse's face. "I'll be a son of a—"

Crow Horse's words were lost in an avalanche of sound that shook the walls of the shacks and trailers. A dark blue pickup truck wheeled in from the highway, spraying gravel in a high rooster tail behind it. Three Guardians clung to the truck's roll bar, long guns slung over their shoulders.

A second truck screamed in from the opposite direction, then a third and a fourth. Men were packed into the cabs and in the truck beds, armed with shotguns and assault rifles, Jack Milton's tribal Guardians converging on the Little Slum on the Prairie.

Ray threw up his pistol and rapped off two quick volleys, two shots each. The heavy slugs from the Magnum

shattered the windshield of the first truck. Before it came
to a stop, the men in the cab and in the bed had bailed
out in different directions.

"To the car," Ray yelled, digging for the .38 in his
boot.

Crow Horse was already on the move, firing and running and firing again with his worn pistol. Together the
two men charged straight through the ranks of the Guardians.

Their counterattack caught the men flat-footed. The first
volleys from the new shotguns and assault rifles did more
damage to blue pickups than anything else.

Crow Horse lagged behind and fired as he ran. By the
time he reached the Caprice, Ray had grabbed the two
shotguns from the gun locker in the trunk. He laid down
heavy fire with one, then pitched the weapons and a box
of shells into the back seat.

As Ray threw himself behind the wheel, Crow Horse
dove for the passenger side. The Caprice made a wide,
skidding circle and headed back toward the highway. The
Guardian pickups rushed to follow in disordered pursuit.

"Head left, off the res," Crow Horse said over the
sound of the engine.

He grabbed one shotgun from the back seat and checked
the action. "Does this work like the ones you sell to the
Indians?"

"Shit!" Ray said, his eyes fixed on the road ahead.

Crow Horse looked up from the shotgun. A dark brown
Diplomat was parked broadside across the highway. Frank
Coutelle stood in the open driver's door, radio microphone
in his hand.

Jack Milton lay across the trunk of the Diplomat, drawing a bead on the approaching Caprice with his shiny new
Browning pump gun.

Ray spun the big car into a bootlegger's turn on the dry
pavement, rubber smoke boiling white and acrid from the
tires. He headed straight back at the Guardians who had
been chasing him. At the last moment, he swung the wheel

hard left. The Caprice slammed through the ditch and out across the open prairie.

With a savage gesture Ray snapped on the FBI radio that hung from the dash. The set came alive instantly, in the middle of Coutelle's transmission.

". . . said, hold your fire. This has to be done right!"

Crow Horse looked sideways at Ray. "What's he mean?"

"No wounds in the back, I guess," Ray said bitterly.

Crow Horse stuffed red plastic shells into the shotgun. "Get me just one shot at that *wasi'cu,* brother. I don't care how you do it. Wouldn't mind taking out Milton, too."

Ray glanced quickly in the rearview mirror. Pursuing vehicles were strung out behind him like a wagon train, FBI and Guardians both. Coutelle's Diplomat was leading the pack. Ray could see the hawk-faced agent lounging in the seat, one hand on the wheel, like he was out on a Sunday drive on the smoothest highway in South Dakota.

"Sal, do you read me?" Coutelle's voice was calm on the radio. "Talk to me. It's Cooch."

Crow Horse stuck his .38 out the window and tripped off two shots.

"Ray, listen to me. Stop the car. You're making a serious mistake," Coutelle came back.

Ray slammed the pedal to the floor. Dust boiled up behind him like a building thunderhead in a sultry summer sky.

Coutelle kept up a steady stream on the radio, as though he were talking to a jumper perched on a bridge or a terrorist with a gun at the head of a hostage.

"Ray, can you hear me? This is futile. You're under duress. There's a lot going on you don't understand, you had no way of understanding. But I can explain everything. Just pull over. That's all I ask you. Just stop the vehicle."

A new voice came on the radio network. "Unit calling on the local net, this is Rapid City," a woman's voice said. "Your signal is broken, unreadable. Do you need assistance?"

Ray had the satisfaction of seeing Coutelle straighten up in the seat like he had been slapped. Coutelle and Milton seemed to argue for a moment, then Ray heard Coutelle come back on the radio, this time on the long-range radio frequency.

"Negative, Rapid City, we don't need backup. Disregard."

Then Coutelle switched to the local net again. "All pursuit units, I want containment at every reservation gate. No media in. None. Do you copy?"

Coutelle is always thinking, always trying to contain the situation. He's kept the lid on for a decade. Hell of a field marshal, even if he's trying to blow my brains out.

A thought came to Ray. He smiled with grim amusement and picked up the microphone.

"You're doing a hell of a job, Cooch, but I just thought you ought to know. Yellow Hawk is going to sing."

Coutelle lifted the microphone to his mouth. The Diplomat dipped and bucked, but it didn't stop Coutelle from talking.

"Yellow Hawk . . . committed suicide at three-oh-six this morning. Now pull over and give it up."

"Negative, Cooch. Yellow Hawk's still going to sing."

Ray took the mike and held it inside his jacket, where his holster would normally have been.

Crow Horse watched, puzzled.

The scratchy sound of a microcassette recorder came as Ray played back the confession of a dead man into the open microphone. Ray's recorded voice was first, picking up in the middle of the conversation.

"You violate parole, you go back to the joint. That's the way it is."

Then came Yellow Hawk's anguished voice.

"What do you people want? I done everything you asked. I blew Leo away with the rifle you gave me just like

*you told me to. You can't send me back to O-Wing, man.
I ain't going back!"*

Crow Horse watched, first in bewilderment, then in
spreading amazement as Ray worked the playback buttons.

*"The men who came to see you in Leavenworth. The
ones who made the arrangement. Maybe I can reason with
them. Who were they?"*

*"Just one. Coutelle. Ask Coutelle. He's the one that set
it all up."*

Ray's fingers moved and words came again: *"You people tol' me I would beat twenty years if I helped you. Well,
I helped you!"*

". . . who made the arrangement."

"Coutelle. Ask Coutelle. He's the one that set it all up."

"Coutelle.

"Ask Coutelle."

"Coutelle."

The Diplomat was close enough now for Ray to see
Coutelle's outline clearly. The senior agent looked like he
was shaking his head in disbelief. Ray caught the flicker
of a white handkerchief. Jack Milton was wiping sweat
from his face.

The tape ended as Ray lifted the mike to his mouth.

"Fuck you, Cooch. Fuck you and Jack Milton, both."
Then Ray asked, "Are you two brothers or just from the
same tribe?"

Coutelle didn't answer.

Ray dropped the mike and drove.

))) EIGHTEEN

THE HIGHWAY TO Nebraska was blocked.

A truckload of Guardians tried to force the Caprice into a small draw where a second truckload waited in ambush. Ray reversed direction and smashed his way out, ramming the big car through an old corral fence and flattening a tar-paper shack that stood between him and the open prairie.

Crow Horse whooped and hollered like a bronc rider and fired at any pursuer who got too close. There was an exhilaration in the chase that freed them of fear or hesitation. It was football, a rodeo, a race, a wild mindless game that had no purpose beyond itself. It was being a brick agent or a tribal cop with no larger purpose than the caper itself.

The exhilaration ended when the temperature warning light on the dashboard began flashing. It was a harsh red reminder that after the game came the reckoning.

In front of them, the Stronghold loomed out of the dust and shimmering heat waves like a medieval castle in the middle of an inland sea. One look in the rearview mirror told Ray the rocky crags were their only refuge.

He also knew that Coutelle would kill them to keep them from reaching that safety. So would the truckloads of Guardians. There would be no one to stop them; the other FBI agents had fallen off the chase or had been sent to cover the reservation exits.

"What'll it be?" Crow Horse asked, looking over his shoulder. "Coutelle or the Goons?"

"Who cares? Dead is dead."

"If it's all the same to you, hoss, I'd just as soon be killed by Coutelle."

"Yeah?" Ray pumped brake and wheel, whipping the Caprice around an outcropping of stone. "Why?"

Crow Horse braced himself on the dashboard and ceiling just as the Caprice hit a bump and jumped like a deer.

"Coutelle's tricky and mean as a shedding snake," Crow Horse said after the Caprice landed, "but he's by damn a warrior. The Goons are just assholes with automatic weapons."

Ray laughed and swerved around a thicket. "I'll be honest, man. I'd rather kill them all and let God sort it out."

"Amen, brother." Crow Horse grinned as he shoved bullets into his pistol. "A-*men.*"

When he was finished loading the pistol, he stuffed the muzzle in his belt, picked up one of the shotguns, and racked a round into the chamber.

The red light flashed on the dashboard, monotonously reminding them of engine trouble.

"How much longer?" Crow Horse asked as though it didn't really matter.

Ray shook his head. "Not much, if that corral fence punched a hole in the radiator."

He pushed down on the accelerator, testing. The motor still responded, but sluggishly, telling him that the end was sooner than he had hoped.

He kept the nose of the car pointed toward the wall of rock known as the Stronghold, but the distant battlements seemed to recede rather than come closer.

The radio crackled and spoke in Coutelle's calm, reasonable voice. "Ray, where you going to go? You know you're not going to get off the reservation."

Crow Horse listened, then nodded unhappily and looked sideways at Ray. "I was thinking about asking the same question."

" 'Run for the Stronghold, Thunderheart.' " Ray mimicked Grandpa Reaches's quavering voice. "That's what the old man told me. You got a better idea?"

Crow Horse studied the rock wall in the distance, then glanced at the dashboard lights, wondering whether the car would make it.

"There's a hole in the rock, just about midway," Crow Horse said. "Big enough for a man and a horse, but I don't know about a car. Maybe . . ." His voice trailed off. He shrugged. "It's gonna be tight, hoss."

Ray remembered what Anabel had said a lifetime ago in Washington, D.C. "It's gotta be tight to be good."

Crow Horse laughed and shook his head at the same time. "Then it's gonna be great, man. If it doesn't kill us first."

"That's the problem with traditionals like you," Ray said. "You have no faith in modern technology. Think of the Caprice as the modern equivalent of a magic dog, a big old Sioux pony, and you'll feel a lot better."

"A shape-shifting car, huh? Well, hoss, do your trick."

Ray spurred the Caprice. The motor growled, faltered, then growled again as the revs climbed.

Crow Horse looked over his shoulder, shook his head, and began checking the loads in both shotguns.

The pursuing pack began to thin out, but that only spurred the remainder on. Coutelle was still in the lead, with Milton beside him. The federal sedans had fallen away and been replaced by a battered, tough pack of Guardian pickups and civilian junkers.

Ray pushed the Caprice to the breaking point and held it there. From time to time somewhere in the caravan an overheated engine would explode like a grenade or a speeding pickup would catch a tire in a deep rut and cart-wheel over. Six miles of plains were strewn with wrecked and abandoned automobiles.

Survival of the fastest.

Then came survival of the fittest. Ray didn't know how much longer he could stay on the surviving side of the

equation. He remembered the vision when he had tried to
outrun a mounted warrior. He had lost, then.

He would lose now, and there would be another rusting
wreck to mark the spot. Not that anyone would notice.
Most of the land was so wild it was never visited from
year to year by man.

*That's how Cooch got away with it so long. The reser-
vation is an island in time and space. No one knows what
happens here. No one wants to know.*

Another dead Indian face down in the dirt.

The savage caravan bounced and slithered down the
slope to a dusty depression and then bucked and fishtailed
up the other side. When Ray stared through the dusty
windshield to the battlements ahead, he felt a flash of hope.

"We're gonna make it," he said to Crow Horse. "Look
how close we are!"

The ramparts of the Stronghold were closer, almost
within range, but Crow Horse felt no exhilaration. He was
staring at the dashboard with the eyes of a man reading
his own death sentence.

Ray's glance swept the dashboard. It was a sea of red
and orange flashing lights, oil pressure failing, coolant
overheating, fuel low, brakes gone. The engine still
screamed, but it was a metallic death cry rather than the
growl of a healthy machine. The moving parts would seize
up and quit at any moment.

Crow Horse put his hand on the dashboard, urging the
struggling engine on with a soft Lakota chant. Ray didn'
think it would help. It wouldn't hurt, either.

The car started down the last long slope to the Stronghold. At the bottom lay a shimmering pond, a mirage of
heat waves, an illusory barrier between themselves and
safety.

The Caprice flew down the long slope. The needle
touched one hundred and stayed there, shivering like an
overworked muscle. The suspension was gone. Sitting inside was like riding a runaway jackhammer. Ray looked

beyond the failing car, beyond the twisting mirage, to the Stronghold wall, seeking a break in the rocks.

At the last instant, Ray realized the pond at the bottom of the slope wasn't a mirage. The shimmering heat waves gave way to a sea of cattails and marsh grass. He swerved hard, trying to skirt the wet ground in the depression.

The car jerked and slewed sideways as tires lost traction in the mud. The Caprice went broadside into the marsh, throwing up a curtain of muddy water that shrouded the entire vehicle.

The engine stalled during the skid. Ray snapped the shifter into neutral and turned the key. Nothing, not even the coffee-grinder sound of the starter. The pursuers were seconds behind. Ray could hear their straining motors in the sudden stillness of the plains.

"Out!" he ordered. "Run!"

The battlements of the Stronghold were just beyond the opposite edge of the little marsh. Ray and Crow Horse piled out of the car and crashed into a screen of tall marsh reeds.

The pursuit vehicles fanned out on a broad front, pinching in on the flanks, trying to contain the fugitives in the marshy ground. Coutelle slewed to a stop beside the Caprice and bailed out running. The camouflage green of the Remington .308 rifle in his hands matched the cattails perfectly.

"Ray!" he shouted. "Give it up."

The two fleeing men broke from the reeds and splashed into knee-deep water. Mud clung to their feet like training weights, slowing them, making them stagger just to keep their balance.

Coutelle fired a warning shot. The bullet threw up a geyser of mud directly in front of Ray and Crow Horse. They whirled and stared into the muzzle of Coutelle's Remington.

Ray racked a shell into the chamber of the shotgun and waited, staring across the muddy ground at the man who once had been his superior. The rest of the posse was slowly pinching in, making sure that the fugitives didn't escape.

From the corner of his eye, Ray saw Jack Milton hurrying out of the Plymouth, shotgun in hand and murder in his eye. Ray was struck by the difference between the two. Coutelle could have dropped the two fugitives before Milton ever got out of the car, but the agent had only sent out a warning shot.

Milton wouldn't be so reticent. He was armed and ready for the kill.

Coutelle took three steps toward the fugitives. "C'mon, Ray," he said quietly. "You don't want to hang around here any longer. Let's go talk somewhere, just the two of us."

Ray kept the shotgun at hip level, trained on Coutelle's belly button.

"What's to talk about, Cooch? Red Deer Table?"

"Among other things," Coutelle said evenly.

"Too late," Ray said in a flat voice. "We should have talked a long time ago."

Coutelle lowered the .308, but he still kept his finger inside the trigger guard. From where he stood, Ray could see the Day-Glo orange dot that indicated the weapon's safety was off. The rifle was ready to fire.

"You want to talk about Maggie, too?" Ray asked savagely.

"I don't know what the hell you're talking about," Coutelle said.

"I'm talking about why Maggie's laying up there dead. Why Leo Fast Elk was killed in the first place. What did they do to us? What did we do to them? *Why are they dead?*"

Coutelle pointed the muzzle of the sniper rifle toward the ground. "What happened to you, Ray? What are you doing to yourself?"

"Nothing that's half as bad as what you've done to yourself," Ray retorted, "and nothing as bad as what's being done up on the table."

Expressionless, Coutelle listened.

"And for what, Cooch? For the 'national interest'? Chrissake, the world already has more uranium than it knows what to do with. How many lives is another few grams worth?"

Coutelle looked around. The Guardians and the two FBI agents whose car had survived the chase were still out of earshot. They wouldn't be for long.

"I did what I had to do," Coutelle said calmly. "The traditionals don't want the reservation to change. They want to turn back the clock, go back to the time of demons and shamans. They want starvation winters and Ghost Dances. They want to eat shit and die—and they want every other Indian to do it with them."

"So you decided to kill them outright instead."

"No. I did what I could to bring this place into the twentieth century."

"You need a reality check, Cooch. The twentieth century is ancient history. The future belongs to people like Maggie and Leo Fast Elk and Grandpa Reaches."

"All that belongs to them is the dirt they're finally buried in," Coutelle said contemptuously. "Are you one of them, Raymond Little Weasel?"

"I've pitched my tent," Ray said. "It's up to you to decide what camp I'm in." He drew a deep breath. "How much does Dawes know about all this?"

Coutelle smiled coldly. "It doesn't matter. He'll do what he has to do to protect the Bureau, particularly against a bunch of half-baked charges coming from a renegade agent who's gone native."

"What will he do with the tape?" Ray retorted. "Weren't you the one who told me about cases being built on tape? How are you and Dawes going to explain that?"

Coutelle's rifle came up. "I'm not. And neither are you, Tonto."

The first of the support troops rushed to the edge of the marsh. They lined up behind Coutelle, guns at the ready. Coutelle took a step forward and held out his hand.

"Give it up, Ray. You can't put your interests ahead of the country's."

"What about the truth?"

"The truth—whatever it is—will end up in a 302 burn bag or a shredder. And so will the lies."

The words were intended for the other agents. Both Ray and Coutelle knew it.

"Hey, fed," Ray called. "Listen up. You turned a bunch of badge-heavy Goons loose on people whose only crime was to be born Indian."

"We came here to apprehend a murderer," Coutelle said clearly. "We did it. Case closed."

"We mopped up, all right," Ray said sarcastically. "Operation Powwow. How many of these guys even know the name?"

"That's restricted data."

"Restricted data!" Ray's voice was bitter. "Isolate and eliminate, right?"

"Whatever works." Before Ray could speak, Coutelle asked, "What do you really want, fed? Supervisory special agent? ASAC, maybe? I can arrange that, in time."

"How about resurrection? You good at that? You'd better be, you bastard. Maggie had media contacts. They'll be doing more than writing her obituary. It's over, Cooch. You lost. There's not a damn thing you can do to stop it."

"Listen to me," Coutelle said softly, urgently. "I can help you . . . or I can send you to hell. What's it going to be?"

Ray looked at Coutelle, then at the line of gunmen behind him, blind patriots and Guardians and a few federal agents who were as blind as he once had been himself. Their faces seemed hooded, hidden, the faces of executioners. Each of them held a weapon that could kill a dozen men. Every weapon was aimed at Ray.

Surrender or death.

Coutelle's weapon wasn't raised. The senior agent wouldn't be one of the executioners. He had meant what he said; he would pay any price within reason for Ray's silence. So would the Bureau. So would any self-respecting group, tribe, or corporation. The life of the individual was secondary; survival was all that mattered. That was the way the game was played.

Ray took a deep breath, savoring it, knowing it would be among his last. The stately, elemental rhythm of the heartbeat drum pervaded him. Slow, measured, muffled like the military tympani on the black horses in the Arlington Cemetery parades, the drumbeat transcended man's divisions of time and tribe and place.

He hoped Maggie had heard it before she died.

Ray lifted his eyes to look at his executioners. His glance stopped on Jack Milton. He would be the first to fire because he had the most to lose if Ray lived.

"Ray?" Coutelle asked. "What'll it be?"

"See you in hell, Cooch."

For a long, stretching moment, there was only silence. Ray stood without moving, wondering if the guns had been fired so quickly that he hadn't heard them, hadn't felt the bullets slam into his flesh, hadn't felt himself die. Slowly, Ray turned his back on Coutelle and walked away, heading for the cool shade of the Stronghold wall.

Crow Horse stood and stared while Raymond Levoi turned his back on death and walked away. Crow Horse steeled himself against the sound and impact of shots, but he didn't turn away. He had promised himself that he would kill the first man who fired.

Silence stretched, then shattered over the sound of Jack Milton racking a shell into his shotgun. The sound came back from the wall of the Stronghold, but not as an echo.

A single, lonely figure with long dark hair decorated by an eagle feather stood silhouetted against the blue high-plains sky. The figure was armed with a pump shotgun. Slowly he brought the gun to his shoulder, taking aim at the lawmen below.

Ray still did not see the man on the wall. The FBI agent turned to face his executioners.

The sound of shells being racked into firing chambers

came again and again, distant thundering warning of a coming storm, silence shattering as weapon after weapon was readied.

But none of the attackers had moved.

Ray turned and faced the Stronghold. The single figure was joined by two more men, then by other figures, men, women, and children, a ragtag army of irregulars. Each person was armed with a long gun and the will to use it.

The ranks grew into a solid line along the lip of the Stronghold's wall. Some of the warriors Ray recognized; the traditional youth who had been roughed up at the first roadblock, the working man whose dog had been shot by the Guardians, the dancers he had seen at the powwow, the storekeeper who had sold him the jeans.

Some were ARM activists in full regalia, with red and black clenched-fist shirts and savage eyes. The rest were strangers, people from the housing projects and the rough camps along the Little Walking River. They were the quiet people who sat on their sagging porches, unmoved by the modern world and unyielding in their timeless dignity. They were people who were slow to anger; but once angered, they would not stop short of victory or death.

They were the separate beats that together formed the invincible medicine drum.

A stooped, frail figure rose up and made his way to the center of the rank. Grandpa Samuel Reaches carried a shotgun that was almost as long as he was. He slowly lifted it to his shoulder, wavering under its weight; but the muzzle didn't waver. It was pointed straight at Jack Milton.

Milton stared at the weapons arrayed against him and slowly lowered his own gun. His mouth worked dryly, the gesture of a man chewing dirt. He tried to speak, to bark some order, but the words stuck in his throat.

Silently Coutelle stood and counted the guns on the rim above him. His forces were outnumbered three to one, and the enemy held the high ground. When he looked down from the rim, Ray was standing in front of him again.

"We could kill a lot of people," Ray said, "or we could have a little powwow of our own."

Coutelle stood, listening.

Ray touched the jacket pocket that contained the tape recorder. "Leave them alone, Cooch. Let them go to heaven or hell in their own way, in their own time."

"Or else?"

"There will be a lot of dead Indians face down. And you'll be one of them, Cooch."

Coutelle looked through dark, narrowed eyes at the Sioux lined up against him. Motionless, as though listening, he stood for a long time. Then he turned and walked away without looking back.

Ray wondered what the drums had told Coutelle. He didn't ask. He knew Coutelle would deny having ever heard them.

"Son of a bitch," Crow Horse said, watching Coutelle go. "What are you going to do now, hoss?"

Ray stood motionless, as though he was listening, too. Then he turned and walked away.

Crow Horse stared, then stared again. A three-legged reservation dog danced happily at the heels of the man called Raymond Thunderheart.

))) EPILOGUE

THE FIRST BREATH of autumn had broken the steamy spell of summer on the high plains. The cottonwoods beside the little graveyard were at their green zenith, as though they somehow sensed a change in the air. A breeze played through the tall grass and rustled the leaves softly, a reminder of lives that were present but not seen. Raymond Levoi knelt on the bare, brown soil beside the newly covered grave and draped a string of tobacco ties across the fresh white paint on the small cross that bore the name of Magdalena Eagle Bear.

There was something strange yet familiar about the ritual, Ray thought. Perhaps that was the strength of ritual; it was a reminder of the connection between the living and all those who had performed such acts in the past. It was a reminder that life is human and so is death.

"What will happen to Hobert?" he asked aloud.

Walter Crow Horse stood beside him staring down at the fresh grave. The big Indian wore his tribal police badge on his shirt pocket. The metal star was bright and shiny now. Crow Horse wore it openly, as though challenging Jack Milton or anyone else to take it from him.

"I will raise him," Crow Horse said. "So will the other men of the tribe.

"He will be your son, too, if you want him to be. A good man has many fathers, in the end."

"But only one mother," Ray said, adjusting the string of tobacco ties so that they moved freely in the breeze, carrying the sweetness of the tobacco to the spirits of the air. "Make sure that Hobert remembers his mother. She was very special."

Crow Horse nodded, his eyes suddenly filling with emotion. He drew a deep breath and let it out in a long, heartfelt sigh. Then he straightened himself and looked away, out toward the prairie. "The people are already talking about their vote for the new tribal prez. They want to vote for Jimmy, when he finally gets sprung."

Ray stood up, brushed the soil from the knees of his jeans and put his new white Stetson on his head. It had been a present from Crow Horse. Not a trade but a gift. "If you're going to be the sheriff, you'll have to start dressing like the fucking sheriff," the tribal officer had said.

Together the men moved down the dusty path that led back to the main gate of the little graveyard.

"What about the water?" Ray asked.

Crow Horse lifted his hands, palms up in a gesture that said he was uncertain. "The Mother has a way of healing herself if she's given time," he said. "You bought her some time, *Kola*. Ain't never gonna be over, but you bought her some time."

Ray glanced at him thoughtfully. "Yeah, but was it Indian time?"

The Indian officer gave Ray an appreciative grin. "Let's hope so, hoss," he said, "because in the end, that's the only time that counts."

They reached Crow Horse's battered Triumph motorcycle and stood uneasily for a moment, not sure what more to say. Finally Crow Horse offered his hand. They shook straight-on in the white man's clasp, then shifted to the grip of Indian allies. They held tight for a moment, eye to eye.

"Where you gonna go?" Crow Horse asked.

Ray let his eyes rove the arid landscape, falling on children playing in junked cars beside settlement shacks across the road. Beyond the little collection of houses, the land fell away toward the horizon, changed little by man's presence. The last summer breeze felt good on his face, a sign and a benediction. Finally he answered the question the only way he could.

"I'll have to see what the visions say before I decide," Ray said with a sad hint of a smile.

"You didn't have another vision, did you?"

Ray made a gesture that didn't answer the question, as though he wasn't sure himself. "Time will tell," he said. "You take care of yourself, Crow Horse." He turned and started toward his car that was parked in the shade of a small stand of cottonwoods.

"If you ever need a place to come back to, a place to listen to the trees a little, we'll be here," Crow Horse called after him. "We'll be here . . . brother."

Ray stopped and turned back. His face showed how deeply Crow Horse's words had touched him. He seemed to search for words until the Indian officer held up a hand, palm forward. "Ain't no word in Lakota for goodbye," he said. Then Crow Horse threw his leg across the motorcycle, kicked it into life, and rode away without looking back.

Ray watched him go, then turned back toward the dusty, road-battered Caprice. He heard the soft sound of a prayer song even before he rounded the car. The quiet chant was as familiar to him now as a childhood lullaby.

The singer sat on the trunk of a fallen cottonwood, his back to Ray, his eyes fixed on the far horizon. But Ray recognized Samuel Reaches's bony shoulders and hunched back as though the old man were his own grandfather.

Ray watched the old man for a moment, reluctant to disturb his devotions. Finally, he came around the end of the fallen tree trunk and sat down on it, content to listen and wait. Grandpa's prayer song finally faded away softly and was finished. He turned and his eyes focused slowly on Ray, as though he was faintly surprised to find the younger man there. Ray met his gaze for a moment. Then he stood up, rolled his sleeve back, and stripped his Rolex off his wrist. He handed it to the old man without a word.

Grandpa accepted the watch gravely. He held it up to the sun, letting the light glint off the crystal face. Then he buffed the shiny stainless-steel band against his shirt and admired it. He dropped the watch into his pocket, then gave Ray a brilliant smile and made a flat-handed gesture that said it was a done deal.

Ray was a little surprised that Grandpa offered nothing in trade but he let the matter go. They nodded to each other, then Ray turned and went to his car. Grandpa stood up and trudged down the narrow footpath toward the open prairie. He stopped once and looked back before he shuffled off toward the setting sun, content with his world.

Ray knocked as much dust as he could from the windshield of the Caprice. The antennas had been snapped off in the chase. Now the car looked as though it was just another late-model reservation-beater. Ray had decided that, no matter what, he didn't intend to turn it in as he had turned in the rest of his FBI trappings.

He got in, rolled down the window, and twisted the key in the ignition. The engine had been abused. It didn't start until the third try. While the car warmed up, Ray stripped the pistol from his belt and went to lay it on the seat beside him. That was when he first noticed . . .

Grandpa's sacred *caanunpa*. The pipe. The symbol of truth. Ray looked out of the window. Grandpa was a distant figure on the path. Ray tapped the horn ring of the Caprice once. Grandpa turned and looked back. Then he raised his hand and made the flat, done-deal sign again. Ray repeated the gesture, put the car in gear and drove off.

The sun was settling in the west as he pulled onto the main highway and headed for the edge of the reservation. Remembering the playing children, he slowed as he passed the cluster of houses. Then he saw something that made him brake to a sharp stop.

The three-legged dog sat patiently at the edge of the pavement, tongue lolling, eyes bright, waiting. When Ray opened the passenger door, the dog hopped nimbly into the passenger seat and sat down as though he owned the car. He stared straight ahead out the windshield, ready to go. When Ray didn't start immediately, the dog gave him a look that seemed to say, "What are you waiting for? Let's roll."

Ray put the battered car into gear and started up. Somewhere in the recesses of his mind or memory, he heard the slow, deep throb of the heartbeat drum again. He knew it would show him the way.